Splinter City

"*Splinter City* is an action-packed homecoming tale with a satisfying twist. Dan Parrish, ex-con, ex-football star, is a fascinating, complex character who braves the prejudice of a small town that may not be ready to forgive his alleged sins."

—Deborah Shlian, award-winning author of
Rabbit in the Moon and *Silent Survivor*

"Thomas Wolfe said, 'You can't go home again,' but haven't we all gone back, or wanted to? If you haven't, you can go back vicariously by reading *Splinter City*, a fine new novel by established authors Shawn Corridan and Gary Waid. Travel with Dan Parrish as he deals with homecoming, heartbreak, and small-town football."

—David Bishop, author of
The Third Coincidence

"When a former local football hero returns home to a small Kansas town after eighteen years in prison he discovers even the secrets have secrets, and the forces that tried to ruin his life are still there, now more powerful, ready to finish the job. Highly recommend."

—Mike Pace, author of *One to Go*

"Corridan and Waid spin a masterful tale of redemption with surprises at every turn. A great read."

—Robert B. McCaw, author of the
Koa Kane Hawaii mysteries

SPLINTER CITY

ALSO BY SHAWN CORRIDAN & GARY WAID

Gitmo
Goliath

SHAWN CORRIDAN & GARY WAID

SPLINTER CITY

DOWN&OUT
BOOKS

Down & Out Books
3959 Van Dyke Rd, Ste. 265
Lutz, FL 33558
www.DownAndOutBooks.com

Cover design by JT Lindroos

ISBN: 1-948235-39-0
ISBN-13: 978-1-948235-39-6

*With gratitude to Coach J.D. Bobbitt
and his loving widow, Mary.*

*And the Corley brothers, Andy and Kurt,
as tough as they come.*

CHAPTER 1

I killed John Henry.

Dan Parrish stood in a cloud of dust and waved to the driver of the departing pickup, then slackened his shoulder and dropped his duffel in a heap on the side of the road. Sweat ran down his face and the back of his neck and into the lining of his shirt.

He was used to discomfort, though. He was used to a lot of things most folks weren't used to.

I killed John Henry.

In Kansas, during the last days of August there is a relentless heat that comes in subtle increments, introducing itself a degree at a time through white afternoons of cloudless skies. So when the little Ford pickup slowed and stopped to deposit Dan, the taciturn old farmer had been almost apologetic as he turned and nodded to him.

"This is fine," Dan Parrish had said. "Thanks for the ride. I'll just get off here."

As if here was anywhere.

But he recognized it. He knew the landscape—the washed-out colors and the broken fences and the miles and miles of sameness. He could smell the land and feel the grit between his teeth and inside his socks. He was in wheat country. Amber waves as far as the eye could see. He closed his eyes and sighed.

I killed John Henry.

There was a dilapidated billboard in the near distance with a utopian image of a farmer standing in front of a silo. On the top right there was a sun-bleached outline of the United States, with a star superimposed on the spot near where he was standing: Lebanon, Kansas, Center of the Continental U.S. Someone had put a ragged cluster of twenty-two rounds into the sign, no doubt aiming, without success, for the star.

If Dan were to look at a real map of the United States and work out the exact center of everything, he knew that the actual location of that spot on the grid would be here or maybe a nearby field. The town of Lebanon should not be faulted for boasting its location with a billboard. A lot of Kansas could be labeled and filed away—Bleak City or Hoxie or Hope or Last Laugh, or a hundred other tiny dots on the dusty, dun colored prairie covered in grass and grain and littered with too many broken dreams.

So Dan Parrish wasn't just standing in the middle of nowhere. He was standing in the middle of *somewhere*.

The heart of the Heartland.

He squinted into the dust and wiped his face. Road grit had worked its way into his eyes and he dug at it with a thumb and forefinger. He was not a kid anymore—thirty-six and counting—but blessed with the same chiseled, athletic frame that he'd had as a youngster. He'd been notable for his physical talents back then, and the evidence was still there. Except now, part of the reason for the strong legs and the shoulders that rolled and swelled was not because of his Kansas history or his genes, but because of personal circumstances. His jaw was square beneath his beard, too, and his teeth were white, his nose straight and his flaxen hair was thick and long, hanging in a rope to the middle of his back. His eyes were as blue as the ocean he'd never seen and more troubled than he ever imagined they'd be.

Everybody knows I did it.

He stepped to the sandy berm, bent down and picked up a

2

handful of rocks. He began throwing them at targets as vague and unfocused as watercolor shadows, something he'd done since he was a kid.

The day was getting on, the heat turning the soles of his old Chuck Taylor's sticky. The laces were so rotten he'd had to double them and use a square knot to keep them on his feet. His jeans were pretty sad, too, and his Sears chambray shirt had faded to a whitish shade of lilac. He hadn't worn any of these clothes in years. Now they were all he had.

The whole town knows.

He picked up another handful of rocks and threw them one at a time at a beer can thirty yards distant. The sun was overhead, so it was at least noon now, maybe later. With the last rock, he hit the can then looked up into a sky that hadn't seen a cloud in days. He wiped his hands on his pants then bent and opened his duffel bag and searched the insides for his water bottle. When he found it there was only enough for a swallow, so he sipped, replaced it and sealed things up and stacked the baggage on the berm. It was an old bag, older than the clothes he wore, labeled with his father's name: SGT. CARL PARRISH, in faded black stencil across the top. Below that, DA NANG. It was a possession he was proud of.

There was barely a breeze at this time of day. The only sound came from the wheat fields crackling and hissing in the dry heat. He continued throwing stones gathered from beside the road. He flung a stone at an imaginary opponent. He saw movement in the brush and fired. He stood in the middle of the road and scanned the nearby area for more targets. There were always targets. Always. A jackrabbit. A Hackberry tree. Prairie chickens. Everything. Anything. He threw. Then threw some more. And continued to throw for the better part of an hour. Finally he dropped his handful of rocks and looked away into the distance.

I shouldn't go back.

Two hours later a speck appeared on the horizon, warped

3

by the heat radiating off the pavement. When Dan stuck his thumb out, the driver downshifted and the air breaks engaged. The tractor-trailer stopped right beside him. The driver was no doubt breaking company rules about hitchhikers. Dan opened the door. Before he climbed in, he reached down and grabbed a last rock, oval, like an egg. He rolled it around in his hand, took aim, and flung it at a green roadside mileage sign sixty yards away, a sign that gave material substance to middle-America Kansas—*PHILLIPSBURG, NORTON, ATWOOD, ECHO*—all small towns on the prairie. The rock landed with a loud metallic twang on the name *ECHO*. A sixty-yard shot, easy.

Dan Parrish climbed up onto the seat and shut the door.

"Nice arm," said the driver.

"Thanks," said Dan.

The air breaks hissed, the truck and its cargo began to move.

It's crazy to go back. Suicide, they said. I was warned.

But there's something I have to do.

CHAPTER 2

Hours later on that same August date, a Lincoln Town Car made its way down a rural road, stopping in the weed-choked entrance to a sharecropper farmhouse set back amidst a copse of stunted oaks. The driver killed the headlights and the world was suddenly black as tar. Only an outline of the dilapidated shack was visible, a post-and-beam, tin-roofed relic of small farming, leaning in on itself, held together by the dry friction of time. A single light glimmered from a kitchen window, failing to penetrate the night.

Inside the Lincoln, behind the wheel, sat a man whose hair glistened with pomade. He was in his thirties and displayed the handsome-if-unctuous mien of someone with money. His suit was Italian silk and his boots were made from the skins of caimans. He wore a bolo tie in a clasp studded with diamonds, and clamped in his teeth was a diamond-headed, gold toothpick bequeathed to him by his father. When his dash-installed police scanner burst into life, spewing cop data, he coolly reached over and silenced it. Outside, a cadre of lightning bugs swirled like embers. A mournful whippoorwill pleaded its case.

The man removed his toothpick and tucked it away in a top pocket. He took a flask from his coat and tilted it to his lips. Then he screwed the lid back on and slipped it back beneath the flap.

"So, we all set?" He wiped his mouth with his forefinger.

There was a pause, too long, before an answer floated out

5

of the darkness, angry and defiant. "Yeah. We all set."

In the passenger seat Brenda Price, nineteen and simmering with rage, sat in her pink, second-hand dress and matching pink rubber flip flops, shrouded in the dark. Another silent moment passed. The clouds parted and the moon appeared, revealing her high cheekbones, close-cropped Afro, full lips and fierce, clear eyes. Despite her clenched teeth she was beautiful.

The man must have expected her to leave but she didn't. He sighed and took out his wallet and removed some crisp C-notes, offering them to the girl. She slapped them to the car seat in a sudden, violent movement. Her nostrils flared with quick, heavy breaths.

The man shook his head. He picked up the bills and tucked them away. He retrieved his gold toothpick and stuck it in his mouth, trying not to snort his derision.

"You people..." he said, not finishing the sentence, but allowing it to hang in the air like a malodorous cloud.

The girl still did not move, so he leaned his shoulder and arm across her chest and threw her door open. He sat back, eyes straight ahead, fixed on nothing but the darkness that had retaken the night. He surely felt her eyes on him, but refused to acknowledge it. He looked at his watch. His hands were narrow and clean, with perfect nails.

Brenda turned away and put her feet on the ground and stood herself out of the car. She could have slapped the man, clawed his face, screamed. But she didn't do any of that, not here in Punch Town. Not to a boss from across the tracks. She stepped back and slammed the car door shut as hard as she could. The dogs began to bay, and she stepped backward, turning and stumbling over a root, falling to her knees in the mud. Brenda Price rose up then, but she'd lost a shoe and had to go back down to find it. Her dress was covered in dirt. She could have cried, but saw him looking at her, taking aim with his lidded eyes, disgusted. He wasn't going to get out of the car,

6

but still she was frightened by the look: white-on-black mean.

He threw the Lincoln into gear and gunned it, racking gravel, dust and mud onto her. He rocketed up the road, back the way he had come. The police scanner came back on, spewing voices into the night.

Brenda clutched her belly and stifled a sob, refusing to cry. She watched the car disappear into the darkness, red taillights like living things, demon eyes growing smaller, blurring through the glyph of tears. Her dress was a mess. Her glistening skin now covered in a fine layer of dirt. Her life had shrunk once more into the sterile obscurity of the Punch Town people.

She brushed herself off as best she could. Her father would have questions. He would be mad at her. She could make out his profile in the kitchen window.

Yet as she wiped away the grime, she listened, and from far away she could hear the car's big V-8 accelerate, back toward town, across the railroad tracks, away from the squalor. And she made a promise to herself.

A promise she would keep.

CHAPTER 3

*Sometimes when the quiet man closes his eyes he can see it.
He can see the body lying on the ground, the blood on the
clothes, the look of shock and even sorrow in the dead stare.
He sees it all.*

He glanced down at Puck in the passenger seat. "Let's take
a break, boy," he said, reaching over and patting his little dog
on the head. A minute later the quiet man pulled over and
parked his Ford Focus in front of the blinking *VACANCY*
sign. He'd been driving for hours, but now the rain had
caught up with him, a hard, late-summer storm that had come
over the Cascades, lightning flashing, illuminating the peaks
and dells, thunder booming. The highway was plagued with
switchbacks and long straightaways that were filling with
flumes of rushing water, which meant his tires were losing
traction. He had a thousand miles to go, at least, but night
driving was impossible in weather like this. He pushed his hat
back and sat, waiting for a lull in the storm. When it came, he
jumped from the car and ran under the awning.

He rang the buzzer.

Ten minutes later he and Puck sat on the bed in his little
room. He unpacked his new pistol, a Glock 9mm semi-
automatic, and held it up, feeling the weight of it. The dealer
at the gun store said it was a good personal protection weapon,
easy to master, with three safeties, so there was little chance
of an accident. The dealer sold him three fifteen-round clips,

8

too, and four boxes of ammunition. Together, he and the dealer loaded one of the clips and seated it into the weapon, then released it. Over and over, putting a bullet into the chamber each time, then ejecting the bullet. Over and over.

He would need to practice with his new gun. That's what the man said. Maybe he'd find a gun range tomorrow or the next day. God knows they were everywhere. He would have to teach himself a few basic things before he got to Kansas.

The dog began to whine. He'd been cooped up in the car all day and needed a walk. The quiet man got out the leash took Puck out into the surrounding woods as the rain slanted down, soaking them both. After a hundred yards or so, he stopped near a cluster of Sequoias. Puck looked up at him expectantly. The quiet man waited for another peal of thunder then pulled the trigger.

It wasn't his dog anyway.

Dan Parrish thanked the truck driver and waved goodbye to the back of the rig as it powered up and disappeared. He stretched his body this way and that, working the kinks out. He would have arrived earlier but the driver had run out of hours on his time sheet and had to stop and eat and then sleep. So rather than take his chances on the lone stretch of highway in the wee hours of the night, Dan decided to stay and listen to the guy's asthmatic snoring for hours.

He scanned the near horizon. Across the highway was a large, rustic wooden sign atop hand-stacked-and-mortared boulders. The sign read WELCOME TO ECHO and beneath it a smaller WELCOME TO ECHO and then a third, even smaller, WELCOME TO ECHO...

Dan smiled in spite of himself. Years ago someone with over-inflated expectations had insisted the sign be placed here. They extended the city limits, too, ostensibly so that rabbits and prairie dogs could have a post office box in town. He picked up his duffel bag and walked to the back corner of the sign and stared down at the cornerstone. He stood there for a minute, remembering things past, and shot a quick look around. There were no cars on the road and the sun was dying. Nobody would see him.

He quickly dropped to his knees and tugged on the stone, pulling away a loose chink of mortar. The rock came away and he placed it off to the side. He reached into the hollow and felt around for the package, his heart racing. The hole was smaller than he remembered and now filled with insect dirt and debris. He stabbed his hand in deeper. When he wiggled his fingers he got a hit, a flap of plastic sticking out from the rest of the detritus. He drew the little Ziploc out of its cave, his treasure, ignored all these years.

Dan Parrish opened the baggie and retrieved his class ring, awarded to him in 1998. It was engraved with the Echo High School monogram, the words *State Champs* emblazoned over the stone in the middle. He shirt-shined it then slipped it on his finger. It fit perfectly.

He fumbled in the Ziploc bag and pulled out a faded photograph. He raised himself to his feet then drew a deep breath. He examined the photo, the first time in eighteen years. The image drew him in, a blow to the solar plexus. For a moment he forgot to exhale.

She was everything—long, dark hair and slightly crooked nose and expressive blue eyes. A body that defied gravity. A smile that took my soul and carried it away.

Katy looked out from the old picture, posing in her cheerleader outfit. And he knew the smile was just for him.

Everything she did back then was just for him.

Dan wiped the photo on his shirt and pocketed it. He stood and slung his duffel over his shoulder and began walking.

Outside of town, at an old cemetery called God's Little Acre, Dan set his bundle down. The sun was dipping below the tree line and stars were beginning to emerge, making ready for the Kansas night. Dan stood outside the rusty gate. He could smell flowers. Someone had put gardenias on one of the graves close by. The heady scent reminded him of a long dead past, a vague recollection of his mother in the backyard garden.

The lightning bugs would soon emerge, and the still night air would begin to dance with their tiny industry. The cicadas would make a racket. The bats would appear and begin to hunt. It had been so long since he'd seen the place, and it hadn't looked like this eighteen years ago. It seemed larger back then, and less encumbered. Death had taken its toll. He retrieved his bag and opened the gate and entered, dropping the bag inside. He made his way to the back of the lot, passing tombstones marked with names he hadn't thought about since he was a boy. There were some that had been around since the 1800s, many his father and grandfather had known. He wondered if he would be buried here.

Then he found it. In front of Dan a tiny, weed-choked gravestone leaned backwards into the dirt. The inscription was indecipherable through the overgrowth. He stood for a time, staring down at the marker, his blood beginning to boil. He scuffed his feet into the ground and bit his lip and noticed he'd unconsciously balled his fists. His eyes swam.

Speechless, he turned and hiked back to the gate. He snatched up his duffel and stood on the road in the purple and blue light of the emerging moon.

CHAPTER 4

The fire-engine red Jeep raced down the road at almost twice the speed limit. Behind the wheel Chip Hunter peered into the night and blinked away the wind in his face and the whistling in his ears. He drank deeply from his beer bottle then wedged it back between his legs. Beside him his girlfriend, Darla Finch, clenched her teeth and prayed a raccoon, dog or deer wouldn't jump out in the road. A wreck was imminent. At least it felt that way. It always did with him at the wheel.

Chip was worth the risk, though, she thought. He had that special something that spelled Big Man on Campus, and later he would surely end up owning things. He had the blond hair and the blue eyes and the granite jaw. He was tall, too, and "hunky" according to all the other girls, including her own mother. He was also the starting quarterback for Echo JC. Her grandmother called him a keeper.

Plus his dad ran things in town. Nothing wrong with that, she decided, because the father also recognized Darla's potential assets. She could tell. The old man would lock his eyes on her teenage breasts and her perfect bottom, and he'd smile like the devil every time he heard her say "Hi, y'all!" with her Kansas twang. She knew that the sprinkle of freckles on her nose made her look younger than her nineteen years. She also knew the old man was a bit of a lecher, too, but she didn't give a whit. The son was all that mattered. And he was cool. And he liked to have a good time. Darla raised a beer to her lips and drank, pulling the bottle off to the side when she did so she could see how she looked in the rearview mirror.

Chip watched his girl admiring her image in the mirror as she drank. He snorted and took another long pull on his beer and stuffed the bottle back in his crotch. He took his foot off the gas and feathered the clutch, downshifting for the blind curve that was approaching. It was a little too early, but he'd been drinking and he didn't trust himself to pull a Jeff Gordon, power-sliding into the cemetery curve and shifting out of trouble in the nick of time. After all, he'd just gotten the car. He didn't want to test the roll bars yet.

"Why you do that?" he groused, watching Darla examine herself again.

"Do what?" She turned to him and smiled. She took another long drink, checking her reflection.

"You know what. You *look* at yourself every time you take a sip."

"Is there a law against it?" she asked, reaching out, tickling his ribs, causing him to squirm. Give her credit, she didn't deny she was doing it.

"If there ain't, there ought to be," he said, slapping her hands away, retrieving his beer, driving with his left elbow as they approached the curve.

They were still a few miles from Echo proper, so when Chip suddenly slowed down she was on it, seeming to follow his eyes just in time to see a man with long hair and a beard moving off the edge of the road in front of the old cemetery.

Chip idled down and flipped on his sidelights and took in the scene, locking eyes with the stranger. God's Little Acre— he knew the place well. And judging by the man's looks, he had probably been snooping around inside. Chip glanced over at Darla, who was staring at the guy, blinking her baby blues and already acting the whore. He scowled, suddenly angry, gunned the engine and swerved the jeep toward the shoulder, hurling his empty bottle at the vagrant. The man ducked his head just in time and Chip yanked the wheel back to the left. The front tires came off the ground and bounced once as the Jeep found the pavement again. Darla the beauty queen flopped like a rag doll and slid across and banged her head on the side of the seat back, then ricocheted back into her door panel. "Hey!"

In his rearview, Chip watched as the man just stood there, staring. The bottle had whistled past, then crashed into the rusty gate behind him, splintering into a million shards of glass. Chip gunned the engine again, popped the clutch, and the jeep lifted away down the highway.

It took Dan's heart a moment to slow as he watched the vehicle tear down the road, swerving across into the opposite lane for a hundred yards until the driver regained control. The beer bottle had just missed his face. An inch the other way and he'd be buried inside the gate of the cemetery rather than standing outside it. So much for wondering how he would be received in Echo. Welcome home, son.

In the Jeep, Chip said, "Gimme another beer." He kept his eyes straight ahead, refusing to look at Darla. The speedometer was climbing into the eighties.

"What is wrong with you—"

"Just get me a damn beer!"

They went over a rise and down between a stand of trees. Chip slowed to a reasonable speed while Darla retrieved a beer. They both took long gulps, not speaking. Darla finally held the cold bottle against her head.

"I'll bet you anything I have a bump as big as a walnut on my head tomorrow."

14

"A head like that *should* have bumps on it."

"Ha, ha, very funny." She took a sip, admiring herself in the rearview mirror again. "What did you go and do that to that poor man for anyway? He never did anything to you."

Chip had no answer. What could he say? "Did you see that guy's hair?" he blurted, weakly. It was the best he could do.

"Oh yeah," she purred. "I saw his hair alright."

Chip recognized that tone. That delivery. He knew what it meant. She'd used it on him for years. To keep him in place. And he hated it.

He stomped on the gas and tore down the road into Echo, finished his beer and tossed the empty bottle into the trees.

CHAPTER 5

Dan Parrish walked for hours around the town, past farms and schools and through the parking lots of rural stores and when he made his way further in, he saw the once-familiar shapes of unlit silos and wide-sided barns. He walked and smelled the great, dark expanses of late-season alfalfa and wheat. Then he crossed over a cattle grate and came to a meadow where, on the near side, cattle grazed and on the far end, an empty feed lot squatted, sullying the air during most of the year, when some local company fattened beef for slaughter. Then he hiked past the ramshackle sharecropper dwellings and the tumbledown outbuildings and he noticed that, as a whole, not much had changed. A few Latino families had moved into the outlying neighborhood—Punch Town, they called it—competing with the poor blacks for the available work. He saw kids playing in the side streets, black silhouettes or small eager shapes speaking Spanish in the dark.

He passed the old meat packing plant, now closed. He'd read the story a couple years back. At one time a man could earn a living wage there, but no more. The prior owner, Lamar Paris, had been driven to sell out and the new owners came in and fired everyone, then opened back up using undocumented labor at seven dollars an hour. In no time, the government stepped in and closed them down. No more Kansas Star Meats and no meat packers' float in the Christmas parade. Everybody loses.

When he crossed the railroad tracks he passed a sign: Echo, pop. 9,980. An increase since he'd left. The junior college had brought more people in. Another sign gave the route number and invited travelers to "Enjoy our Shopping District and Restaurants."

By the time he reached Main Street, the sidewalks were starting to close up for the evening. People were still about, men and women finishing up late chores or simply enjoying the evening cool-down. A few families strolled together, too, the kids scrubbed and healthy-looking, red cheeks and white teeth and clean clothes. School would be starting soon.

Dan kept walking, his head down but on a swivel, his eyes everywhere. His pattern was anything but random. He was in fact getting closer to the place he'd been thinking about for years.

The front door of the bakery had the *Closed* sign in the window. He remembered they always closed in the afternoon, then opened again in the wee hours. If you lived anywhere on their block the aroma of fresh baked breads and cakes and other goodies would wake you before dawn. Next door was Bern Carney's coffee shop, open all night, and down the street at the next corner an Italian restaurant—Smitelli's—that had been slinging pizzas and stuffing cannellonis for fifty years. Echo still had a bookstore, but judging by the window display, its days were numbered. And there was a Chat n Chew, a Dads n Lads, and a beauty parlor called Mane Street.

Clever, thought Dan. Mane Street. On Main Street.

One more block took him past a steak house that he didn't recognize and a barber shop—Mutter's Barber Shop—that he did. The laundromat was on the corner and it still sported a bulletin board, surprising in a day and age where everything was digital. He stopped to examine the yellowed index cards, some of which were in Spanish. Somebody had scrawled Lern English! directly onto the corkboard beneath them. There were lawn mowers for sale and trucks and appliances and old furniture and bedding. Someone had puppies they were giving away; someone else wanted fifty dollars for a bowling ball and bag. An outdated SLR camera was offered, and a motorcycle and various tools.

Dan left the laundromat and shifted his pack over to his other shoulder and turned left off Main Street onto Elm.

Just past ten o'clock, he reached his destination and stood outside a clapboard house that had once been modest, but was now just plain ostentatious. Beside him an ornate mailbox read *HUNTER* on its flank in large gilt lettering. He looked around. None of the neighbors had a mailbox so extravagant. Most of the neighbors couldn't afford such gingerbread. In fact, they were probably asleep or getting ready for bed. The following day was Friday, a work day, and in this part of the country your labor and your daily bread were taken seriously. He turned his attention back to the house, sizing up the place as best he could in the dark. Where once there was a little front porch, now there was a wide, elaborate veranda. The front door was gaudy, too, with cut glass mounted in white oak. It was flanked by big palms in potted profusion, each vase painted a different pattern of southwest style hieroglyphics. The old front window had been replaced by a single pane, and Dan could see the light was on behind the curtain in the front room. Moths circled in frenetic ecstasy around the porch light. In the driveway, a black Town Car and a white BMW sat side by side, a display that made him notice that every other car on the block seemed to be a truck or sedan.

He could feel the bile rising with his heartbeat.

At once a silhouette walked into the front room, a female form, backlit by the soft lights from the interior. Parrish stood frozen, his heart hammering in his chest. He quickly stepped into a deep shadow and watched as a man's outline appeared, grabbing the woman, shaking her. A muffled argument ensued while Parrish stood there, hands balled into fists again, watching, helpless. After a moment another figure moved into view, a larger shadow, separating the two. "Knock it off, you guys!" The words echoed in Dan's ears as the three shadows fell away and back into the diffused amber glow of distance.

Dan realized he'd been holding his breath. He let it out with a rush and picked up his duffel bag and stepped back to leave. He backed toward the street, almost tripping over a pair of extended deer lights mounted on the bumper of a brand-new, red Jeep Wrangler, partially hidden in the deep shadows between their property and the next door neighbors'. Parrish examined it as closely as he dared. The license plate read *BLU CHIPPR*. The back seat floor mat was wet with melted ice and littered with beer bottles, the same brand as the one that had narrowly missed him outside the cemetery.

He shook his head then backed out of the shadows and stood on the cracked sidewalk. Insects sang in his ears.

A few blocks later he stood outside an old board-and-batten affair hiding inside high thickets of overgrown yard plants. There was a sad picket fence and a prodigious willow tree that wept over the squalor in the front yard.

There was something else in the yard: a *ROOM FOR RENT* sign.

Dan dropped his bag and scanned the house. He saw two stories of chipped paint, torn screens and sagging beams. When a light came on in the kitchen, he viewed it as a sign, an omen, and decided now was as good a time as any.

CHAPTER 6

Millie Slocum stood in the dim halo of porch light and examined Dan Parrish. After a moment she turned and led him through the kitchen and into a short hallway connecting to the garage. She seemed much older than Dan, forty-five going on sixty thanks to years of cheap vodka and unfiltered cigarettes. Her face was a leathery wickerwork of failed girlishness when she turned and smiled at him for the first time. "You said your name is Dan?" she asked. Her baritone voice had been dragged through the smoke house for too many years.

"Yes, ma'am," he said. "Dan Parrish." He held his breath, worried she might recognize the name.

She smiled again, and blinked her painted eyelids. "I'm Millie," she said. Her teeth were as yellow as a sunrise, her body a swizzle stick. She wore a faded housecoat gaping open at the throat to reveal paps like empty grain sacks.

A moment went by. When Dan didn't respond to her overtures she reached out and flipped a light switch in the little hallway, the single dirty bulb revealing an open door. Inside the door, Dan could see a cot with clean sheets and a pillow with an army blanket folded on top. It sat amid a garage diorama of rusty tools and bric-a-brac: a bike, a lawn mower, a bench with a vise and various greasy tools, a pile of rakes and hoes and shovels, a broom, an old barbecue grill.

Any other person would have seen squalor. Dan saw opportunity.

"You use the downstairs bathroom just past the kitchen." She pulled a cigarette butt from a pocket in her housecoat and lit it with a Zippo. "Fifty a week," said Millie, "due every Friday night. No checks, no chicks, no problems."

"You need some kind of deposit?"

Millie sucked smoke into her lungs and looked Dan up and down, devouring him with her rheumy orbs. "We'll work it out," she said, flashing a K9 smile. She exhaled spirals of smoke through her nostrils and into the air in a way that she had probably come to believe was sexy.

It wasn't.

For the second time Dan refused to take the bait. Somewhere outside, a barn owl hooted. Dan decided to move past her and examine his new quarters. As he did, she stopped him with a spatulate hand to his chest. "Uh uh, Romeo," she said. "The fifty bucks." She snapped her fingers for emphasis and Dan was reminded of a television show he'd seen, a nature program displaying a reef of angry Fiddler crabs, clicking their claws. She took another drag and the smoke curled up into her left eye. She clamped it shut, unintentionally giving Dan her best Popeye imitation.

"It's only Tuesday," he replied.

"Yeah, well, it'll be Friday soon enough."

Dan dropped his duffel, dug out his dog-eared wallet and paid Millie Slocum. She tucked the money into her loose bosom, and as he tried to squeeze past her toward his new bed, she swelled like a cobra to get a feel of him going by. Then she stood in the threshold, ogling him like newly acquired property. Dan found another light, a bulb on a wire hanging down from the rafter above the cot. He pulled the string. The light came on. Millie's face warped into shadows and disappeared when he coolly shut the door with the heel of his foot.

He waited for a time until he heard Millie's footsteps pad away, then he sat down on his dilapidated mattress and tested the creaky springs. He nodded to himself, thankful the whole thing didn't buckle and jackknife from his weight. He lifted the blanket to his nose. It was rough and smelled of mothballs and cigarette smoke, yet would keep him warm enough during the upcoming fall evenings. The sheets were threadbare but clean, and at the head of the bed there was a discolored pillow in a Charlie Brown pillowcase.

Dan stood again and took in the rest of his surroundings. He noticed the dusty cobwebs and empty cocoons. When he began to pry a little he found a rusty sickle inside a little, red Radio Flyer wagon that had been marking time under a fake Christmas tree and a pile of Christmas decorations. He raised the sickle and tested the blade with his thumb. Rust never sleeps, he thought. He took special inventory of the tools on the work bench and came away with a hand rasp. He sat back down on his cot and began to sharpen the blade. He wasn't tired. He was antsy and rejuvenated by finding the sickle. There was a full moon tonight. Plenty of light for what he had in mind.

He ran the rasp over the hardened steel until it was razor sharp. Then he stood and left through the side door, the sickle hanging at his side.

CHAPTER 7

Dan stood on a sidewalk in a wash of moonlight, surveying the immediate scene. When he didn't detect anything unusual or hear anything but insects, he stepped toward the tall pine tree in front of the Hunter house a dozen yards away. He stood in the dark shadow of the tree trunk, turning the sickle slowly in his hand. The night was so hot he was sweating. He could smell the pine and the muggy rot of a nearby irrigation ditch that bordered the field behind the house. The pine tree and the mud odors and the night sounds all brought back memories from his youth.

A car sound intruded, motor idling. When the beat-up sedan approached, its headlights cut through the mists. Then the car stopped.

Echo was not a late-night town. So the young black man, Belden Ferguson, didn't make a habit of driving around at this hour, especially not in this neighborhood, and especially not in front of this particular house. There were unwritten rules, and one of them was related to prowling in the dark where he didn't belong. Except he hadn't been able to sleep and he was worried about his financial situation, and he had been at the coffee shop and made things worse visiting with Shyla, the waitress, and pouring caffeine down his gullet. So now here he was, stopped on the road, eyes bugged and brain on steroids from the caffeine. And he thought he'd seen someone or something, but wasn't sure. He'd better not stay too long like this, though. He was young—twenty-five—and alone. Even though he was dressed for work, people around here immediately thought trouble when they saw the likes of him in their neighborhoods at night. Unless they knew him from the feed store warehouse or the gas station.

Still, if he was right, someone else was lurking, and whoever it was, carried something that had a long handle and something metallic that reflected the moonlight. He shoved the vehicle into first and his transmission clunked. When his gears caught his back wheels screeched as he drove away, the sounds loud in the empty night.

No, sir, it would not be good to be caught out here at night.

No, *Suh.*

Dan stepped from the shadows and watched the car move away, the sickle spinning in his hand. Then a light came to life deep inside the Hunter house and Dan knew a porch light would soon follow. An old car that clunked and squealed would wake a light sleeper. He took a last look at the mailbox, then folded himself into the shadows and began to trot. He was in good shape; he could run for miles.

By the time he reached God's Little Acre his shirt was drenched with perspiration and his eyes were stinging with fatigue. He leaned against the fence a while, catching his breath, then opened the gate and retraced his earlier steps through the property. He stood once more in front of the headstone. He fell to his knees and began to cut the weeds away. The solitary chore made him think. And on this most lonely of nights, despite his best efforts, he grew emotional. A few minutes later he stood to examine his work.

The little marble slab that read *JOHN HENRY*, nothing

more. A tear ran down Dan's cheek, escaping into the dir his face, leaving a trail of infinite sorrow. He hadn't crie many years, even during the times when he'd had ample son to. Letting the world see his pain was not in the ca and he'd be damned if he was going to let it happen in pub

He closed his eyes tight and used the back of his arn wipe away the evidence. Then he found his sickle in the d: gripped it by its handle, snapped his arm back and slung sending the worn tool in an arc that wolf-whistled thro the damp night and embedded itself into a brooding oak c side the cemetery fence.

He started off for Echo. It would be a couple hours bef he reached his new home. He wanted to be there before s up. He had to win over the new landlady and her tenants.

And he knew just how to do it.

CHAPTER 8

Hot-water steam erupted from the bathroom faucet and fogged the vanity mirror. Millie Slocum squinted into the cloud and squirted a dab of shaving cream into her palm. She daubed the lather between her eyes, taking care to go by the lines she'd drawn with an eyebrow pencil. A bristly shadow had marked the center of her uni-brow, and it was time to clean things up a bit. She placed the razor on the right hash mark above her nose, and slid it across...

...just as her dog silently bounded up onto the toilet seat ring and yapped his approval.

Millie started, lurching upward. One of her canary yellow mules slid across the tiles, making her twist around and bump into the wooden wall rack that held six of her tattered, hand-washed brassieres. Her elbow thwacked into the edge of the shower door and she sat down hard on the toilet seat ring that her dog had just vacated. When she stood and regained her composure, she caught her image in the mirror and didn't like what she saw. A half-inch of left eyebrow was gone.

"Damn you, Larry!"

She snatched up a jumbo-sized can of Aqua Net, turned and bombed the little Jack Russell now standing in the threshold. The hair spray temporarily blinded the dog and forced his frizzy hair to spike.

Millie retrieved her cigarette from the ashtray on the toilet tank, took a drag, and checked her image in the mirror again.

She took another drag, pulling the smoke into her lungs and blowing it out. There was nothing to do but shave the other side to match the screw-up. She bit down on the cigarette, pulled her hair away from her forehead, and was just about to deliver the *coup-de-grace* when she smelled something. She began sniffing the air like a bloodhound picking up a scent. She frowned. On her way out the bathroom door she kicked at Larry and expertly flicked her butt like a comet into the toilet.

In the kitchen she found her new boarder serving something to her other two tenants—the twins, Booker and Baker—eighty years old but still spry and mischievous. They'd been living in her house for almost ten years now, and never caused much of a problem unless someone gave them beer, which brought out the twinkle. They must have been hungry, because they were chowing down with gusto, at least until they saw Millie.

They both looked up and smiled—eggs between their teeth—guilty as hell. If they were a dance team they'd get the gold.

She practically ran across the kitchen and confronted her hunky new sleep-in. "Who are you, Bobby-frickin'-Flay?" She looked down into the skillet. Some sort of omelet look-alike presented itself.

The twins nudged each other. Millie shot them a look, catching her image in the cabinet glass. Shave cream still decorated her occipital ridge. She wiped the telltale lather away with a swipe of her hand and glared at the old brothers. They looked away, clearing throats, trying not to laugh.

Her new tenant said, "It's just eggs, ma'am."

Millie took a closer look into the pan. Along with the eggs, there was a strata of colors that included lumps of sausage, with red and green peppers, scallions, white button mushrooms, and a couple of different cheeses.

"Eggs, my ass," Millie squawked. "What is it?" She picked up a fork and poked at the concoction like it was a dead rat.

Booker spoke up. "It's a *frittata*. It's I-talian. Like an omelet..."

"...but with a PhD," finished Baker.

The twins regarded one another.

"Good one, Baker."

"Thank you, Booker."

Parrish looked away, smiled.

"A frittater?" Millie asked, butchering the word.

"Yes, indeed." Dan pulled up a chair for her to sit. He poured her a cup of coffee and set a plate in front of her. She sniffed, took a mammoth bite and her face lit up.

"Damn."

She took another bite.

"A woman might could get used to this," she said. Her mouth was full, so it sounded like a bunch of vowels strung together. She continued to eat.

After she swallowed, she tried again. Mae West, not Millie, should have delivered the next flirtatious line to Dan. She said, "A woman might also wonder what other, uh, skills a man such as yourself might possess." She looked up and winked at Dan.

The twins coughed in unison.

Dan raised his eyebrows. He held his breath.

Millie was unfazed by the long pause. *Maybe this guy needs a little push.* She stood and turned to face her new tenant. She leaned forward into his space. "Mmm," she said, "I-talian frit-ta-ta. The *sausage* is what makes it. Nothing like a good sausage." Her robe yawned open and her sad topside swam into Dan's view.

Dan blew air and blinked. He decided to act dumb. "You bet," he squeaked and quickly turned away.

Millie sighed. Defeated, she sat back down.

Dan went to the sink and started washing dishes. He smiled to himself.

I'm in, he thought.

CHAPTER 9

Echo Junior College was an unremarkable facility whose red brick buildings sprawled over fifty acres in the middle of town. On this day, the first of September, the sidewalks bustled with young men and women involved with registration and book buying and all things matriculation. Some of the students gathered in groups, comparing schedules. Some sat beneath the trees, fussing with new-fangled educational apps. Some were already starting to worry about the moment their professors would hand them a syllabus for the semester, forever spoiling any free time they'd planned over the next few months.

Registration took place in the old Echo JC gym, a cavernous chamber appropriately named, smelling of pine and sweat, sounding like blower fans in need of new bearings. It was filled to bursting with student enrollment. A few were dropping classes, others were picking up new ones, and some were just plain flummoxed.

Dan Parrish was one of the latter.

He sat by himself at a bench, in front of a school computer, not willing to speak, vexed by the process and intimidated by the technology he'd never experienced. He was way behind the curve and knew it. Dan watched as the new students moved in and out of the computer kiosks like they were born to it.

And they *were* born to it, committing their keyboard circumnavigations as they learned to walk and talk. But Dan was older, maybe the oldest student in the building, and he'd never been good at following coded instructions and tiny icons that kept secrets from being revealed. The academic staff was there to help, but they also spoke in technology riddles. All but one.

"Need some help?"

Dan looked up. A young woman smiled at him. She was thirty maybe, with auburn hair and a lithe figure and a summer weight suit that said staff. And she had dimples, a feature Dan had always been a sucker for.

"It's that obvious, huh?"

"Let's just say I've seen the look before." She took a seat beside him, close enough so that he could smell her perfume. Their shoulders touched as she reached across and opened his folder. His heart began to beat a little faster and his face felt hot.

"Okay, what's the problem?" she said, slipping a pair of reading glasses over her nose to study his paperwork. When Dan didn't respond right away, she turned and faced him.

When he found his voice he said, "I'm trying to decide between English Lit or Communications 101."

"That's easy," she said. When she smiled her dimples came to the fore. "Take English Lit with this professor." She leaned into him to underscore a name with her felt pen. Dan smelled her fragrance again and he felt the warmth radiating from her body. A wisp of her hair tickled the side of his face as it tumbled from her shoulders. He noticed her slender neck and her green eyes and the freckles on her arms.

Then he read out loud the name she was pointing to in the book. "Agnes Stankowiecz." He looked up. "Yikes. That's old-school ugly."

"Yeah, but she's really good." The woman capped her pen.

"With a name like that she better be." He smiled, loosening up a little, warming to his helper.

She beamed at his joke, then added, "Well, you know what they say. 'What's in a name? That—'"

"'—which we call a rose, by any other name would smell as sweet,'" he finished, feeling just a tad silly.

The woman sat back, hands folded neatly in her lap, impressed. "A Shakespeare aficionado, I see."

"Shakespeare? Nah. I pulled that from *The Flintstones.*"

She grinned again and stood. "Cute." Then she pointed at her watch. "Gotta run. See ya 'round." She gathered her things, waved, and just like that she belonged to the mists...

...while the rest of the world intruded: the students swirled and eddied like bees, the pine and sweat smells poured into his nose, the fans rattled and echoed off the rafters like ghost noises in a cathedral, the computer screen asked for him to CONTINUE or GO BACK...

...and the best looking girl he'd seen in ages walked out between the tables and into the confusion.

Dan watched her backside navigate the crowds. He wished she hadn't left so soon. Except that he was also relieved she'd left so soon. He was puzzled. Maybe he wanted her to leave, or maybe he wanted to talk more. It had been so long since he'd done anything like that. The overriding rule where he'd been was to always keep your thoughts to yourself. Or else.

He caught a last glimpse of her retreating form as she slipped from the gym and wondered if he'd see her again. He stood and headed for another door on the opposite wall. Recess was over. Time to buckle down. So far, the day had been a mild success. He'd managed to do most of his enrolling into the local junior college. Good for him. And he would for sure sign up for Ms. Stank-o-Witch's class. Advice from a girl who had been here for a while and who was so easy on the eyes was not to be ignored. But there was something more pressing he had to turn his attention to. Something he needed badly if he was going to make a go of Echo, Kansas.

He needed a job.

He worked his way through the masses and left the gym. He followed the sidewalk to the Administration Building and soon found the Financial Aid office, where he spotted a bulletin board under a heading that said ON-CAMPUS EMPLOY-MENT. He ran his finger down the glass, scouring the listings.

Within a few moments he discovered this list was not for him. There were job titles like Graphics Design Consultant, Computer Repair Tech and Digital Programmer this and that. One ad said Opportunities in Laser Optics and Liquid Flow Modeling Characteristics. He was invited to join the Games Development and Diagnostics Research Staff if he qualified.

He didn't even know what a USB port was. He thought for sure somebody has misspelled BUS. And who the hell was Skype?

There was nothing he could remotely understand on the board. No mowing lawns or mopping floors or what he was really hoping for: cooking. The list was from a world as foreign to him as hybrid cars and cell phones. It spoke in a language he didn't know. The whole country now floated around him in code words and symbols he'd never contemplated. What was an e-trade? A byte? An app? What the hell was virtual sex?

He took a dog-eared document from his pocket and unfolded the single page. It was time stamped and notarized. It said:

KANSAS DEPARTMENT OF CORRECTIONS
Required protocols for newly released inmates.

Near the bottom of the page there was a heading regarding employment. He had fourteen days to secure a job. His whole life depended on getting that job. There was no way he was going to go back.

No way.

* * *

In Cheyenne Wells, Colorado, the quiet man fired off two

boxes of shells in the Shots Fired Gun Range on Highway 40. The targets were paper silhouettes of bad guys. He loaded his own clips, and ejected them, and went through the safety-on, safety-off drills. And hit the bad guy silhouette in the middle of the chest. He bought two more boxes of ammunition before he left.

He thought about the dog. The way he looked up at him. Puck.

What a stupid, stupid name.

CHAPTER 10

Dan lay on his cot in the soft light provided by an open dormer window over the outside door. His hands were folded behind his head as he stared up at the dirt-spackled rafters above. He'd been trying to fall asleep without any luck, and for the past hour he'd given up, learning the locations of the overhead spiders, watching as they went about the business of food gathering and home rebuilding. He glanced across the divide at his alarm clock, a wind-up version he'd found in a trash can. He winced at the late hour, but there was nothing to do about it except to try to relax and take things as they came. Everyone else had a routine; maybe he would have one soon. Be a spider, he said to himself. But then he started thinking about the past again. He had so many years to recover, and so many sorrows to reconcile.

He heard a click and saw a ribbon of brighter light beneath the door to the kitchen. Somebody was awake, maybe one of the twins heating up a glass of milk or sneaking a midnight bite of the chocolate cheesecake he'd made earlier in the week.

Or maybe it was Millie, cadging another shot of rotgut because she couldn't sleep. It was that time of night, the time when the booze stopped anesthetizing and a drinking person's world began to vibrate behind the eyes. Millie sometimes needed a little hair of the dog to make it through till morning. Dan couldn't begrudge her that. Who was he to try to proselytize? *Your life's in the dumpster, Millie.* Yeah, right. Coming from him? What a joke.

Millie stood in the kitchen and gripped her cheap vodka. A cigarette burned in the ashtray. She poured a double shot. Then she set the bottle down and picked up the glass and drank it down, peeling her lips away from the sting. It was the middle of the night, but she still had her makeup on, and if she had any guts at all she'd knock on Dan's door and go in and climb into his arms and show him what a real woman could do. She picked up her cigarette and drew.

She could tell that he was shy, although she didn't know why. There was nothing wrong with him; she could see that. But for some reason he backed off at any sort of approach, and she knew she wasn't as young or pretty as she used to be, but hell, for medicinal purposes only, it couldn't hurt to experiment a little. Men, she knew, could overlook the lack of beauty for the useful. Her old boyfriend had been like that. Always grousing and running away, until she grabbed him by the pecker and made him sit and roll over.

That was twenty years ago.

Millie looked at her reflection in the glass of one of the cabinets. She smiled at the image. *Screw it*, she thought. *I'm in my nicest, shortest nighty. My assets are front and center!*

She strode down the hall and flung the door open...

...Dan Parrish was gone.

Dan had given up on sleep. Eighteen years of his life to make up, and lying on a cot pretending to be calm and collected, docile even, was not as easy as he'd hoped. The spiders above him had a plan; everyone that succeeded had a plan. Now, each hour of each day was a challenge. And the intensity of nights, too. You're free, Dan, except in your head.

He stood outside the Hunter house, beneath the low branches of the big pine tree, a tree he had planted with his father a lifetime ago. The clouds had obscured the late moon, forcing an oily blackness to envelop the land. The air was thick with early moisture and gauzed by the mists over the houses. Nothing stirred, not even the crickets. Time slowed and disappeared as Dan gazed at the picture window in the front of the place. Maybe if he hung around long enough he could will the woman to show herself. Maybe he could force a different life, a new outcome, a world that swirled away the dirt and grime like a bathtub drain. A world that offered a new start.

Eighteen years of a man's life should be worth something. Eighteen years where every day was a fight to forget, then a fight to remember. Sometimes the concrete and the wire became too much and the dreams of the girl that was now a grown woman, someone else's woman, would overwhelm him. As he counted off the years he thought about what she would be doing. Kids, maybe, and a job somewhere and Christmas times and summers and the light that shined through her hair in the mornings and made his knees buckle and his heart unravel.

But no matter how badly he wanted to, he couldn't rewind the clock.

Then a gun barrel stabbed Dan Parrish in the side of the head. He'd seen the shadow a millisecond earlier, but before he tried to turn and duck, he was paralyzed by the click of the hammer being drawn back. He exhaled. He relaxed his neck muscles, letting the cold steel push his head into the trunk of the tree.

"I figured you'd show up sooner or later," said Rick Hunter. His hair smelled of the pomade he always wore and he spoke around the ubiquitous toothpick. His words came out lathered with an insouciance inspired by bourbon. Rick Hunter, Dan decided, held a grudge that would never be reconciled, even if he had long ago been declared the winner and had walked away with the prize, the girl, the life…

"Why shouldn't I be here?" he said. "This is my house."

"Was," Rick said. He poked Dan's head with the pistol barrel for emphasis. He gestured across at the mailbox. "Do the math, Einstein," he whispered. "It says Hunter." A light came on in the house. "And that's *my* old lady, now."

"Is that what you call her? Your old lady?" Parrish stared at the front door. Rick Hunter barked a laugh. "I call her whatever I want…*killer*."

Parrish stiffened. His heart began to hammer, the blood rising into his face, hot and prickly with something more than rage. He started to turn, but Hunter stopped him with another poke of the gun barrel, this time to the cheek.

"Just like you to hide behind a gun."

"Funny, coming from a man hiding behind a tree." Another light came on inside the house. Parrish swallowed hard. He'd have to make a decision soon. Fight or flight. Either way was a bad choice. Hunter had the deck stacked. He ran things in this town.

Dan took a swipe at diplomacy. "Look, I don't want any trouble. I just want to get on with things. A man's got a right to start over, doesn't he?"

"Sure," said Hunter. "A *man* does." He let the insult sink in.

Parrish realized he was beat. He had no cards to play. Standing in another man's yard, creeping another man's trophies in the middle of the night. What was he doing here, anyway? Why did he decide that this kind of thing could solve anything? The only result would be bad, an end of everything, and more years of heavy gauge wire and concrete walls.

The two men stood silent, awkward and angry, jaws clenched, breathing the acid vapors of hate. An air conditioner kicked on beside the neighbor's house. A cat yowled from the shadows, then tore through the shrubs and away into the blackness.

"You aren't calling the signals anymore, Parrish," said

Hunter. "I am. So leave. Or I'll send you right back where you came from." He prodded Dan's head with the pistol.

Parrish backed a step and turned and took another step, then another. When he got to the sidewalk he looked back, just as the front door opened and a woman appeared, the light pouring out around her, her face illuminated.

Katy, his Katy, older, as beautiful as ever.

"Who is it, Rick?" she called.

"Nobody."

Rick Hunter took a breath and watched Dan Parrish turn around and walk away. "Just an old drunk is all," he said.

Rick Hunter stood for a minute in the shadows of the pine tree as he watched Dan walk away, swallowed up by the darkness. He realized his knees were threatening to give way. Then he looked down at the gun that had been given to him by his father many years ago.

His hands were trembling.

CHAPTER 11

On the first day of school Dan Parrish was beyond nervous. Even the walk to the campus had panicked him. Barking dogs had made him wince. Even when he passed the bakery, the aroma failed to dislodge his trepidations. As he approached the complex of buildings, the surrounding road, King's Highway, was a traffic jam of cars lined up for blocks, with students vying for parking spots and parents saying goodbye-good luck to their recent high school graduates. They carried themselves with much more confidence than Dan did. They looked the part.

He didn't. Not by a long shot.

He found his first period building without any trouble, but then he had to shoulder his way through a crowd of people half his age, all clothed in understated chic, or outlandish costumes, a group as diverse as any gamut would allow. He had never considered that his jeans and sneakers might be out of place, but these students didn't look like any farm kids he remembered. Guys wore surf shirts from Billabong or Quiksilver. Girls had bare bellies, yoga pants, NFL jerseys, depending on their particular outlook, and the only other person he saw that might have been almost his age sported a crew cut and naked lady tattoos on his shoulders and biceps. And he was a janitor! There were suits and ties and NASCAR T-shirts and golf polos, and if the 4-H Club was extant, Dan couldn't find any evidence of it.

When he crossed the threshold into the classroom door

and sat down, front and center, a nervous Dan had to squint until his eyes acclimated themselves to the fluorescent lighting and the stark white walls. There was nowhere to hide. He felt like a lab rat in a cage. Then the other students began filing in and taking seats. The looks he got made him feel like the main feature in a carnival freak show. Surely this was a first day procession that would deteriorate with time. He literally gulped and sure enough, the girl beside him heard it and looked at him.

A few minutes before the bell, Chip Hunter ambled through the door. Dan recognized him as the kid who threw the bottle, the driver of the red Jeep outside his old house. In a town of ten thousand, in a school of five thousand, Dan had somehow drawn the Hunter card again.

Chip was a big, good-looking kid for sure, but the swagger didn't impress Dan, and the nodding and chuckling and winking at everyone were irritants and an affront to Dan's sensibilities. Even so, he decided to take the high road and look straight ahead. After all, Dan was not controlling anything around here, and if he hoped to do well, to even survive his homecoming, he'd better get used to the idea that other forces were at work, hormone and estrogen levels were off the charts, and the local pecking order didn't include Dan Parrish. He figured that Chip would recognize him, yet the last thing he wanted was a confrontation.

Chip, though, wasn't observing the paradigm. When he spotted Dan he stopped, snorted, and pondered the ponytail. He said aloud to the class, "Yo, check it out! American Idol!"

Dan didn't understand the joke, but when the class burst out laughing he shrunk a little lower in his seat. Then Chip made his first big mistake of the day when he put his hand on Parrish's hair, flipping the ponytail up with a roll of his wrist, like he was allowed to pass judgment and it was all right to invade another person's space if you were a big shot.

In the place where Dan Parrish had spent the last eighteen years of his life, one of the cardinal rules that everyone observed was inviolable: *Never touch another man.*

Never.

What happened next was so lightning fast and skilled, that the populace of Echo Junior College would be talking about it for the rest of the year. Dan jumped to his feet and snatched Chip's arm up so high and tight behind his back that the kid dropped his books and cried out in pain.

A jock buddy of Chip's, a student-athlete named Jimmy Durr, lurched to his feet and took a step toward the older guy who'd accosted his friend.

Dan narrowed his eyes and looked at the potential threat. "Sit down or you're next," he hissed, the first time he'd felt control of anything all morning.

The young man recognized a serious ass-whipping might be in the cards and backed into his seat.

Dan put his mouth to Chip's ear. "You wanna keep this arm?" Chip tried to wrestle his limb free, but it wasn't going to happen.

"What kinda question is that?" he cried. His words had ended on a high note, making the sentence sound like a plea. His swagger had deserted him.

"A rhetorical one," Dan said, giving the arm a little more torque.

"A *what*?" The boy was almost in tears.

Parrish drew a deep breath. Then the suddenness with which he had over-reacted stung him and he looked up to see all eyes paying close attention, watching a crazy older guy fixing to kill Chip Hunter, football star. How did he let this thing happen? Why did he go so crazy at something so slight? He glanced around the room, the kids all blinking and staring, the vacant white walls admonishing, the whiteboard that was supposed to be a blackboard saying *WHOA*, and the ceiling lights buzzing their disdain. He knew he'd placed a target on his back before the first bell.

"Forget it," he said, releasing his grip, shoving Chip to-

41

ward an open desk.

Dan took his seat and looked down at his desktop, refusing to acknowledge the stares, listening to the blood pound in his ears, trying to control his breathing. *Maybe I'll pick my things up and leave right now, before it gets worse. If I can't control myself just a little, just a tiny bit, however long it takes to become a normal person, maybe I'll have to look somewhere else for salvation.*

He had made a promise to his father years ago: *I will graduate from college, Dad. If it's the last thing I do. I promise.* Except he hadn't realized how hard it was going to be. So who did he make that promise to, anyway? The person that was Dan Parrish all those years ago? Or to the man who flips out and accosts a kid for something trivial that in the real world didn't matter a hill of beans?

Dan stayed in his seat. He held his head up and put his blinders on and stared straight ahead at the blackboard, ignoring everything around him. He needed this classroom. He needed this life.

When Darla Finch, the girlfriend of the boy he'd just humiliated, tiptoed in two minutes before the bell, he ignored her too. But she didn't ignore him. She slithered to her desk, shooting looks at Chip who shut her down with one cold hard stare that said, *Don't even think about it!*

Then the woman from registration walked in, and Dan was so surprised, he almost forgot himself and spoke up. She saw him and approached, taking the open seat next to his. She didn't seem to notice when the other students stared.

"So you made it," she said, and there was that smile, dimples and all.

The fire in Dan's heart melted away, and the trepidation in his stomach moderated. He did his best to act as if nothing had just happened. "Yeah," he said, "I'm real, um…excited."

"You look it," she said. "Your face is kinda flushed, Mister…"

"Parrish. Dan Parrish."

* * *

Behind them Jimmy Durr nudged Chip and drew a make-believe knife across his throat. Chip nodded back. He had been embarrassed. He needed to regain some of the mojo he'd lost.

Except in such a closed society it wasn't easy. Especially with entities like Facebook, and all the other invasive, computerized distractions around. With the help of social media, the confrontation was more than likely sweeping the campus like wildfire. Chip's reputation might have huge problems recovering.

Darla had been in the hall for most of the dust up. She'd been able to peek in and watch from the cheap seats, and now she was studying Dan's back, liking the way it looked, liking the way he handled himself. She also liked the blue of his eyes and the square shoulders and the sinew in his forearms as he toyed with his notebook, talking quietly with the lady on his right. She wondered what it would feel like to have those same arms wrapped around her body. She decided to find out before the end of the semester. Old guys rule, she thought, especially when they were as good looking as this dude.

The bell rang. The lady beside the old dude said, "Nice to meet you, Dan Parrish."

"Likewise. And you are—?"

The dimpled lady stood and strode to the whiteboard. She wrote *Dr. Agnes Stankowiecz* across the top. Then she walked back to an abashed Dan Parrish with a stack of documents and a twinkle in her eye. "Mr. Parrish, would you be so kind as to pass out this semester's syllabus?"

Parrish stood and began to distribute the material. He looked confused.

* * *

Later that afternoon Dan sat on an empty bench and watched a squirrel gnaw an acorn into little pieces, reminding him of his own empty belly. After that first class, things had gone a little smoother. Maybe he would calm down at some point, and maybe in the future his mind would step in before his mouth or his fists screwed things up. All he needed was a little dedication, like he'd dreamt about all those years. Or like the squirrel that sat in front of him now. He needed only one thing on his mind; everything else could go to hell. I'm a squirrel and I need that acorn. My whole world is that acorn. And a job. I gotta have that job, too.

He looked up in time to see Agnes hurrying across the parking lot with an armful of books and a valise. He stood and hustled across the yard to cut her off. His feet slapped the macadam as he approached, which so startled her, the handful of books went flying. She spun and raised her valise and ducked her head like someone being attacked.

He stood back, embarrassed. Somehow he'd done it again. First time he insulted her, this time he'd frightened her.

She put a palm to her chest and glanced sideways, around the lot, back to Dan, who was now on all fours trying to gather her things. He felt positively sick when he handed her the disheveled mess that was her study material.

"I am so sorry, I didn't mean to startle you…"

She didn't speak. She must have been still gathering her wits and trying to calm her pounding heart. He held her books and waited while she regained her composure.

He said, "Look. About today in class. Your name. I had no idea…"

She smiled then, and held up her hand, stopping his apology cold.

"Oh, forget it. It was funny. You should have seen the look on your face. Priceless."

"Yeah, but still—"

She stopped and faced him. "I tell you what. Buy me a coffee

44

someday and we'll try not to let it affect your grade. How's that?"

Good. She had a sense of humor. "You got it, Professor—"

"Agnes."

"Yes," he nodded.

"Say it."

"Agnes."

"See? That wasn't so bad, was it?" She got in her car, backed up, waved and drove away. Dan watched until she was a speck in the distance.

"No," he said, "that wasn't bad at all."

The quiet man likes to drive at night. He sleeps all day, then gets into his car and drives across the prairie and thinks about night things—how he looks at night, how to stand and sit and breathe. He imagines the world ending just past the reach of his headlights. No fields, no people, just black.

He'd had no trouble finding his target. Everything is on the internet these days. If he doesn't know an address yet, he'll be patient and investigate. Leg work, they call it. The money he was going to spend on a skip tracer went toward the gun and lease of the rental car. That was smart.

At dawn, outside of Wallace, Kansas, the quiet man pulled into a gas station. He went inside and gave the clerk a twenty. Outside, the quiet man put the nozzle in the tank and triggered it and began to sing a childhood ditty to himself, one he'd learned from his mother whom he loved so deeply it confused him at times.

"From here to there to Madison Square, when I get there, I'll pull your hair. From here to there to Madison Square, when I get there I'll pull your hair—"

Then the pump clicked off, the nozzle shooting gas out the pipe onto his pants, infuriating him. "God damn it, God damn it, God damn it," he said through clenched teeth, over and over again, the first words he had spoken in days.

He tried to pull the handle out of the tank, but the coil on the nozzle hooked itself in and wouldn't come free. He fought and fought, yanking on the handle, getting louder and more desperate with each tug. The only other customer, a local woman, watched the display, mildly amused as the quiet man finally gripped the nozzle with both hands and gave a mighty pull, separating the spigot from his car, landing on his ass between the passenger door and the pump.

He dropped the handle and turned, watching as the woman covered her mouth, stifling her laughter. His face turned red and his bottom lip began to quiver as he rose, dusted himself off and jumped in the driver's seat, tearing away into the sunrise, leaving the nozzle and hose on the ground.

The quiet man could still see the gas station in his rearview mirror when he made a sharp left onto a rural gravel road. He actually shouted when he said, "You stupid, stupid, stupid, stupid man! You stupid, stupid, stupid man!" He pounded the steering wheel, feeling like he was going to cry, pulling off the road beneath a stand of trees. The world was empty, there was nobody around for miles.

He spilled from the vehicle, clutching his head, nearly falling. Then he began pacing back and forth in tight little circles, berating himself for his stupidity. He stopped and stood silently. Above him there was a sound. "Pssshhhhh, pssshhhh, pssshhhh…"

The quiet man looked up and saw a mockingbird staring down at him. Pssshhhhhhh, pssshhhhhhh, pssshhhhhhh. Over and over. Exactly like the sound of a leaf rake being dragged over a driveway.

Mocking him.

He stepped to the passenger side window, reached into the glove compartment, and retrieved his gun. He scrambled to the tree and with both hands on the weapon, just like he'd seen on TV, he emptied the entire clip.

But he missed the bird, which flew to a lower branch and looked down at him again, tilting his head this way and that.

Pshhhh, pshhhh, pshhhh.

The quiet man sat down hard on the ground and hugged his knees to his chest and buried his face into his lap and began to rock from side to side. He could hear his heartbeat in his ears and his face glowed, hot with rage. He could hear his father, his big fat morbidly obese father with the weak chin and wispy girlish eyebrows and who always reeked of cheap tobacco.

Big boys don't cry. Big boys don't cry. Big boys don't cry...

The mockingbird lifted its tail feathers, shat, and flew away.

CHAPTER 12

The sun was well past its zenith when Dan finished his first day and started for home. The heat had begun to lessen and in the west a low bank of black clouds was threatening rain. He quickened his step. He had promised Millie and the twins he would make them a dinner of braised chicken legs with sausage, beans, and cipollini onions that the twins had been growing in the backyard garden. Millie was happy not to have to cook so much, and she'd knocked a little off his rent when he agreed to take care of breakfast and dinner most days. The twins had always paid her an additional fifty dollars a week for their meals, but she said she hated cooking and it tasted that way. Working in the kitchen, she said, reminded her of when she was a little girl. Her father had forced her into a life of servitude, cooking all their meals after her mother had run off.

Dan turned and headed around the back of the gym and across one of the tracks, a shortcut that might take some time off the walk if the rain loomed. Navigating King's Highway around the entire campus then south would push him into the teeth of any storm that was brewing.

Besides, he enjoyed the scenery. Echo JC had a well-respected athletic department, thanks to the patronage of local businesses and the interest of the town fathers, not to mention the surplus of flat Kansas acreage. Inside the training track were facilities for field events and a volleyball practice court. On the other side of the track there was a baseball diamond and another practice field that sometimes served as a parking lot for games, then a twenty-thousand-seat football stadium that lit up the town on fall Saturday nights, though it had never sold out before.

As he walked, though, he couldn't help but think about Millie.

She was rough on the twins. She even admitted it sometimes. Ten years they'd lived with her, and for ten years they'd been loyal. Deep down she appreciated their company and needed their patronage. They ran errands for her and made their beds each day, and helped her fold laundry. Millie was a sad, lonely lady, attached to the bottle. But Dan knew that she was firm in her resolve not to allow anyone inside her head. So he'd do what the twins did. Chill. And mind his own business.

Dan angled around the baseball diamond and headed across the dusty, near-empty, Echo JC football practice field. A figure stood on the fifty-yard line. He seemed to be examining whatever was written on the clipboard he was cradling. Dan approached to within a few feet. Then stopped in his tracks.

JD Bobbitt, thought Dan. *Son of a bitch.* He was the same age as Dan, but with more of a belly and bright red polyester coaching shorts, and a red ball cap with the Echo Cougars logo. One foot was resting on a football. He was so engrossed in what he was doing, he wouldn't have even seen Dan.

"Hey!" Parrish's tone was anything but friendly.

Bobbitt looked up and locked eyes with the intruder. His gaze narrowed. It took him a moment to realize who was standing there. He put his fists on his hips and snorted. "You got some nerve, showing up here."

"Yeah, you think?" In the near distance a row of trees bent with the wind. The rain was getting closer. Debris sailed across the patchy grass and a shoal of blackbirds curled up and away.

Bobbitt took a long slow circumnavigation of Parrish, nodding and sneering. He finished in Dan's face. "I ought to kick your sorry ass," he said, his voice carrying over the

49

sound of the wind.

Parrish curled his lip and took a step back. He opened his arms in a bring-it-on gesture.

Bobbitt smiled, slow and deliberate. Lightning ripped across the sky. Another gust whipped into a circular devil and tore over the field.

Then thunder cracked. Bobbitt dropped his clipboard and bull-rushed Parrish, driving him to the ground, knocking the wind out of him. Dan rose up and snatched the man's ears. Bobbitt screamed as Dan twisted his head around and put him in a head lock, grunting like a pro wrestler, lifting one then the other of Bobbitt's legs up off the ground before collapsing in a heap under the prodigious weight of him.

"You give?" yelled Bobbitt, smiling fatuously.

"You're crushing me, JD!"

"Why didn't you tell me you were home, man?"

"Just got here a couple days ago, JD. I haven't even had a chance to unpack!"

Bobbitt began to laugh. Then Dan started laughing. Bobbitt burped. Dan redoubled his efforts to get loose. Bobbitt's grin was infectious but it was also infuriating. And he didn't act like he wanted to move.

"I can't breathe, JD. Really," he grunted. "I'm gonna suffocate if you don't let me up, not to mention the asphyxiation."

"Aw, you old pussy."

They untangled themselves and Bobbitt rolled away. They both sat up. Bobbitt gestured at Dan's ponytail. "What's with this?" He gave it a swat.

"I dunno," said Parrish, "what's with that?" He thumped Bobbitt's belly like someone testing a watermelon for ripeness.

"That's home cooking, Dan. Looks like you could use some."

They both paused and looked up as the skies cleared and the wind began to subside.

Bobbitt said, "So fill me in, dude. What're you doing? What's up? What's the plan?"

50

CHAPTER 13

Parrish wiped his face and pushed his hair back. These were the same questions that the state of Kansas had been asking. And the answers were getting harder to figure out. It seemed simple at one time, yet now he realized there were complications. Still, he had to go with the plan. He had no other option.

"Simple," he said. "Get a job. Finish school like I promised my dad I would. In that order."

Bobbitt first nodded, then shook his head from side to side. His sadness was genuine. "Man, I'm real sorry about your dad, Dan. Real sorry. All of us were. Hell, half the town was at the funeral."

"Really, JD?"

"Oh, hell yeah, Dan. People loved him to pieces. You know that."

"Yeah, well..."

...but it was true. Dan's father, Carl, was not like anyone anywhere, and most of the town had known it. Carl was the Echo homeboy who forced life into the most mundane of situations. Just when all the neighbors would begin to forget about their irreverent, home grown war hero who wasn't, something would happen to remind them all how important it was to laugh and how a small town's excess reservoir of significance could end up being hurtful. "We're farm stock," he would say. "Let's not torture ourselves over the small stuff." It was the way things were, and it was the biggest source of pride for Dan as a kid—having a father like Carl Parrish. Which might have been one of the reasons Carl couldn't catch a break in the end, after his wife had died. He was well liked, sure, but there was a limit.

"Yeah, well," Dan said again. He couldn't finish, so he looked away. Bobbitt waited for the moment to pass, then tiptoed in with, "Listen, Dan, things have changed—"

"I know. I went by the house."

Bobbitt's face clouded with concern. "Uh...does Rick know you went by?"

"Oh yeah." Dan pointed a make-believe gun to his head. "He rolled out the old Colt .45 Welcome Wagon."

JD shook his head. "Watch out, budro. He will absolutely make your life a living hell. He can do it now."

"Great. Just what I wanted to hear."

"I'm just saying..." Bobbitt trailed off.

The two sat a few minutes, mute. The wind picked up again. The oaks that fronted the stadium thirty yards distant spit leaves onto their ground cover. The grackles began to complain. Dan sat up and pulled his knees to his chest, thinking. JD watched him, his legs splayed out like a twelve-year-old.

Dan said, "Why'd Rick want that little house so bad, anyway, JD? He could've had any house he wanted."

Bobbitt drew a deep breath then let it out. He shook his head. "Any time Hunter gets the opportunity to rub your face in cow flop, he's gonna take advantage of it. You need to know that if you don't already." He paused. "From what I understand, your dad got behind on the medical bills your ma had run up. Then he couldn't pay the property taxes on the house. Hunter smelled blood. He swooped in and..." Bobbitt trailed off, letting Dan fill in the blanks.

"Unbelievable."

"For what it's worth, me 'n Babs tried to snag it for you, but we didn't have the jack back then."

Dan looked up and blinked twice and offered a weak smile.

He patted his old buddy on the back. "Thanks, JD. I know if there's something you could have done, you'd have done it."

They both sat and nodded in silence. Then Bobbitt's nod turned to disgust, head going side to side, face clouding with something like rage. "Man, it's all such a bunch of—"

"Hey!"

Bobbitt stopped.

"Water under the bridge," said Dan. He changed the subject, eager to escape the pity party JD was throwing for him. "So, how's things otherwise?"

Bobbitt sighed, understood. Rolling with the punches was easy for him. "Ah, hell. Good. Real good, actually. Still married. Kids are giants. House almost paid off." He paused, adding, "And then there's this." He swept his arm around the practice field and across to the stadium.

A light flickered on. "You the *head* coach, JD?"

"You think I'd wear these stupid polyester shorts if I wasn't?"

"Uh, yeah."

"That's beside the point." He punched Dan on the arm and they both stood. In the west the sun appeared, white and pink, surrounded by the fading remnants of clouds still trying to roll east.

CHAPTER 14

"When did you score the coaching gig?"

Bobbitt reached down into the grass and tore off a stalk. He jammed it into his mouth. "Not too long after you...y' know..." Again he trailed off, unable to finish or look Dan in the eye.

Parrish nodded, a slow silent tribute to the inevitable process of time passing. A lot had changed. He knew he'd better get used to it. "Congratulations, man." He held up a palm and they slapped five. Yet the gesture was weak, and Dan could see that his friend from long ago knew it. JD felt guilty for his own abundance of good fortune and for Dan's troubles that had somehow spiraled out of control all those years ago.

JD shuffled across to the tackling dummy and dug the football out of the bag. He tossed it to Dan, who deftly snatched it out of the air with one hand and tossed it back.

Bobbitt repeated the exercise. Dan responded in kind. JD stepped back a few feet then cocked his arm as if he was going *r* throw it a little harder. Then he patted the ball. So Dan ̣cked up a foot and they faced off, maybe twenty yards apart, and commenced a tradition that went back as far as grade school, a tradition that played out across back yards and neighborhood streets and playgrounds—anywhere there was open space and a ball to throw.

"You need a place to stay, Dan?"

"Naw. I'm all set. Got a room at a boarding house off Main."

"I know the one," Bobbitt said. The ball fired in and he caught it in his gut. He held it and pointed it at Dan. "Ya gotta watch her. She will attack—"

Dan held up a hand, chuckling. "I'm onto her."

"That's what I'm afraid of."

"She's not my type. I'm holding out for something, I dunno…more human."

Immediately he was sorry he'd said it. *There was never any sense in letting his mouth run on. And there's no sense being mean. I let that happen, I'll end up being a bitter, old, small town bastard, pissed at the world for the cards I was dealt.*

Bobbitt wrinkled his nose and nodded. He took a step back and threw a little harder this time. Parrish caught it. He held the ball up and took a good long look, running his thumb over the threads, caressing the leather. He squeezed it and tested its weight by tossing it between his hands. He brought the ball close to his face and smelled the leather.

"How long has it been?" asked Bobbitt. He'd been watching, imagining the thoughts running through his friend's head. "Since you've thrown a football, I mean."

Parrish studied the ball for a time. He knew how long it had been, to the day. And it saddened him. He hadn't realized all those years ago that it would be the little things, life's little pleasures that would torment him so much. A smell, a color, a game of catch. Not that the larger game itself wasn't important in his life. It was. But there was more to miss than eleven guys lining up in front of eleven guys, and Xs and Os and pads and contact and sweat. There was the act itself, the wind up and the hand behind the ear and the release, a perfect thing repeated time and again. A simple game of catch.

"A long damn time," was all he said.

He wound up and threw, this time with a little mustard on it. And Bobbitt threw it back, then drifted off into a short down-and-out pattern, one of the same old routes they ran as little boys. And when Parrish delivered the ball right on the numbers, Bobbitt caught it and wrapped his hands around it like it was a gift. He threw it back and once again ran his route, this time ten yards longer. Parrish hit him in stride and they both grinned and the years melted away. When he threw it back to Parrish he hollered, "Fade pattern, corner of the end zone," and took off, a middle-aged, stout guy huffing and puffing down the field. Dan smiled to himself. The ball came out of his hand in a perfect spiral, soaring high over the yard markers, hesitating at the top of the arc...and finding JD's outstretched palms at the last possible second before his feet toe-tapped in front of the boundary marker, a kid's dream touchdown in any language.

JD stood in the end zone cradling the ball over his stomach and trying to catch his breath. For a moment he seemed deep in thought. He jogged back up field to Dan and stood in front of him and pitched him the ball, still breathing hard.

"What kind of work you looking for, Dan?"

Dan shrugged. "Cook."

"Cook? You shitting me?"

"I wouldn't shit you, JD..."

They finished in unison. "...you're my favorite turd."

Bobbitt stepped back and they began throwing again. "Cook's wages might cover your rent, but it ain't gonna pay for books and tuition."

"I gotta start somewhere, man." Dan dropped back like a pro, arm drawn back, point-of-ball by right ear, looking like Tom Brady with a beard and a pony tail. He drilled a perfect ball into Bobbitt's waiting mitts.

Once again Bobbitt stopped and pondered the pigskin as if it were a crystal ball. "I got this kid, Dan. A QB. He's good, y' know. But he could be real good. He needs some polish is all."

"Yeah. So?"

"So you wanna help me get him a free ride to a four year school?" Bobbitt chucked the ball to Parrish.

"Gimme a friggin' break, JD, I'm a hundred years old. Besides, I have to get that job—"

"I'll get you the job, Dan. If you help me out with this kid."

CHAPTER 15

Parrish stopped and held onto the ball. A job? His hopes started to rise. Time wasn't on his side with this work thing; there were only so many days that the State of Kansas would wait. He needed a pay stub in the worst way.

Still, he had taught himself several years ago to be circumspect about pledges and promises. Usually they didn't pan out, at least in his own life and not for the last eighteen years. He said, "I dunno, man..." which trailed off into silence. He wound up and tossed a neat underhand spiral to Bobbitt, a ball so tight and with such force and accuracy that the coach had a tough time catching it. Bobbitt was impressed.

"Look, Dan, we just lost a kid, big fast dude got a ride to U of K. Freed up a scholarship. I give it to you, you help me out and—boom—tuition and books are free. Win-win. And the job I get you will cover your other expenses. What'cha think about that?"

Dan looked at JD as if he were from another planet. "Me? On scholarship?" he erupted. "Good one, JD. You should take that routine on the road." He knew it was sounding too good to be true, and this confirmed it. For a moment he began to steam. *Don't play with me, JD. Just don't do it.*

"Not as a player, you flathead. As a coach. An assistant."

Dan stared at him.

Bobbitt said, "I can make it happen. I'm not kidding."

Bobbitt tossed up a wobbler and Parrish made a circus

catch of it, slipping back into his old element with every throw. To him, though, the game was over. There was no way JD Bobbitt was going to be able to solve his problems for him, no matter how much both of them wanted him to.

"JD, you're dumber than you look. And that's saying something. Especially in those pants."

Bobbitt shook his head and shrugged. "Sure. What was I thinking? I mean, what's a long-haired loser like you gonna teach a kid about throwing a damn football?"

Bobbitt waited for Parrish's return throw and wondered if his words were sharp enough to get under his friend's thick skin. He watched Parrish drop back with perfect grace and speed, saw the arm cock back, the point of the ball poised by his ear. He saw Parrish step forward with a perfect weight shift and release the pigskin.

The ball arrived with dizzying speed and sizzled through Bobbitt's hands, hitting him square in the nose and dropping him on his ass. Blood trickled down into his daffy grin.

And Parrish grinned right back.

"Let me think about it."

CHAPTER 16

At the end of his second day of classes at Echo JC, Dan Parrish found himself peering through the front window of the only drugstore in town, Mulligan's. It was hot and Dan was perspiring. He noticed the ancient decal on the glass: *Come On In, It's Coooool Inside...* The storefront looked the same as it had since Dan was a boy. There were old cardboard cutouts advertising faded gems of a forgotten era, things like Boy Scout knives and Walkman radios. And there were also newer messages, printed signs inviting people to use the free Wi-Fi while they waited for their flu shots.

Yet nothing had really changed except maybe the employees. Mulligan's was what used to be called a five-and-dime, a drug store with a lunch counter. Mulligan's also carried anything you might need in a pinch—sunscreen for the summer hay ride, a squirt gun for the kid or a birthday card for Grandma—this was the place to find it. Dan had been thinking about Mulligan's soda fountain for years. And now here he was, face pressed against the glass, staring in at a quartet of empty, red vinyl booths.

Dan entered and meandered over to the fountain. He shot nervous glances around the place, hoping no one would be there from the old days, no one to recognize him. The place smelled the same, like floor wax and vanilla and old wooden shelving. Even the ceiling was the same—sagging wainscot tongue and groove, painted dark green to hide the dust. The neon light fixtures always seemed to buzz. How many Sundays had he come here with his mother and father? How many chili dogs had he wolfed down on summer lunch breaks, or between high school football two-a-days? How many malts had he shared with Katy here? Echo never had a McDonalds or a KFC back then. But they had a Mulligan's. And that was okay by him.

Parrish drifted to the counter, where a pretty young twenty-something sat popping her gum and texting on her iPhone. The name tag on her blouse read *Sandie*. Dan cleared his throat. The girl looked up and smiled.

"Sorry," she said. "I didn't see you there."

"That's okay. Mr. Mulligan around?"

"Oh God no. He died a ways back. Heart attack." She looked around, then leaned in closer. "Poor thing keeled over right there in the ice cream bin, pistachio all over his face." She gave Dan a sheepish grin and shrugged.

Dan nodded. He felt a pang of remorse for the old man. Mr. Mulligan wasn't ever what you'd call sociable; he didn't have an easy smile and a way with the kids. But Dan got along with him and managed to stay on his good side. The guy had been a rabid football fan of Echo High during those years, and Dan had taken his freshman son Marvin under his wing after he joined the team, one time even standing up for him when a group of seniors had come down a little hard. Marvin Mulligan didn't have much in the way of athletic skills, but he was an Echo Cougar nonetheless, and Dan was a team player. For that small act of kindness, Dan decided, he had been given a bit of slack at the store. Old Man Mulligan had even allowed him a free ice cream soda once in a while.

Sandie finished texting and stowed her phone away in her apron. She ran her eyes over Dan, mesmerized by his blue eyes. Dan looked up and caught her staring. He blushed more than she did.

"You folks need some help in the kitchen?" he asked quietly. There were a couple of people in the store now and Dan didn't want anyone to hear.

"Not really. Just hired a hotshot all the way from K.C. Even makes these cute little thingies." She gestured to her left, pointing out a plate with a half-eaten burger, garnished with pathetic little carrot curls and green onion brushes. Parrish picked up a knife, grabbed a radish from the plate and with a few deft strokes turned it into a rose. He set it back on the plate. Sandie beamed, impressed.

"That is so cool! Can you show me how to do that?" she gushed.

"Sure," he said. "You still make malts?"

"You bet!"

Parrish slid his rear up on one of the ancient stools at the Formica-topped counter, smiled, tapped the counter and said, "Set me up."

A few minutes later Dan sat outside of the drugstore at one of three wrought iron tables. Before him was a dented, Waring stainless steel canister half full, and a malt glass overflowing with chocolate malted milkshake—the ambrosial nectar of the gods. Dan wielded a spoon, stirring the often-dreamt-of concoction and salivating. Like he'd said to himself for years, it was the little things that he had missed so much. When he put the straw to his lips, he closed his eyes and took the first sip.

There were many things he'd missed about his home town: the clean air and the smell of burning leaves in the fall, the movie theater on weekends, barbecues by the lake over on County Line. And kissing Katy. Yet the malt he held in his hand had to be right up there near the top. He took another sip and nearly moaned, it was so good. He took another. When his face exploded with pleasure, he sucked on the paper straw until it started to gurgle and collapse. Then he put the tin cup from the blender to his mouth and poured it down, only letting up when there was nothing left.

A voice intruded. "Is it really that good?"

Parrish pulled the cup away. He had a chocolate mustache and the end of his nose was coated. Agnes stood there at the table, arms akimbo, and offered an amused smile.

"You tell me," he said with a sheepish grin. He offered his cup. When she looked inside, it was empty. Without skipping a beat she took the straw and licked the end clean.

"Mmmm, that is good. No wonder you have it all over your face."

Dan quickly wiped his face with the back of his hand. He was really starting to like this girl.

"Mind if I sit?"

"Please," he said. He gave her his best smile. Here came the jitters again. He was well aware of why she made him so nervous; but way back when, he didn't suffer a want of confidence in himself. Now, after all the water under his bridge, a beautiful woman made him stammer inside.

She sat down. He laid his palms flat on his jiggling knees, pressing them down from the underside of the table so they wouldn't bang on the glass. He tried to think of something to say. Maybe a weather pronouncement. *Hot, isn't it?* No. That wouldn't do. That was too lame.

"Hot, isn't it?" he said anyway.

Just then a sleek, black, Lincoln Town Car pulled up to the curb and stopped. Rick Hunter opened the driver's-side door and got out and eyed the pair sitting at the sidewalk table. When he walked around the hood of his vehicle, Dan's uncomfortable smile died as fast as it had appeared.

Hunter lifted a booted foot up over the curb and took two steps to the table. He put his fists on his hips and stared down at Dan as if he were a bug. "What are you doing here?"

"Mulligan malted. Want some?" Parrish offered up his fluted glass innocently. Hunter batted it to the concrete and it shattered into a thousand glittering shards. Agnes gasped.

Dan regarded the mess with a lazy eye. *Keep cool*, he told himself. He looked up. "Litterbug."

Hunter's nostrils flared. He looked at Agnes for the first time. He turned back to Dan. "She know about you yet?"

Dan shot an uneasy glance at Agnes Stankowiecz. He hadn't anticipated this. Even though he knew it was just a matter of time, he hadn't expected to have to bleed out so soon, to lay his history bare and wait for the recriminations and the judgments and all the rest. And he knew Hunter loved Dan's discomfort, catching him unawares. *Blindsided.*

Except Agnes said, "Yeah, I know all about him."

Hunter's smirk disappeared. He frowned.

Dan allowed himself a quick peek and a nod of gratitude to Agnes. She caught it, and in that moment made it clear that she would roll with whatever direction Dan wanted to take this. They were dancing now. And he was leading.

Hunter wasn't done yet, though. Dan knew there was too much hate stored up. After all, Rick Hunter wielded a big stick in this town. So he rubbed his palms on the sides of his creased Levis and tried a little snake oil. With the most saccharine of smiles to the lady, he said, "Welcome to Echo, ma'am. The name's Hunter. Richard Hunter." He held out his hand.

Agnes looked at it for a moment, contemplating her choices. She glanced down at the broken glass on the sidewalk. She looked up at the over-dressed man and noticed he wore makeup on his nose in an unsuccessful attempt to break the sweat shine. She peered into the salon-tanned, perspiring face and saw the capped teeth and the hint of jowls and the publican smile of a deceiver. In the end her trust meter went into the red and she declined the invitation, leaving the man's Rolex-bejeweled paw floating in the air like a painted dirigible, rudderless and confused.

Dan said, "Or as we used to call him in high school, *Dick* Hunter." He smiled up at his one-time nemesis. "Remember that...*Dickie*?"

Hunter's face swelled and turned crimson and his upper lip curled into a snarl. He took a half step around the little round table.

Just then a car horn sounded and they all turned to see Richard Hunter's son Chip and his mom, Katy, sitting in an idling Jeep.

"C'mon, Dad," the boy lectured aloud. "I'm late for practice." He seemed to notice Parrish, but didn't allow himself to stare during the awkward silence that followed. He reached up to the visor and grabbed his sunglasses and put them on.

At that moment Dan Parrish could not have seen Chip Hunter's eyes assimilating the little montage in front of Mulligan's Drugs and Sundries. Because all Dan saw was Katy. In the daylight he noticed the changes, the hairstyle not as young, the laugh lines more pronounced, the figure a little fuller.

But she was lovely all the same, and when he looked at her he felt once again the old passions, and their words of fidelity. And he could hear the promises they had made to each other so many years ago. He looked at her and he could see that she didn't yet recognize him. He was older and bearded now with hair half way down his back.

But he sure did her, and it killed him. And Rick Hunter had to know it.

Meanwhile, Agnes was amused. She had no real stake in this little drama, at least not yet, so she drank it all in, watching the strange dynamic play out in a series of exchanged glances and mental transgressions that vibrated the air around them. Hearts were hammering and what was *not* being said was more important than anything that actually was.

Hunter leaned over and brought his face to within inches

of Dan's. "Better light a shuck, Danny Boy." He stuck his gold toothpick in his mouth. "Or else," he whispered, flashing his teeth around the diamond post. He turned and nodded to his family and strode to his car, climbed inside and started the engine. When he pulled away he refused to make eye contact with Dan or Agnes.

But then a strange thing happened. Chip had been sitting in the driver's seat of the idling red Jeep, seeming to pay close attention to the little drama in front of him and to the words his father had said. He must have been wondering who Dan Parrish really was...

...while beside Chip his mother had come alive. She must have recognized Dan. It hit her hard. She stifled a gasp and tried to cover her face, as her son stepped on the gas and sped away.

Agnes and Dan sat at the sidewalk table, an uncomfortable hush hanging in the air.

Agnes broke the spell. "Light a shuck?" she asked. Her voice jolted Parrish and he blinked.

"Just an old redneck expression his father was fond of."

"Meaning?"

Dan took a deep breath and looked off down the street at nothing. "Get the hell outta Dodge."

"You're kidding, right?"

"I wish."

"Where are they?" she asked.

"Who?"

"John Wayne and Gary Cooper? I mean, Jesus, talk about a scene right out of *High Noon*!"

Dan allowed himself a wry grin.

"Seriously, what's this all about, Dan?"

Dan shook his head.

Then a voice spoke up from behind them and a few feet away. "It's about Splinter C-c-c-city." Agnes and Dan turned in their seats to see who had spoken.

CHAPTER 17

On Tuesdays, Belden Ferguson didn't have to show up at Echo Feed & Seed, until after six, long past the day shift guys had left. Even then, his job was to take one of the trucks to the rail head and load up from whatever box car had their delivery order and requisition stamp pasted on the door. Usually his Tuesday night duties took a few hours, unloading pallets of goods, then loading them into the truck, driving back to the warehouse and unloading again. So he had every Monday night off and all of Tuesdays until late afternoon. Then there was the work at the family-owned filling station. If he had time before these shifts he liked to go to Mulligan's for the special: Salisbury steak with gravy and parsley potatoes. Belden was pretty predictable in that regard. As he walked up the street he had watched the tail end of the drama that had just unfolded. And he'd recognized Dan.

"Belden Ferguson? Is that you?"

Belden nodded, spreading his lips in an embarrassed smile. He was a big guy like his father, and his faded denim overalls fit tight around the middle.

A huge grin spread across Dan's face. He stood and extended his hand, which Belden ignored. Instead, the man snatched Dan up in a bear hug and squeezed, taking him by surprise, forcing the air out of his lungs in a heartfelt act of joy. This was the sort of greeting Dan had dreamt about but didn't dare consider.

Belden tried to speak, except when he was excited his stutter was more pronounced. "W-w-when did you g-g-get—"

Dan stopped him with a hard look and an eyebrow wag toward Agnes, silencing Belden before he gave up the ghost. Belden understood and zipped his mouth shut. He stood back and beamed as Dan took him in.

"Look at you, all grown up! How the hell are you, Belden? How are things?"

The young, black man looked away, unable to meet Parrish's eyes. He took his faded green hat off and wrung it in his big hands. "Th-th-things are…"

He didn't finish. His hands twisted the old hat until Dan thought he was going to rip it in two. Then he started to cry.

"I thought I'd n-n-never see you a-g-g-gain, Danny!" He backed away and stared down at the ground, his shoes kicking some of the shards of glass atop the pavement.

Parrish shot a puzzled glance at Agnes. What was this all about? Eighteen years ago Belden was a little boy—a nice kid from a nice family. But Dan had no idea his leaving had meant anything to the little guy.

Dan patted Belden on the back. "It's okay, man. I understand."

Belden wiped his face with the back of his hand. "No you d-d-don't. B-b-but you will." Belden looked down again. "I owes you, Danny. I owes you b-b-big time."

Dan ran his eyes up and down the street, looking for anyone who might be with Belden Ferguson. He exchanged looks with Agnes, but was unable to clear things up or answer her unstated questions.

"What are you talking about, Belden?"

"I gotta go n-n-now," he said. "I gotta go to work." He looked resolute, even nodding to himself. He'd clearly made a decision of sorts and began to step away. He was leaving Dan's question to hang in the air between them. And he was doing it on purpose. "G-g-good to see you, Danny. And d-d-don't you listen to Hunter. This is your t-t-town. You belong here. Y-y-you'll see." He turned to go, but hesitated and stepped back around, giving Dan another hug. Then he hurried away down the sidewalk.

Agnes looked down at her arms. "That gave me goose bumps."

"Me, too."

"What do you suppose he meant by all that?"

Dan followed Belden's retreating form. "I haven't the vaguest idea."

She watched Dan watching Belden. "Well, you heard the man, Dan. You can't leave. You belong here."

Parrish gave her a dubious look.

"Besides, you wouldn't let a *dick hunter* run you out of your own town, now, would you?"

Agnes Stankowiecz winked and walked away, smiling to herself.

At this late hour the Echo JC men's locker room was dark save a single light burning in the coaches' office. JD Bobbitt sat at his desk studying game film, stopping and starting the celluloid over and over. Forward. Reverse. Forward. Stop. Jot down notes. Again. He heard footsteps and looked at the open door to his office. A tired grin spread across his face and he tossed his pen aside and folded his hands behind his head. Dan Parrish stood in the doorway.

"Hunter's making it hot for me," Dan said. His face was grave.

"Surprised?"

"I just thought that by now—"

"You always were a naïve s.o.b." Bobbitt rubbed his face and ran his hands through his mop of brown hair. "The sad fact is, he's in a position to mess with you now." Then a mischievous smile spread across his face before he added, "With

69

you, that is…but not with *us*." Bobbitt stood and gestured at a picture on the wall. It was a black and white photo of Parrish and Bobbitt as high school seniors in gridiron garb, arms draped over shoulders, teammates, pals.

And two-time state champs.

"Remember what happened last time you and me teamed up? Remember where we sent that sucker?"

Parrish remembered all right. "Splinter city," he answered.

"You're damn right."

Parrish stroked his beard, thinking. He had come here for a reason—to talk to JD yeah, but also to find out if he was still considering what they'd talked about. To find out if he was serious. "That scholarship offer still good?"

"What do you think?"

"And the job?"

"Way ahead of ya," Bobbitt said and handed Dan a slip of paper. "Meet with this guy tomorrow at noon. Don't be late."

Parrish folded the paper twice and pocketed it. "So, what kind of hell are you gonna catch for this?"

"Don't you worry your pretty little head about it."

Parrish took a deep breath and let it out. He walked over to study the photo on the wall. There they were, two old friends, in the prime of their lives, feeling immortal, with the best part of their lives before them. Or so he thought. That was eighteen years ago, when Dan Parrish had the world by the tail. Now it was different. The world had him. Now he was nothing, a bearded, long-haired, washed up has-been begging for scraps.

But scraps would have to do.

"Where do I sign?" he asked.

CHAPTER 18

Sam Blevins sat in his upstairs office behind his battered, gunmetal-gray tanker desk and scowled at Dan. He was well past the normal age of retirement, Dan guessed, and his white walrus mustache and wide red suspenders over checked shirt made him look like a logger just home from the Great Northwest. He was a fixture at Echo, hired to run the JC cafeteria and cleaning staff when the place was new and tiny, and still here doing the same thing after thirty years.

He looked down and perused Dan's résumé, wrinkling his prodigious nose like he smelled dirty diapers, holding the pages down on the desk with a single forefinger. Dan could tell that Blevins wasn't impressed. Who would be? Dan and JD had spent two hours the night before writing the thing. Check that, *concocting* the thing. And no amount of proofreading and margin adjusting could fix such a document. No amount of gerrymandering could cover the huge hole in the middle of the timeline.

Parrish sweated it out as his potential boss studied the document. Dan had his pen out like he was ready to sign something, but all he could do was click the button and watch the point appear and then hide. Time slowed. Soon it stopped altogether. He put his left hand on his knee to keep it from jiggling, and tried to look engaged. Click went the pen.

Click, click, click, went the pen.

Sam Blevins raised his eyebrows and shot an annoyed look

at Dan's hand.

"Sorry." Parrish put the pen away.

A minute later, Sam leaned back in his chair and examined Dan. For a time the two men regarded one another. Then Blevins picked up the resume by a thumb and forefinger and dangled it over his desk. He shook it, like he was waiting for something—anything—to drop out. But nothing did.

"Am I missing something?" he asked. His voice rolled and grumbled like far away thunder.

"No, sir."

Sam leaned back in his chair again and studied Parrish some more. Then he took off his glasses and polished them, saying, "More holes in this application than a pound of Swiss."

Parrish remained mute, both hands on both knees. He'd learned long ago that it was better to let things happen without his editorial help. Where he had been, you did a lot of sitting there acting like a head of cabbage.

"You want to talk about it?"

"Not particularly, no."

Sam nodded. He pretended to reexamine the application. He laid it aside, then placed both his hands palm down on the desktop.

"Your boy Bobbitt is vouching for you, you know. Going out on a limb here."

"He's a good man, JD is."

Sam narrowed his eyes and gestured at Dan's ponytail. "You gay?"

"No, sir. You?"

Sam's face erupted in a huge grin. "I suppose I asked for that." He clapped his hands together, rubbed them and sat forward. "The job's yours." Sam stood and extended his hand, which Dan grabbed and pumped like it was a lifeline and he was drowning. "Gotta warn ya, though. It ain't gonna be easy. And you've got a tough crew to deal with." He gestured toward the glass wall that looked to ground level, his

domain. Twenty feet from the foot of the stairs a confrontation was unfolding. Four cranky-looking cafeteria ladies were
howling at a skinny gang-banger wanna-be in his twenties, a
spirited Chicano who seemed to be vocal about his amuse-
ments. The guy was plugged into an iPod, rapping and dancing in place to music only he could hear. He seemed oblivious
to their *a cappella* shrieks of derision. Parrish couldn't help
but smile.

"You're smiling now," said Blevins. "You won't be for
long."

"Who's the kid?"

Sam drew a deep breath and sighed, long and rueful.
"That's Jorge. He was sent by Satan to torment me." Blevins
shook his head and stared through the window, down at
Jorge dancing like a whirling dervish while the ladies continued to berate him.

"He's Echo JC's president's kid—in town they call him
Jalapeño—and he's lazier than furniture." Sam pointed a finger at Dan. "Just keep him out of my hair. That's all I ask."

Dan nodded. The idea of a Hispanic bureaucrat as top dog
must have been a new demographic in the state of Kansas.
They both watched as Jorge commandeered an industrial-
sized ladle and worked it into his dance routine. He looked up
at the window and hit both men with eye lasers of loathing.
He sure enough scowled like a gangster.

Dan looked at Sam. He turned and sat and exhaled again,
a lumberjack's sigh of defeat. "Still want the job?"

Dan stepped closer to the glass and looked down at the
dated kitchen, scarred by time, the corners coated in a crystal-
lized patina of ancient grease. He saw the outmoded utensils
and the inefficient layout, the cantankerous old ladies staring
at him like a scene from a zombie movie. He saw the troubled
slacker covered in tattoos, wearing his slick-backed hair and
gold tooth like a badge of discontent. Sam Blevins was right:
this job wasn't going to be easy.

73

"Oh yeah," he replied.

He couldn't wait to get started.

The quiet man lies on his bed in the little room. Sometimes, in the middle of the afternoon, when his eyes are closed and after the maid has given him his clean towels and a new bar of soap, he visits imaginary people and tries to explain things to them. Analytically. So they'd know. When someone wrongs you, when they've destroyed your life and made a laughing stock of you...

...you respond. Death as a rational solution.

He stood and went to his little table and sat. He began to clean his gun. You couldn't do anything without a clean gun. The dealer had told him that.

CHAPTER 19

Dan hurried down the sidewalk, his stomach rumbling with nervous energy. He'd nearly made it through another day of junior college. He still had one more class, then he was going to coach football for the first time in his life. And not just the game, but one of the important skills, maybe the most important skill on the field. He felt like he knew his subject. After all, he'd been a student of the position half his life. And, while dealing with young egos might be a challenge, he had a good memory.

He turned a corner and almost ran into a young man wearing what looked like a skirt, sitting on his book bag, his back against the bricks, snacking. He had a broad, flat nose, wide cheekbones and dark skin. Dan looked down and mumbled his surprise.

The kid took a bite of his lunch. He looked up and smiled through the food. "How's it?" he said. While he chewed he pointed at Dan's hair. "You get some sack wearin' hair li' dat around dis place."

Dan smiled. "This from a guy in a skirt?"

The guy flashed a big, bone-white smile. "Ain' no skirt, brah, it's—"

"—a lava lava."

"Hey, how you know dat?" The kid seemed impressed.

"Did a lotta reading where I came from," said Parrish. He pointed at the kid's lunch. "What's that?"

The young man looked down at his lap, where the remains of a giant chunk of rice was topped with Spam and wrapped in nori, the seaweed stuff of the gods. "Spam musubi," he said. "Like try?" He offered up the *pupu* to Parrish, who took a bite. A minute went by while Parrish chewed, assessing the flavor. "Hmm. Let's see…Spam, rice and…is that some kind of kelp?"

"Close. Nori. Brah, you're good."

"This is some good eating," Dan said. "Delish."

"Ono."

When Dan gave him a quizzical look, he added, "It means delicious."

"Ono it is, then." He offered his hand. "Dan Parrish."

"Ku'uipo Kawananakoa. Friends call me 'Ipo." They shook hands.

"So what's a Hawaiian kid doing way out here in West Kansas?"

Ku'uipo looked up, then his eyes ran away across the horizon, settling somewhere out on the wide Pacific. "Brah, only one thing can drag me away from my islands." He turned his shoulder and revealed a tattoo. It was a picture of a football superimposed on the map of the Hawaiian Islands. He checked Parrish to see if he was buying it. The fact was, at five nine, Ku'uipo must have known he wasn't exactly college football material. Maybe a buck sixty-five dripping wet. Not counting the size of his heart.

"Wide receiver," said Dan.

'Ipo's face lit up. "How'd you know?"

Dan held out his hand and they shook again, this time Dan measuring the grip. "Good hands." He smiled and walked a few steps and turned around. "Aloha, 'Ipo."

"Hey, right back at ya."

Dan started off then stopped and turned again. "What does Ku'uipo mean, anyway?"

'Ipo sighed. He gave Dan a long hard look, his eyes sliding right and left before riveting front and center. He answered,

"It means 'sweetheart.' And if you tell anybody around here, I'll kick your *okole*."

"No need to ask what *that* means," Parrish said with a grin. He turned back around and began to walk, a slight spring in his step now. It was nice to kick it with someone who would never wonder about your history.

Or care.

CHAPTER 20

What hit Dan first was the eye burn of liniment. The menthol, clove and camphor of Tiger Balm. Beyond it, he smelled the cold steel of the lockers, the sweat, the musty odor of the always-dripping showers mixed with the overwhelming redolence of bleach. All around him the Echo Junior College Cougars were strapping their gear on, preparing for the first day of fall football practice. Dan and JD moved through the young warriors as they told jokes or discussed the day's events—classes, cars, girls. On the first day of organized practice there were always the guys who knew they were on the team, mixed with a couple dozen walk-ons with aspirations beyond their high school senior seasons. Some of them would make it, meeting the challenge and growing into the next step. Some wouldn't. First days were public trials, and for some, private disappointments. Dan felt like a walk-on for sure, no matter the scholarship.

"Let's go, guys!" Bobbitt shouted. "Five minutes!"

Parrish walked past Ku'uipo, who looked up, surprised.

"Hey, brah, wha'chu you doin' here?"

"Not sure yet, tell you the truth." He and Bobbitt continued to the far corner of the locker room. Two players were dawdling, their backs to the others.

Bobbitt pointed to the one on the left. "This," he whispered, "is your new protégé." He cupped his mouth and hollered at the two prima donnas. "Hey, ladies, get a move on!"

78

They both turned and faced Dan and their head coach. It was Chip Hunter and Jimmy Durr. The trio exchanged looks.

Bobbitt offered a voice from outside the circle. He said, "Chip, meet your new quarterback coach, Dan Parrish."

The awkward silence told its own story. Parrish's eyes felt out of focus, like he was examining his own ruin. At that moment, Dan was sure of one thing: *I do not belong in this locker room.*

Chip pushed past Parrish and JD and headed out to the field with a phalanx of other players, Jimmy Durr hot on his heels. A trio of coaches—two young guys wanting to learn the ropes and a middle-aged student of the game—went with them. The equipment bags were already outside, with ball boys and the ancient team doctor and a quartet of students, two boys, two girls, so-called team managers, who had volunteered to nurse the cuts and scrapes and hydrate the players if they could wear the jerseys and travel with the team.

Parrish watched them exit, then turned to Bobbitt, arms crossed, one eyebrow arched suggestively. The locker room was empty, dead quiet, a chamber of understated echoes.

"What?" said JD.

"You know what."

"Water under the bridge. Those were your very words, Dan."

"This is different and you know it." He turned for the exit. Things *were* too good to be true. He knew it.

Bobbitt asked, "Why? 'Cause he's Hunter's kid?"

Parrish stopped. "Uh, yeah!"

"So let me get this straight. You're gonna punish him because his dad's a dick? You've come back here to pick up the pieces and finish school but you never imagined it included any of the hard stuff? The suck-it-up stuff?" He paused to take a breath. "You gave me your word, Dan. A deal's a deal."

Bobbitt didn't wait for a response. He turned and headed for the field.

Parrish stood in the gray light and tried not to shout at the walls. Yes, he did think about these first few weeks in Echo, of the trip home and the people who might recognize him and all the rest, the innuendos and the denials and the way he would have to turn his head and ignore the whispers. It hadn't been so bad up until now. Not bad at all. No one except the Hunter family had tried to pigeonhole him. Except now he would have to be an impartial arbiter and forget the history. He would have to judge another man's son while carrying his own baggage inside, forgetting the kid's father, the pomade-scented ass who only a few days ago threatened him, who just yesterday told him to leave Echo "or else," forgetting the fever of retribution that took eighteen years of his life and flushed them down the toilet.

He heard a whistle. Out on the field Bobbitt was gathering his players. Dan took a step toward the open door, then another. When his feet hit the grass he began to jog and then to run out onto the playing field.

CHAPTER 21

Dan and JD stood in the middle of the field watching Chip and another young quarterback perform passing drills. In other areas around the grounds, parts of the team were engaged in their own exercises: running backs, defensive backs, offensive linemen and defensive linemen. Off in the distance a kicker practiced field goals and a punter sent booming spirals toward a ball boy. The entire practice field was charged with activity.

Dan watched as Chip and the other kid repeated the five-step drop, set the feet, then passed to a pair of receivers running short routes, over and over. Chip partnered with Durr on every snap. It wasn't clear why Chip was first string, though. The other kid, a guy named Chad Stone, had a big arm and a rocket delivery. He was a good-looking prospect: decent size, great footwork and big, strong hands. When he dropped back, he looked as sharp as Chip. In some respects, even sharper. Dan wondered why he wasn't the starter. He also wondered why neither quarterback threw the ball to Ku'uipo, who tirelessly ran crisp routes, despite the fact he wasn't getting the ball.

Parrish leaned across to JD and gestured toward Chad. "Who's the kid?"

"Chad Stone. Our backup."

It was Chad's turn. He took a snap, dropped back, and threw. His form was textbook and the results were, too—a fifty-yard bomb that landed soft as a dove into the receiver's hands.

"Damn, JD. Pretty good for a back-up." The tone all but suggesting maybe he should be the starter.

"Yeah," Bobbitt said, "but the guy's all arm, no heart. He's really a great kid, but he ain't got the killer instinct. He gets hit, he folds. Out of the pocket, he's a defensive back's wet dream."

"What a shame," said Dan. "With those mechanics and a name like Chad Stone, he could go places."

"Don't I know it," said Bobbitt.

Once again it was Chip's turn to throw. He crouched over center, barked a single "Hut!" then dropped back, planted, and threw to Durr. He overlooked Ku'uipo again, and was unapologetic.

Bobbitt looked to Parrish. "Well? Whattya think?"

Parrish stroked his beard, going over what he just saw. "Strong arm. Sloppy footwork, though. And that three-quarter delivery's gotta go."

Bobbitt smiled then arched his brows. "Remind you of anyone we used to know, Dan?" When Parrish's face suggested a smile, he asked, "Think you can fix it?"

Parrish watched as Chip took another snap, dropped back and threw again.

"Sure," he said, squinting into the heat. He was starting to sweat. "Like fixing a mirror, JD."

Bobbitt clapped Parrish on the back. "That's just what I wanted to hear." He blew his whistle. "Yo, Chip!"

"Yes, sir?"

JD and Parrish strode across to the nucleus of players standing with Chip and Chad. "Coach Parrish thinks you could sharpen your footwork some," said Bobbitt.

Dan looked Chip in the eye. "And maybe lose that three-quarter delivery," he said.

Hunter and Durr exchanged a look. It was obvious they didn't take to the new guy. "Oh yeah?" said Chip. There was an edge in his voice.

Dan stepped forward, eager to explain, forgetting for a moment who he was talking to. "It's just that your crossover and depth steps are—"

"Don't tell me." He flipped the ball to Parrish. "*Show me...Coach.*" His voice dripped sarcasm.

The last time Dan had heard a player use that tone when he spoke to his coach was years ago, in junior high school. The kid's name was Timmy Peacock, and Coach Hodgin lined him up, then promptly broke his nose with a forearm shiv as boy came out of his three-point stance.

Dan didn't have that luxury.

Hunter and Durr stood, arms crossed, waiting to see what their new mentor would do. By now the entire offense had noticed. They were watching, waiting to see how things would play out. So Parrish shrugged. He assumed the QB position without a center. He felt the eyes of the team on him and he was nervous. After all, it had been the better part of two decades since he'd thrown a ball for real, much less demonstrate the proper technique on *how* to throw it.

His voice, when it came, was calm and commanding. "Your first step is the six o'clock pivot step. This is where you begin to gain depth." Parrish took one step back and stopped. "Then your crossover step—" as he crossed his feet over, "—then the depth step—" as he completed the depth step, "—then the short crossover, leaning slightly forward with the upper body..." As he said it, he leaned forward and completed the five-step part of the drill. "Then the set-up in good throwing position, feet shoulder-width apart. Try to look away from the intended receiver during drop back. Then you just..." Dan feigned a pass and was more than a little amazed at his recall. He tossed the ball back to Chip, impressed with himself.

Except Chip Hunter tossed it right back, unimpressed. He'd decided to up the ante. "But *sayin'* ain't *doin'*, is it, *Coach*? I mean, who can't *walk* through a drill?"

"Yeah," added Durr. "Who?"

And there it was, the gauntlet. Thrown down by the son of the only man Dan ever hated.

But this kind of thing shouldn't be happening. Chip Hunter should have learned some things when he was younger. When Timmy Peacock had challenged their coach all those years back, Coach Hodgin had taken offense. And Hodgin had been a bully, at least in Dan's eyes. He broke clipboards over helmets. He wrung kids out by their facemasks. He kicked over coolers of Gatorade during sweltering-hot two-a-day sessions. He was a grown man, a big ex-jock redneck getting in the face of an eighth-grader, making the kid line up, showing him how he was supposed to get under his block. And Peacock didn't have a chance. The boy's mother came and took him to the hospital, and for days he wore a nose splint around school, like a badge, reminding everyone that he'd bawled like a baby on the football field. Dan would always remember Timmy Peacock, and the pounding he'd absorbed. And he was not going to be that kind of coach, ever. Still, if Chip wanted to play games, Dan would have to do his best, never mind the rust.

Bobbitt leaned in close to Dan and whispered, "Game on, old man."

Dan whispered back. "I'm gonna kill you for this, JD."

Dan, heart pounding, called for the center and his two receivers, Durr and Ku'uipo, and they lined up on the imaginary line of scrimmage. Everybody, even the punter and kicker, was watching now. Dan's throat went dry when he crouched under center. He took a deep breath, then yelled "Hut!" and the ball smacked his hands with force. He began his five-step drop as Durr and Ku'uipo streaked downfield.

Dan completed his maneuver with perfect, coordinated agility. Durr ran a deep sideline route, hoping to test the arm of the bearded old man, and Ku'uipo ran a deep fly route up the middle of the field. Parrish eyed Durr the entire way, then suddenly wheeled and fired a fifty-yard rope to the blazing

Hawaiian, who hauled it in with both hands outstretched, running like a mad man, then spiking the ball in the end zone and jumping high, tapping the goalpost crossbar and shouting "Toughdown, brah!" to a cheering throng of sweaty football players, three assistants, four team managers, two ball boys and JD Bobbitt, grinning through his whistle.

Jimmy Durr was obviously angry at the wasted run and the snub.

Chip Hunter was obviously angry at the insult, this time in front of the entire team.

But everyone else was ecstatic. And no one had a broken nose. Maybe one a little out of joint, but not broken.

Ku'uipo jogged back and flipped the ball to Parrish. "Nice ball, Coach," he said. And Dan Parrish handed the ball to Chip, who snatched it away with an angry flourish. When the team resumed drills, Dan walked back over to Bobbitt. The head coach had been hiding his smile behind his clipboard.

Dan said, "Like riding a dang bike, JD."

"Well, I guess, *Coach*," said an amused Bobbitt.

Dan crossed his arms and looked around. He'd passed his test. He didn't feel like a walk-on anymore. For the first time in a long time he was looking forward to whatever came next.

CHAPTER 22

Bobbitt blew his whistle. "Alright, circle up, men!"

Players and staff alike turned and grouped around him. They'd been at it for almost three hours and by the looks on some of their faces, they would feel it deep in their bones, the aches and pains of the first day of practice. The sky was layered with early evening colors, yellow feathers of clouds in the west, shot through with orange and deep violet. A breeze had come up, promising to cool things down.

Yet even though the heat was beginning to diminish, the young men that grouped around their head coach weren't contemplating the weather or feeling the beginnings of sundown. Their minds were full of numbers and moves, and their bodies were talking to them. No matter how hard you worked to prepare for it, the shock of hitting the sleds and running through drills made plenty of guys not want to show up the next day. As they gathered around, Dan Parrish closed ranks with them. But Chip Hunter and his receiver buddy, Jimmy Durr, kept to the fringe, deciding not to mix with the others.

Bobbitt noticed and called them out. "You two got a problem?"

"No," said Durr. His voice was flat.

"No, what?"

"No, sir."

Bobbitt looked at Chip. "You our starting QB, son?"

"Yeah," he responded. The sullen tone was evident. "Yes, sir."

"Then act like it." Bobbitt stared at him hard and let it sink in. He turned to face the others. "Guys, listen up. Today's practice was okay, but we got a long way to go before the first game. Only one week away. Remember, the more you sweat in peace, the less you bleed in war. Now we—" He stopped in mid-sentence when he noticed one of his linemen sitting. "Diamantis, what'd I say about parking your ass on your helmet?"

The boy looked down at his helmet as if seeing it for the first time.

"Gimme a lap."

Diamantis sighed. He raised himself up and started to jog, a painful circumnavigation of the whole field that would take him ten minutes. Bobbitt watched him, shaking his head. He turned his attention back to the others. "Anyway, you probably noticed this hippie here." He gestured to Dan. "His name is Dan Parrish. Coach Parrish to ya'll. He's going to be working with the QBs and receivers. You give him the same respect you give to the other coaches, you got that?"

"Yes, sir," chorused the team. Ku'uipo shot Parrish a *shaka* sign. Durr and Chip exchanged another look and shook their heads.

"Awright, hit the showers."

As the team headed for the locker room, Bobbitt called out, "Chip!"

The Echo Cougars' starting QB stopped and turned.

"I want you to throw a little with Coach Parrish." Bobbitt tossed Dan a ball, turned and walked off before either could protest.

As the shadows began to lengthen, the breeze had freshened and the oaks by the stadium and the pine trees on the north end of the practice field moved in the air currents and rustled with the promise of another autumn's approach. Dan could see Diamantis, the big tackle, running along the tree line. Bobbitt was making an example of him—every move a lesson. But Bobbitt was also trying to teach Chip Hunter a thing or two about respect and teamwork and all the rest. Dan was the tool he'd chosen to use. He turned to the boy and smiled. He decided to slice the first wedge out of Bobbitt's cow pie. "Let's do it," he said, and drew his arm back to throw.

Except Chip wasn't playing. He stood fifteen yards away, helmet in one hand, both arms hanging down at his sides. *Screw you.*

"Drop the helmet, Chip."

He didn't move, so Dan threw a bullet right at his chest, forcing him to drop it. And so it began. The two started throwing to one another, Dan with form and force, Chip with a bitterness that made his balls tumble and his velocity pale, throwing like a petulant child, throwing like a high school hero whose palliative coddling had been pressed into his psyche and taken root.

"Up here," Parrish said, demonstrating a proper release.

Chip ignored him, throwing another three-quarter stinker.

"Up here," Parrish said again, and after another throw, yet again, trying his best not to get angry.

Except Chip's lobs grew even more lackluster until Parrish caught the ball and held it.

"Is this how it's gonna be?"

"I guess so."

Parrish turned and began to walk to the locker room.

"Wait. Where you going?" neighed Chip Hunter.

Parrish stopped. "I got a life, kiddo. I got better things to do than waste my time on a guy who can't throw." Dan could almost see his words crawling under the kid's skin.

Chip threw the ball to Dan, this time the correct way. "There, is that better?"

Dan didn't answer at first. He threw the ball back. They continued the game of catch for a while, now twenty yards apart. "Look, kid, I'm here for one reason." He drew back and the ball left his hand and spiraled into Chip's.

"What's that?" Chip threw the ball back.

"I promised Coach Bobbitt I'd help you get to a four-year school."

Chip laughed. "Oh yeah? How?"

"By teaching you how to throw a football." He tossed the ball again.

Chip caught it and guffawed. "No offense, but what are *you* gonna teach *me* about throwing a football?"

Parrish refused to be offended. He remembered his own childish pride at a similar time in his life. He remembered what it was like to be told over and over how special you were, usually by people that didn't matter. And he knew, because his coach and later his own father had taught him all those years ago, that a lot of pride is misspent and goes by the way when it counts. So a lot of this boy's mouth was nothing but lip. Besides, he knew he could still hold his own. He'd proven it already. And he could tell that, despite the bravado, Chip was curious.

"I'm gonna teach you the Big Three, Chip. Delivery. Accuracy—" he delivered a ball right on the numbers with a perfect spiral, "—and the big V."

Chip tossed the ball back. "The big V? What's that?"

Parrish answered by drilling Chip in the gut. He threw the ball hard, a bullet from behind the ear, straight into the solar plexus again, knocking the wind from the boy and making him gasp.

"Velocity."

Chip glared at Parrish. Dan stared back, the hint of a mischievous grin twisting at his lips. *What do you think about that, boy?* Chip slowly gathered his breath back. Then gripped the ball, planted his feet and fired right back at Parrish.

After that, it was on. The two of them threw back and forth to each other. Check that: *at* each other. You could hear the ball sizzling through the air, smacking into their hands. You could also hear the crack as one of Dan's fingers was jammed and sprained. There was the thud of the ball when it slipped through Chip's hands and into his gut. There was the on-the-numbers rifle that almost put Chip on the ground, and the on-the-numbers missile that almost dropped Dan. But through it all neither of them backed down or showed any pain or weakness, except in the cords of their necks and the lines on their foreheads.

A half hour later the two were still gunning the football back and forth. The sky had grown dark—you could barely see the ball anymore—yet testosterone meters had pegged and the world had shrunk to a small circle of pride. When they ended it, the world was black and the bats were circling in the pines.

Later, in Bobbitt's grungy office, JD looked up from his notebook and examined Dan standing in the doorway. The lights had dimmed; only one shower was on and all the players had left. He rolled a wheeled chair across the room, opened his small refrigerator and offered Dan a Yoo-hoo.

"No thanks," said Dan. His smile was warped by fatigue.

"Don't know what you're missing," said Bobbitt. He cracked the bottle open and drank it all in one pull.

"Yeah I do. About a thousand calories if I remember correctly."

Bobbitt tossed the bottle into a trash bin. He regarded Dan. "How'd it go out there?"

"That kid needs a serious trip to the woodshed."

"So did you at his age."

Parrish held the palms of his hands up, facing them toward the light over the desk. They were red, almost raw. And one of his pinkies was swollen to twice its normal size.

"What'd I tell ya?" said JD. He stood. "Lemme get you some ice—"

Dan stopped him with a look. He cleared his throat and

held a finger to his lips. "Not till our boy leaves." He gestured through the office window at Chip, just exiting the showers, scowling at Dan as he walked across to the lockers.

Bobbitt turned away from the window and stared into the wall of photos, letting his eyes go fuzzy. "Tell me you didn't let him walk all over you."

"Oh, I dunno..." Parrish grinned when he glanced through the window at Chip. The Echo QB was standing in front of his locker, bare-chested, looking down at his torso. It was covered with red welts. "...I'm pretty sure I made an impression."

That Saturday the Echo Cougars won their opener, a less-than-impressive one point win at home. The ground game was lackluster, Chip's performance was so-so but the defense was solid. To JD it meant they had a lot of work to do.

To Dan it meant they were undefeated.

CHAPTER 23

On Friday nights, Dillon's bustled with paycheck activity. Mothers bought groceries for the week, single fathers stood at the frozen foods section ogling the plethora of mac 'n' cheese options, while teens roamed the aisles, cobbling together dollars to buy whatever they could afford with respect to Madison Avenue's latest, greatest, teeth-gnashing glut of caffeinated energy drinks. Or beer if they had the requisite fake ID.

Katy Hunter stood behind her half-full cart at the cereal aisle. The Friday evening ritual was not hers. She did most of her shopping on Saturday. Except now, with the advent of football practice and the possibility of small-town tailgate parties and Chip being front and center, she decided to get things done a day early.

"Buy one, get one free on Cap'n Crunch," said a voice behind her.

She turned and gasped, recognizing the voice and reacting before she could control herself. Dan Parrish stood three feet away in his weathered Goodwill khakis, sneakers and tee. There was a pause. "What are you doing here?" she demanded, flustered. Her voice was more breath than sound. Her hand suddenly—inexplicably—went to the top button of her blouse as she looked around to see if anyone she knew was watching.

Dan's smile vanished. "Nice to see you, too, Katy."

She turned away and began to push her cart, forgetting why she'd come to the cereal aisle, forgetting everything. Dan watched for a few seconds and must have made a decision. He rushed the dozen or so feet up the aisle and blocked her way.

"Katy," he said, "what the hell? What's going on—"

"Dan, not here, not now." She tried to push past him.

"Oh yeah?" Dan's voice rose a few decibels in volume. "Then *when?*" He tried but failed not to sound shrill and somehow desperate.

Curious people turned to look. Katy shrunk. There was no way she was going to do this here. Not after so many years.

She said, "How about *never*, Dan. Is never good for you? Because it's really good for me." Her hiss had become something like a choking rasp.

He lowered his voice and said, "I kinda figured that when I didn't hear from you for eighteen years. What I never figured out was why."

At that, Katy's eyes became slits. She bared her teeth. Dan Parrish, this man from her past, was trying to open old, deep wounds, trying after all these years to dredge up a moment in time that had long been buried. After all, life goes on. The world turns. People change. And the characters in Parrish's orbit don't even exist anymore. Out came an index finger, pointed in Dan's face. "You know why!" she said, the words coated in a rime of insinuation.

"Don't give me that," he said. "I see the way you take care of his grave—"

She cut him off with a hard slap to the face, the sound of it ricocheting down the aisle and across to the sundries, making heads turn as far away as the bakery section. All of a sudden people that had no business knowing anything about Dan and Katy were engaged. Cell phones came out. Tongues began to wag.

A stock boy summoned his courage and approached. "Mrs. Hunter, you need help?" He stared at Dan with more bravado than actual bravery.

"That won't be necessary, Scotty." She looked straight at

Dan. "He was just leaving."

Dan leaned into Katy's face and said, "*Mrs. Hunter?* Shame on you, Katy." He turned to leave.

She reached out her right hand and grabbed his shoulder and spun him around. All of a sudden it didn't matter to her that the stock boy was there and it didn't matter that people were listening. This stranger with his scripted rejoinders had decided who she was and what she was.

"What did you expect from me, Daniel? To *wait?*"

"Yeah, I guess I did."

She stared at him.

"Ya know why?" he said.

Yes. She knew why.

Of course she knew why. Except she'd be damned if she'd admit it to this man from her past, a past that didn't matter anymore.

So he reminded her. "Because you said you would."

Dan turned around and started walking. He had to concentrate not to hurry. One foot in front of the next; eyes forward. His ears rang and the edges of his vision were blurring. The sounds of his shoes squeaking on the tiles made him worry that his feet would fail him. He didn't want to stumble.

He looked once over his shoulder and saw the once-upon-a-time girlfriend watching him go. Sounds of life returned. Someone on the store speakers announced a pork rib two-for-one promotion. Then, "Clean up on aisle six," because someone had spilled a gallon of milk.

In the cereal section the overhead neon lights made Katy Hunter's skin pale and her eyes recede.

The tears on her face sparkled like someone else's diamonds.

CHAPTER 24

Hours later, Dan couldn't remember the route he'd taken on his walk home. He must have left his groceries at the store, too, because he was thirty dollars short and there was no evidence in the refrigerator that he'd filled out his grocery list. No receipt, either, so he hoped there was a way to fix things.

Money doesn't grow on trees, Danny Boy.

He felt sticky with sweat and he knew that his cheeks were stained from hot tears.

He hadn't expected Katy's anger. From others, yeah, but not from Katy. And the vitriolic outburst. The slap in the face. He was an idiot. For years he had pictured their reunion. They would fall into each other's arms and she would be warm to the touch and her lips would invite him into her life again. They would pick up where they left off. Things would be like they were before.

Eighteen years ago.

What a dope. The real world was a desperate place filled with desperate people. Katy took what she could get. She made do. She found a provider and decided to settle for that. He couldn't blame her for that.

He climbed under his wool blanket. He'd changed the light bulb over his bed, yet still it seemed dim and the unarticulated space around him a haven for shadows. No one lived like this. *No one lives like this.* Was it any wonder that Katy didn't want to speak to him? Who could blame her? Where was his head?

What was he thinking?

He threw back his blanket, sat up and grabbed his jeans from the floor then reached into the back pocket and extracted the old picture of Katy. If he tore it up he'd be sorry. He'd lived with the memory of it for so many years now that it had become part of him, like a promise from the outside world. He couldn't believe how much the old Katy looked like the new. She was still everything he loved. She was still his ideal.

He reached across and put the photo on the workbench. He pulled the overhead string to turn off the light. When his eyes adjusted to the darkness he lay back down and covered himself again. He hoped he would be able to sleep.

The next day Echo JC got off their busses after a four-hour drive across farm country and won in a rout, 34-6, against an uninspired team from Oklahoma.

The quiet man knows a few things now: a possible street address, the way the neighborhoods look at night, the lack of noise at night. A gunshot would echo off the little houses. Two or three or a fusillade would wake these people up, so he'd have to think about a proper timetable. He'd have to do some daytime recon. The neighbors shouldn't become part of this.

That next morning, the quiet man decided to drive by the campus. He circled the place for the better part of an hour. He had to roll up his windows and turn on the air conditioner. It was too hot and too dry for him. He wondered how anybody could live here.

But he knew exactly how somebody could die here.

CHAPTER 25

At 4:59 a.m., Dan's hand reached out and slapped the top of the old Westclox alarm clock with the glow-in-the-dark hands that he'd found buried in a box in the rafters. He threw the covers off and rolled up, dropping his feet onto the concrete. He reached over his head and pulled the light cord and his world was illuminated. *Time to get up. A new day is here.* He rubbed his face and ran his hands through his hair. Then he groped down by his feet and found his pants and toed into them. *Lots to do today.*

At the same time, three blocks away, Professor Agnes Stankowiecz slid open her kitchen curtain in the gray light and studied the world outside from her place behind the sink. This time of day was always the worst for her. But she observed nothing out of the ordinary: no parked car on the curb, nobody lurking in the shadows. The yards were deserted, the sidewalks empty, the houses along the street dark. Most of the sky was a haze. Satisfied, she pushed the opaque cloth aside, clicked the light on and faced the new day.

A minute later, Dan Parrish pedaled by on his rickety old Schwinn. He must be going to work, she decided. His first day. Good. She hoped he wasn't going to be another of her bad calculations when it came to men. She had to be careful; she'd been wounded too many times. If truth be told, she should probably steer clear. Yet there was something about Dan Parrish that she couldn't deny. The attraction was definitely there. Speaking with him one-on-one made her heart go fluttery and her brain fuzzy. He was shy, he was careful, and he acted as if he liked her. So if warning lights flashed, it was a function of her past mistakes. Nothing wrong with that. At least she'd begun to learn from her mistakes. She poured the rest of her coffee into the sink, turned, and padded into her little bedroom to get ready for work. Another day, another surprise.

Dan stood behind the steam counter and peered over the glass at his nearly empty cafeteria. It was noon and the place should have been crowded with students. Instead he could hear the echo of a dozen or so instructors and a small gaggle of bag lunch youngsters using the tables and the condiments, but nothing else. Maybe they had been too busy or too involved in classes to run off to the McDonalds, but Dan knew that neither the smells nor the displays were a draw. Beside him one of the cafeteria ladies shuffled from pan to pan, eying the offerings with a jaded expression, one that told the whole story. The other three ladies sat at the cutting table playing cards. Jorge had planted his rear on a stool in the corner trying, and failing miserably, to juggle potatoes. The peeler was clutched in his teeth like a pirate.

Parrish reached over and snatched a spoon from the woman manning the pots. She was startled and turned and backed away a step. He dug the spoon into what was supposed to be gravy, tasted it, spat it out. It hit the floor and fanned into an eccentric blob of goo. "Jesus," he said.

The lady didn't say a word. She turned to her two compatriots and sniffed, and three sets of eyes stared at Daniel Parrish with contempt. Whose fault was this, anyway? It certainly wasn't theirs. The menu was posted. It hadn't changed in years. Nor had the tired, old recipes. *So now who is going to clean up this mess on the floor?* Dan wrote something in his notebook and ignored his now-disgruntled staff.

A minute later, as Jorge was in the act of pitching another trio of potatoes high into the air, he noticed the side door opening and a girl coming to the counter. The potatoes fell to earth and rolled across the tiles. Jorge wiped his hands on his apron, put the peeler in his pocket, and looked up to wink at Tiny Lopez, a young Latina with a shy smile and formidable breasts that spilled out of her V-neck bodice like over-leavened dough. Anyone could see that Jorge was in love. To him, she was two hundred pounds of wonderful, and on this day a vision of loveliness in her tight jeans and puffy pink sweater. She wore bright fuchsia lipstick that she had just touched up in the ladies room, and her eyes were lined with what looked like gold-specked butterfly dust.

"Hi, Tiny. How's it going?"

"Oh, hi, Jorge. Pretty good, I guess." She hadn't noticed his infatuated stare, or at least acted as if she hadn't.

Jorge followed her eyes to a steam pan filled with dead gray meatloaf. It was next to the tray of dead brown broccoli spears and behind the soup tureen filled to overflowing with yesterday's noodle surprise. He tripped over himself getting to the table and grabbed an empty plate from the top of a stack. Before she could point and select, he had already begun piling on the meatloaf. It was an offering to the gods of surplus. The pile became a mountain and Tiny Lopez giggled despite herself. Jorge snatched up a ladle and dipped it into the gravy. He was about to smother the meatloaf when Parrish grabbed his wrist and stopped him. If looks could kill, Dan would have been dead on the floor.

"Whatchu doin', man?" he hissed through clenched teeth, glaring at his new boss.

Dan ignored him. He looked at Tiny and smiled his most unctuous smile. "The gravy is all lumps today, ma'am." He gripped Jorge's wrist like a kung-fu master. He turned to Jorge. "Isn't it, Jorge?" He let go the wrist and the brown globule fired up into the buzzing neon lights and stuck on one of the ceiling panels. *Thuck!*

"See what I mean?" he added. "The mashed potatoes are a sin and the mystery dessert is three days old." He looked at her again. "Come back tomorrow, though, and Jorge will whip you up the best *huevos rancheros* you've ever had. Right, Jorge?"

A very confused Jorge nodded.

Tiny beamed. "Ooh," she purred. "For me?" Then, "I love *huevos rancheros!*" From her side of the counter she looked deep into Jorge's eyes. Then she, too, leaned over onto the sneeze guard. Her boobs pressed into the fogged glass like cartoon thought balloons erupting from a levee of pink fuzz. Steam floated up when she batted her eyes. "Bye, Jorge, see you tomorrow." She turned and left.

Jorge watched her go, speechless. When the door swung shut behind her, he shook his head and turned to Dan, palms to the sky. His eyebrows arched and his upper lip rolled onto his teeth. Dan thought he looked like he might cry.

"What the—?"

"You want her or not?" Dan asked.

He wiped his eyes with the back of his arm. "You *seriousity*, man? Tiny Lopez is totally *beaugorgeous*, homes!"

"Speak English."

"Yes, I want her."

"Cool. You help me, I'll help you."

"Oh yeah? How?"

"Be here. Every day at 6 a.m. Don't be late."

Then Parrish walked off to examine the kitchen mop closet. The place needed a top-to-bottom cleaning. And he decided to put the ladies to work taking inventory from corner to corner. He had to know what he was dealing with. No more card games. He also had to get the grill working and compile a food buying list and work up a new menu. No more glop. To hell with the glop. New menu coming right up!

The gravy on the ceiling released with a glort and plopped down on Jorge's forehead.

CHAPTER 26

Back in the early 1920s the highway running through Echo was only a farm road of gravel and dust. And on that road, a half-mile north of the city limits, a local man named Jackson Buck and his wife, Harriet, opened a place to serve ranchers and other hard-working folks. Over the years Buckhouse BBQ became a fixture.

It now sported memorabilia-covered walls of rough-hewn pine, blackened and sap-hardened, smelling of hickory smoke and the millions of meals that had been served over the decades. The floors were also hardened, heart oak that had been littered with peanut shells every day and scuffed by a zillion boot heels sauntering in and out on their way through local history. The place was eternal. There was no side corral anymore—the 1947 tornado took that along with two pit bulls and a litter of cats—and the outhouses in the back had been replaced, thank God. But other than those two small blips on the screen of time, the Buckhouse remained the same. It had survived the stock market crash, the Great Depression and the dust bowl. It had stuck it out through at least three wars, integration, and the not-so-great recession after the millennium. George Washington never slept there, but two heavyweight champions had eaten at the counter. There was even a haiku scrawled on the men's room stall that some said was penned by Jack Kerouac. The Buckhouse was such a constant in the area that the Buck family once petitioned the city council to declare it a building of *historic* significance.

They were refused. Turned out Jackson Buck had taken a run at one of the Councilmen's wives one New Year's Eve and that was that.

No matter, said the Bucks. Jackson Jr. claimed he was going to run for office. He said he would go to the state house for recognition next time.

At the front door, barrels of peanuts were offered *gratis*, and at the bar jars of pickled pigs' feet and pink rubber eggs served to keep the peace until the real food was delivered. During the lunch hour Junior's daughter, Emma, slid ice-cold beers to tired men who worked long hours outdoors. And at night his other daughter, June, kept station, taking care of the families.

Agnes and Dan sat at a cozy corner table, hunkered down away from prying eyes, soaking up the ambiance and listening to Guitar Slim or The Hudson Dusters on the jukebox. They ate from the same plate, a huge feast of ribs that had become the Buckhouse claim to fame over time. There was also slaw and garlic bread and something fried that the house called cow toes, but wouldn't tell anyone what they were made of. The place was crowded, yet nobody recognized Dan or knew Agnes. So, except for the occasional gawk due to Dan's hairstyle, the two were, for all intents and purposes, invisible.

Agnes held a rib with both hands when she bit down and ripped a big chunk of meat away. "Omigod," she said through her teeth. She'd been saying omigod for the last fifteen minutes.

Dan smiled and reached over to dab some sauce from her face. "Good, huh?"

Agnes closed her eyes and nodded. When she smiled her dimples took control of her face.

"Good enough for a third date?" said Dan.

Agnes nodded over the food. She took a sip of her iced tea. "Fourth, actually, if you include the Slurpee at the 7-Eleven."

"That doesn't count."

"Does to me," she pledged. At once she was sorry she'd

just exposed herself. She added, "And yet, here I am, four fabulous dates later and I still don't know a thing about you."

"You're not exactly an open book," he responded. "Which is saying something, seeing as how you're a literature professor."

Agnes placed her finished rib into the plate. She poked her finger around, searching out a possible tidbit or cow toe. "Well, then maybe tonight we can go back to my place," she said, "and do a little, um, *reading*? Wink, wink." She arched her brows and leaned into her leer, almost touching Dan's nose with hers. A kiss was just around the corner.

Except something caught Dan's eye. "Uh, oh," he said. "Here comes Frick and Frack."

Agnes turned to see Jimmy Durr and Chip Hunter swagger across the room, drunk. They spotted Agnes and Dan, nudged each other and giggled like kids. They headed straight for the little corner table.

Durr spoke first. "Well, well, well. No wonder you been getting' straight As...*Coach*."

Agnes' face turned red. Before she could defend herself, Chip piped up, singing a little ditty from kindergarten: "Coach and Teacher sitting in a tree, K-I-S-S-I-N-G. First comes love, then comes marriage, then—"

In a blink Dan was up and in the boy's face. His voice was quiet and controlled and angry when he said, "Cool it, Chip. Now. I'm serious." He wanted to snatch the kid by the scruff of his collar and lead him out the door, but it was too late for that. The entire dining room was watching.

But Chip had a harder head when he was drunk. And there was nothing he liked better than an audience when he'd had a few. Clearly, he hadn't learned his lesson. He said, "Ooh, Big Man is mad. What's Big Man gonna do now? Five step drop?" He mimicked the field drill, stumbling backwards with an air ball and a drunken grimace that was meant to be comical, yet became pitiful when he bumped one of the tables and spilled a beer on a man's lap, a man that was entertaining his family. Somehow Chip had managed to upset one of the plates on the table, too, which alarmed the guy's children. They jumped up and backed into the wall.

Normally, Chip wouldn't get a rise from a guy ten or fifteen years his senior. After all, Chip was pretty big and athletic, a college football player with all the substance and marrow implied in the title.

Except this guy didn't give a damn. And he was big, too. And, judging by his haircut, fresh from a hitch in the Middle East. He clinched his jaw and looked down at his wet lap. He said, "You damn little punk."

The man exchanged looks with his wife. He raised his eyebrows at his kids. They opened their eyes so wide their foreheads disappeared. He took a deep breath then decided to forget everything and let it go.

But Chip couldn't help himself. "Shut yer ass, fat boy," he said, smiling across at Durr.

So Fat Boy lurched up and hit Chip in the mouth. He punched him so fast and with such power that the intensity invested in the punch surprised everybody in the restaurant. But it couldn't have surprised his wife, who knew all about her husband's hair-trigger temper. They lived on a farm west of town, and were not inclined to pay attention to who-was-what in the world of local football. And she'd seen her husband knock a steer to its knees at the State Fair. So this big smart-mouth boy was just an appetizer.

Chip fell to his own knees. His eyes rolled around in his head. *Oh yeah?* He got up. Jimmy Durr headed for the door. Dan raised a hand and said, "Awright, let's just calm down here and—" Chip took a tepid swing at Fats and got three quick shots to the face for his effort. Chip fell onto the oak, into the peanut shells, over-and-done in less-than-one.

Most of the people in the room roared. Even though the Cougars had won their third game in a row, the townsfolk had yet to commit to their star. Getting behind Chip in any meaningful way depended on his skill, yes, but also his smarts. He had thrown three touchdown passes the night before, which wasn't too shabby. But many of them knew the soldier. And knocking out a steer meant more to these people than bumping pads with a linebacker. So the folks in the Buckhouse didn't let up.

Parrish jumped to his feet. "Okay. That's enough," he said, just loud enough for the people close by to hear. "He's through."

The big soldier had other ideas, though. His lap was soaked with beer and his meal was all over the table and floor and if there was anything he couldn't stand about the younger generation, it was their propensity to pop off. He glared at Chip. Then reached down with a big hand to snatch Chip up by his collar. "Yeah, but I'm not," he said.

Parrish took a step toward the man and grabbed the arm of the offending hand. "Yeah. You are. Trust me."

At the bar, June set her work down and motioned to her waitresses to back away. Across the room everyone grew quiet. Agnes's dimples disappeared. Chip squinted into the overhead and held his breath. Parrish might have been scared, but he didn't look it. He didn't look like anything except a man with a thousand-yard stare as poisonous as an adder's.

Then the soldier did something he surely wasn't accustomed to doing. He stood down. He looked at Chip, nodded to Dan, and stood down.

Something in Dan's eyes must have forced him to reconsider.

Dan stood on the Hunter veranda beneath the yellow bug light and spoke to Katy for the first time since the incident in the grocery store. Neither looked the other in the eye. In the distance the sky rumbled and lightning flashed, exposing a bank of rainclouds over the prairie. "He's alright. Couple days he'll be good as new."

Katy took a while to respond. Under the lights in the side yard there was a plastic bag overflowing with beer cans. She looked at the mess and her right hand went to her face. "Yes," she said, "until the next time."

Dan stood silent. The western sky was blistered with bright lines of energy. He put his hands in his back pockets, an old reminder he learned from his father not to get emotional. Then, "Where's Rick?"

"Passed out." She forced a smile. "You know what they say, 'like father, like son.'" She stole a glance out at the car that had delivered her son. Agnes sat in the driver's seat, quiet, patient. The two women exchanged looks. Dan noticed.

"Girlfriend?" Katy said, and dropped her eyes. She almost tittered, but no amount of casual pleasantry could disguise the veil of sorrow or the stirrings of jealousy. How could you not be jealous of such a simple thing? How could you not be sorry at the way things had turned out? And she had cursed Dan a thousand times, but now, in the middle of the night, standing alone, holding things together, a façade, in front of a house that used to be Dan's, she must have felt like the world was caving in.

"If I play my cards right." His words were so quiet she could barely hear them.

Katy looked across at Agnes then back to Dan. "You will."

There it was—a semblance of closure. You can move on, Dan. Everything's okay between us...but will never be the same. He looked at her to see if he'd heard her right. She smiled wanly. He had.

Dan turned to go.

"Dan—"

Dan stopped and turned back around to look up into the porch. Katy stood in the front entrance, under the pale light. The edge of the door covered part of her face. She was the young girl he remembered and the older girl he could never hold again.

"Thanks," she said.

Dan nodded. "Just don't let what happened to me, happen to him."

The door closed. The porch went black.

The quiet man sat in his car a block away.

I've seen everything, now. There's no possible way this thing can end except through the barrel of a gun.

CHAPTER 27

The fall days became a pleasant blur for Dan Parrish. Every morning at six he worked with Jorge, showing him the ins and outs of commercial kitchen work, starting with a mop and bucket, steel wool and elbow grease. Within a week the entire kitchen was as spotless as thirty-year-old equipment could be, and Tiny Lopez became a regular for Jorge's lunch surprises. After a while the cafeteria ladies were impressed with the new energy around the place, too, and began to show up earlier, adding their two cents to the new and ongoing menu debate. When the grill began to work for the first time in several years and the milkshake machine became usable, the new wall menu began to reflect the changes. Jorge took to his cooking lessons, and with Dan's help, breathed new life into the old standbys: uninspired, gray hamburger became cheddar burgers with balsamic onions and chipotle ketchup. Limp french fries became crisp, slow-fried morsels of flavor, smothered in garlic. The turgid grilled cheese was transformed using crust-less bread, roasted bell peppers and Asiago cheese. A big tureen of southwestern chili con carne was suddenly hard to keep full. The mashed potatoes now got a kick from creamy horseradish. Mayonnaise gave way to an aioli made with the house twang hot sauce. Taco Tuesdays was a huge hit. Fruit salads flew out the door. Dan's Caesar salad got Honorable Mention in the local newspaper contest that he didn't even enter. By the middle of October, the Echo Junior College cafeteria was firing on cylinders it didn't know it even had.

But at two o'clock every afternoon the glass doors were locked, the place was cleaned, and preparations were made for the following mornings, so that by three Dan could leave Jorge to the slicing and thawing and steaming and baking. He had to go to the practice field, where he was fully engaged with his other challenge, working with Chip on his timing, his reads, his delivery and his footwork. The Cougars had won two more games. But what was more important, ever since the debacle on the floor of the Buckhouse, Chip had become more attentive, forcing his teen angst to back off so that Dan could teach him some of the throws it would take to succeed at the next level. The snide remarks and eye rolling had ceased, much to the chagrin of Chip's sidekick, Jimmy Durr. And after the last game, a fourth-quarter, last minute comeback in which Chip had excelled, there was no arguing Chip's new skills had become a bright spot that the whole town was talking about.

For Chip, now, sound mechanics had become his primary goal. That and a little recognition. He wanted out of Echo, except he wanted to do it on his own. He explained to Dan that if he accepted assistance from his father, he'd never hear the end of it and would be beholden forever. So for the present, he was willing to let Dan help him help himself. And the more he listened, the more he learned. And the more he learned, the more he began to respect his teacher. More importantly, Chip seemed to trust him.

Between practices, classes and his job in the cafeteria, Dan could often be found at Mulligan's with Agnes, noshing on the diner food and drinking the coffee. They always sat in the corner booth to avoid the stares. For some reason, long hair and a beard made people look twice. Dan knew he stood out—Echo hadn't changed much in the last couple decades with regard to the hippie look—yet so far nobody had confronted him for his new or old sins, and for that Dan was grateful. One of the promises he'd made to himself was to stay off everyone's radar. You couldn't get in trouble if you were invisible.

Every evening when he got home, Dan made supper. He had been delighting Millie and the twins with his cooking— braised short ribs one evening, catfish picatta another—and as a result they were willing to do the shopping, relieving him of that chore. By the time he was finished in the kitchen, he was worn out. Good food wasn't random, it took effort, and the food was undeniably good. Even Millie had begun to put on some weight. Color was returning to her cheeks. Dan showed her how to make pesto—using her window-grown basil and swapping walnuts for pine nuts—and she was plopping dollops of the green stuff on everything, including her eggs. She was even drinking white zin now—albeit with dinner only— and reading about cabernets.

Then before bed, when Dan put his schoolwork down, he would study the Echo JC playbook. He needed to know everything front to back. If coaching was a test, he would know every play in the offense book, and every defensive scheme that was thrown at them. Besides, it was fun to get his head into football again, a state of grace that few people could appreciate. And the team had been a surprise to many in the state. They weren't just good now, they were very good.

One evening after a dinner of rosemary-crusted porterhouse steaks in red wine sauce, and potatoes-au-gratin with goat cheese, Dan was washing dishes, watching Millie and the twins squabble over dessert. He smiled to himself and thought about his life now, how simple it was and how happy he could be with the way things seemed to be turning out. He had begun to get his groove back. The last decades were beginning to recede. Things were looking up for him. It had been ages since he could say that.

* * *

But on the other side of town, in the house that Dan had grown up in, Rick Hunter and his son Chip sat at the dining room table with no pleasant thoughts and no moments of grace. Chip wolfed his food down with his eyes focused elsewhere.

His father watched, swirling ice in his empty highball glass, the ill-fitting Rolex on his wrist sliding left and right in counterpoint to his agitated state. The world had not been treating him with respect, it seemed to him, and he wasn't happy about it. His kid was becoming a hero in town, but who was responsible for that? The answer was more than he could bear. Even the thought made him sick.

Katy entered from the kitchen hallway with another scotch for her husband. She placed it before him on the table and stepped back. He frowned.

"What'd I tell you about this much ice?"

Chip stiffened. He stopped eating but did not look up.

"I'll work on it, dear," said Katy.

Chip looked at her and she sneaked a wink at him. He shook his head, no doubt disgusted with his father for treating his mother like chattel.

Rick saw the gesture but chose to ignore it. "How's school, son?"

Chip shrugged without commitment and shoveled a fork full of spaghetti into his mouth.

"Grades?" said the patriarch.

Chip gave his father a so-so gesture, wagging his hand in the air, mouth working, eyes on the plate.

Hunter took a long pull on his drink. "Mediocrity won't cut it at KU, Chipper. How many times do I have to tell you that?"

Chip looked up. He realized his strategy to silence the questioning was failing. He swallowed hard and put his fork down and sipped his iced tea. "I told you, I'm not going to KU."

"Oh, you're going," said his dad.

"Why? Because you went there? Because grandpa went there?"

"It's called tradition, Chip." He locked eyes with his son. "You got a problem with that?"

Chip had to pick his battles carefully with his father. Now was not the time, with the old man's belly full of scotch, to start something that could never end right. "I just want to make my own way," he replied softly, averting his father's gaze, staring down at his dinner plate. He picked his fork up and began to move the food around. He hoped this would be the end for now.

Hunter gulped the rest of his scotch and banged the tumbler down on the table. He leaned forward in his chair and put his elbows on either side of the empty glass. He must have decided to call Chip's bluff when he said, "So, I assume you have a plan for financing this, uh, independent streak of yours?"

Chip was trapped. He didn't want to explain himself. He couldn't talk with his father and keep a civil tongue. Sharing ideas with the man had always been impossible. Any kind of discourse was insufferable and fraught with wracking diatribes on both sides. He just wanted to hide. He just wanted to leave the table and walk away and never look back. But he knew that wasn't an option. Instead he answered. "I got prospects," he said.

Hunter snorted.

"I'm serious. There've been some scouts at the games. They've talked with Coach Parrish—"

"NO!" Hunter slammed his hand down hard on the table. His glass fell over and the dinner plates rattled with the concussion. Ice slid onto the floor. "What did I *tell* you about *that* name in *this* house?"

In the kitchen Katy turned away from the sink and hurried to separate the two before the quarrel snowballed.

"What's the big deal?" said Chip. "The guy knows a lot of

stuff. And he can—"

Hunter stood up so fast his chair fell over. He pointed a finger at his son. "Shut up, Chip! Now!" He turned and walked down the hall, then kicked open the screen door and exited from the side of the house, the door slapping like hands to the face. Chip and Katy watched him go.

"Mom, what's going on?"

Katy didn't answer. She couldn't look at her son. He would see it; he would see the truth; he would know. So she stared at the hole in the house, into the echo of the slapping screen door...until she heard another common liturgy of sounds—the car door slamming shut, the engine revving, the squeal of tires on the pavement...*Damn Dan Parrish for coming home. Damn him for coming back and making us do this. Damn him for destroying my charade.*

"Dad's gonna ruin everything," Chip said. "I just know it."

CHAPTER 28

Twenty minutes later, a drunk Rick Hunter stood on Coach JD Bobbitt's porch. The shrubs that lined the front of the place were trimmed and tidy. A jack-o-lantern grinned with the golden glow of candle power from the other side of the living room window. Plastic spiders hung from the eaves of a house that relied heavily on pride of ownership for its charm. The sun had sunk below the horizon and the air had become brisk with a new evening coolness. Fall was in the air and the chill winds of winter weren't far away.

Bobbitt leaned against the railing and nodded his head. He'd been listening for five minutes to an unrelenting diatribe about his quarterbacks coach. He nodded and nodded. This man was out of his mind with anger, he knew, and Bobbitt allowed him to vent, no matter that he was full of baloney. And judging by the fumes, scotch. Hunter was actually threatening him with *immediate termination...*

"...unless this loser is no longer allowed to poison the waters of this respectable community and this respectable institution of higher learning, and he *will* be fired immediately or" yadda, yadda, yadda...

Bobbitt interrupted. "I don't have time for this, Rick. My supper's getting cold." He turned around and reached for his doorknob.

Hunter grabbed his shoulder from behind and spun him around, not an easy thing to do considering Bobbitt's size.

"You're not hearing me, JD. Get rid of that loser or I will."

Bobbitt slapped Hunter's hand away. "You do that and your kid will be riding the pine. Is that what you want? Huh? Your kid on the bench during his last year of JC ball?" His lip curled with contempt. "You can't imagine what that can do to a kid, Rick...or can you?"

Those three words. The way he said it. "You wouldn't dare," Hunter said.

"Try me."

Hunter spat on the ground. "I'll do more than that," he said. He turned away and aimed his unsteady feet toward his idling car. He barked something else, but JD Bobbitt didn't hear it. He watched as Hunter fell into the front seat, picked his gold toothpick from the ashtray, and jammed it in his mouth.

He threw the car into reverse and pulled away with an angry flourish.

CHAPTER 29

The Smoky Hill River is a six-hundred-mile-long stretch of water traveling through the Great Plains of North America from Colorado to Kansas. The river got its name from the Smoky Hills region of Kansas through which it flows. Native Americans living along the Smoky Hill considered it and the Kansas River to be the same, and their names for it included Chetolah and Okesee-sebo. Early maps of European explorers called it the 'River of the Padoucas' because its source was located in what was then Padouca or Comanche territory.

There were other names for the Smoky Hill River: Fork-of-the-hill Buckaneuse, La Fourche de la Cote Bucaniere, Man-oiyohe, Pe P'a, Sand River, Shallow River, Smoky Creek, and Rahota Katit Hibaru, among others.

Chip and his friends didn't care much about the river itself, nor its name. The only place that mattered was The Bluff. On a Friday night they could be seen entertaining themselves on the hoods of their cars or wrapped in horse blankets, drinking beers and making out with their girls.

So on this cool, late-October night, Chip was sprawled out on a blanket on the hood of his Jeep with Darla. Together they watched as a million stars paraded across the sky. On the horizon the lights of Echo blinked, appearing and disappearing like a burn off at one of the fields, golden and smoky and platted in squares. Nearby a dozen car radios spat out tunes from New York or L.A., and if one could listen in to the con-

117

versations beneath the radio noise, one could hear a dozen boys wailing to girls who didn't believe their tales of desperate love. Friday nights were an investment if you were a boy from Echo: a gallon of gas and a six-pack for a chance at love or ridicule. Or sometimes both.

A meteor arced across the sky as Darla popped a beer tab, the gush of foam and the sound of metal on metal destroying what had been, for Chip, sublime. When she thrust the beer in his face, he waved it off.

"You a beer queer now, is that it?" She put the can to her lips and gulped the tepid offering.

"I have a game tomorrow night. Is that okay?"

"Since when did that stop you?" She had irritated him lately. But apologizing wasn't part of her DNA. She took another huge gulp, knowing it would bother him. "That new guy's got you doing all kinds of crazy stuff," she said. She rolled onto her side and her ass pushed up off the hood as she brought her knees together, accentuating the creases in her tight blue jeans.

There was a pause while Chip sighed. He tried to turn his attention back to the stars. *How do I respond? This thing is a lot bigger than she thinks. It's everything for me.*

"That *new guy* has me at five-and-oh. He's got me setting the conference on fire. He's got scouts calling me. He's got me believing in myself—"

Darla rolled her eyes.

"—and he's got me a chance at a full ride."

"Who cares? Your daddy's got you covered wherever you decide to go."

"No. He's got me covered wherever *he* decides I go. Huge diff, Darla." He calmed himself when he saw some of the other couples looking over at the two. "Don't you see? If I'm successful, I'm a chip off the old block. I'm someone who had all the breaks. If I'm not successful, I'm a discredit to my family. It's a no-win proposition."

Darla said, "So?"

Chip couldn't believe his ears. He sat up, turned and looked her square in the eye. "What's it like?" he asked.

Darla sneaked a peek at herself in the mirror. "What's what like?"

"What's it like on Planet Darla?"

She shrugged and continued drinking.

Chip sat back against the windshield and stared up at the stars. He crossed his arms against the chill. There was a certain amount of understanding that just wasn't there anymore. Maybe it had never been there. Or maybe he was seeing a bigger picture. At any rate, when she finished both beers and burped like a baboon, the sound of it resonating down the bluff and across the river to die amid the trees lining the bank, he closed his eyes and shook his head and wished he was somewhere else.

CHAPTER 30

Aside from the annual Christmas parade, there was no bigger day in town than game day for Echo Junior College football. The feeling was electrifying, so much so that the entire community shut down. Nobody wanted to miss the game, and the hoopla and tailgating that went on before the whistle blew. But the merchants shut down also, because there was no business to speak of in town. A small community on the prairie tended to do things together. And in Echo, during the football season, the game was the focal point of everyone's plans.

Coming in to this night, the Echo JC Cougars were riding a five game winning streak, undefeated thus far and already halfway through the season. It was no secret that game six would provide a little more pre-game excitement than in past years. Little boys were wearing Chip's jersey, little girls were dreaming of becoming Echo JC cheerleaders, and townsfolk were exchanging tailgate recipes and quaffing more beer than usual, piling into the stadium or filling the parking area hours early, milling about discussing the pros and cons of the pistol offense, the excitement of the 4-3 blitz packages and the need for a Starbucks on Main Street.

The locker room was abuzz as well. Early on this Saturday afternoon players began to stream in with the hint of a swagger, unaccustomed to the adulation they'd been receiving from Echoans of every stripe, from the banker to the grocer to the underage girls that followed their favorite player's exploits and wore their numbered pins in their hair or on their sweaters. The Cougars logo was plastered all over town. Banners over Main Street proclaimed them demigods and pennants in all the windows were full of pre-congratulatory lauding and boasting. If you were fortunate enough to be on the team, odds were you'd get an extra scoop of ice cream in your milk shake or more french fries with your burger. Girls that had ignored you in class were now taking the time to say hello, and even some teachers, it was whispered, would raise your grade a notch if you scored a touchdown or recovered a fumble.

An hour before dusk, Oak Springs, the visiting team, along with their cheerleaders and band, arrived in five yellow school busses. The players streamed across the field into their locker room, receiving a share of catcalls, boos, and the occasional smattering of applause from the handful of fans that had traveled across several counties to watch their sons, boyfriends, or in some cases husbands do battle with the surprising Echo JC juggernaut.

Back inside the Cougar's locker room, the team prepared for battle. Coaches weaved through the young men, barking words of encouragement, giving last minute instructions and helping players strap it on, getting ready for war. The mood was upbeat and confident. Chip's eyes were clear and bright and his body was as fit as it had ever been as he laid his gear out and with single minded concentration donned each piece, making sure everything was just so. Some of the guys tried to make small talk with him, but his answers were mostly monosyllabic grunts. He was so focused he couldn't have heard anything, just the roar of inextinguishable energy and the murmur in his brain that surely repeated each setup, each play, each timed step in the drop, each read, and each route his receivers would be running on the field. He could probably close his eyes and see the man on the other team who would be assigned with the task of stopping him from taking off with the ball. He wasn't worried. In fact, he was champing at the bit.

He envisioned himself carrying out every one of his assignments without a mistake.

At 6:25 p.m. the sun dipped behind the corner of the visitors' stands as the day morphed into evening. The distant prairie was golden with dust and the western sky was ablaze with ropes of red and yellow. It was almost Halloween, so some of the kids in the crowd were wearing cougar suits. The trombone players in the band wore Cougar paws, the drummers wore Cougar snouts and Cougar fangs in their mouths. At the concession stand the ladies from the Episcopal church tried to sell Cougar dogs to people who'd been eating all afternoon, while two of the soda vendors in the stands had been caught up in the euphoric drive to win and were drunk, stumbling, spilling the Jaycee's super Cougar lemonade all over their aprons as they tried to keep it together. The members of the Echo High School Cougars football team were special guests for this game, sitting together in their team jerseys, many of them hoping to one day play for Echo JC on their way to greatness with the Jayhawks, then the Chiefs. Various small-market media crews were busy setting up at multiple points around the field. The parking area was now full to bursting with cars, the tailgaters abandoning their stations and their still-glowing grills to stream into the stadium. Among them Jorge and Tiny, Darla, Millie, Sam (who was the proud overseer of the school's now-busy cafeteria), even the twins, who'd taken a special interest this year, considering their housemate was involved in the coaching of the team.

When the parents of the quarterback, Rick and Katy Hunter, appeared, many in the crowd fell away and allowed them to parade by, the scene reminiscent of royal pageantry, the pomp of the local high school homecoming king and queen from twenty years ago. They waved and smiled, stopping in front of a life-size statue at the stadium gate. Newspaper camera shutters whirred, selfies were clicked, teeth sparkled in the artificial light. The statue, a verdigris-layered, he-

roic, robed figure, stood over the throng like Moses on Ara-
rat, its bronze plaque reading:

THE HONORABLE JUDGE HARRISON HUNTER
"JUSTICE PARAMOUNT, DUTY
AND HONOR ABOVE ALL ELSE"

Judge Hunter was the stadium's namesake, of course. He
was the one who had arranged for the land acquisition—some
called it a flat-out land grab—from the state and the one who
had schmoozed with then Governor Babbington for the money
to build it and the statue. So HUNTER FIELD was the name
of the place.

Harrison Hunter was also Chip Hunter's grandfather. In the
past Chip had displayed a pretty elastic view of the man. On
the one hand he was an unjustly venerated paragon whose
bronzed effigy had inspired life-long, over-the-top rants from
his alcoholic father. But on the other hand, he was dead and
deserved some respect for his accomplishments, in spite of his
father's totem-pole ideology. If one of the reporters standing
by were to go into the locker room and ask Chip for the truth,
he would say that both his grandfather and his father were
symbols of greatness. If he were to be more candid and perhaps more erudite, he would offer an aside, not for publica-
tion, declaring one of them a fossilized, scheming, blackmail-
ing gas bag, and the other a lick-spittling, propaganda down-
spout. There was anger in Chip's heart that he could not deny.

Except Chip had been sober and uncharacteristically in-
tense during this last month, and happened to be the big man
of the moment, which should have given him some food for
thought, and at the very least some ancestral breathing room.
As yet, he probably wasn't sure if things were working out.
He wasn't sure if things were better or worse.

* * *

A still-smiling Rick and Katy Hunter moved on, soon finding the center aisle and their seats on the fifty-yard line. On their way they passed Agnes, who watched the proceedings with beetled brow and a touch of humor as she tore off pieces of cotton candy and stuffed them into her mouth. Earlier she'd examined the statue and the plaque. It was always wise to learn some local history. Especially when it might concern her place in the scheme of things.

Across the field, on the seventh row of the visitors' section, the quiet man sat in his own nimbus of distaste, surrounded by what he thought of as corruption. He'd never attended a football game in his life. Things have changed, though, and in this stupid little town in Kansas, his reconnaissance patrols had led him to this deceit. Home tickets, he learned, were impossible to find. So he sat where he sat, and pulled his hat brim down and closed his eyes, pretending he was holding his Glock out over the idiots, forcing them to pay attention to real life.

Sometimes when the quiet man thinks about it, the colors fade and he sees everything as it should be—a gray display in a gray tunnel, black shapes looming in the margins, silent, no noise at all, no noise except when he fires his weapon and the echoes reverberate.

Echo. Echo. Echo. Ha ha.

And the people close their eyes because they're frightened. They know there is no real football game. It isn't about a football game. It's a sham, a gust of dirty wind. Someone else's dream. Not his.

CHAPTER 31

Inside the stadium's home team locker room, Coach Bobbitt's loud voice echoed off the tiles and painted concrete, instructing his players to gather round. It was time to finish the pregame pep talk, a sermon that began hours ago and culminated with the head coach's tragic, Shakespearian exhortation that everyone knew by heart, a plea that encompassed life, death, and the value of doing your best even if it killed you.

The room grew quiet as the man talked. He mentioned mothers and proud fathers, weeping girlfriends, the Stars and Stripes and God. He called them all good boys. He proclaimed the upcoming contest part of a crusade to greatness. He was biblical, citing Ecclesiastes. He was poetic, quoting Robert Frost. He even managed to paraphrase Ghandi at some point.

"Guys, we're five-and-oh. Half-way home. Half way to the Heart of Kansas Bowl Championship!"

The team hooted and whistled and ad-libbed agreement. Bobbitt waited for their jubilation to die. He gave them all a long, hard look in the eye.

"You know what you want," he whispered. "You know how to get it!" he bellowed. "Now—"

"Take action!" they all yelled in unison. Chip's heart raced at the oft-repeated mantra. He clenched and unclenched his jaw. He was ready to shred the Oak Springs defense. He couldn't wait to take the field, to hear the crowd roar, to win the game.

To please his father.

He looked over at Coach Parrish and their eyes met. He nodded. Parrish smiled and gave him a thumbs up. Chip returned the gesture. Across the locker room Jimmy Durr watched and shook his head, disgusted.

Bobbitt wrapped up his speech. "One, two, three—"

"Hustle! Finish! Win!" they all yelled, and charged out of the locker room, testosterone meters pegged out.

Dan and Chip exchanged one last look of solidarity just as Durr was passing by. "Geez. Get a room why don't ya?" said the insolent wide receiver.

"Shut up, Jimmy," Chip shot back. He strapped his helmet on and headed for the door.

Outside the crowd was already whipped into a frenzy. The team captains from Oak Springs met at midfield with Chip as Echo's sole captain. They shook hands and the referee tossed the coin and Oak Springs won, electing to receive the kickoff.

The whistle blew, the ball was kicked with a resounding WHUMP and sailed into the evening sky. And it was on—a war on the prairie.

Dan and Bobbitt paced the sidelines, their respective stomachs churning as the game took shape. During the first quarter it was clear that neither team was playing close to its capability: passes were dropped, balls were fumbled, tackles missed. Chip soon settled down, though, and on his third possession went six-for-six, mixing it up with three of his receivers including his tight end, driving his team all the way down the field for a touchdown. Oak Springs answered with a series of plays capped by a fifty-yard bomb all the way to the end zone. The score was tied, 7 all.

After the ensuing kickoff, the Echo offense took the field and Chip led them downfield again, mixing passes with running plays and even taking off on a mad dash himself for a twelve-yard gain. He was methodical, unmerciful and confident in the huddle as he led his guys through punishing third-down situations and one heart-stopping fourth-and-one on the sixteen. Two plays later they were in the end zone again, the score now 14-7. The Cougars were ba-a-a-a-d ass.

When the quarter expired, the air in the stadium was charged. Cheerleaders danced on the fifty, bands played fight songs, mothers worried about everything, their hearts filled with the unstated promise of perfection, or in Oak Springs' case, an upset for the ages. On the sidelines, both teams reflected the energy of twenty-thousand fans screaming their lungs out. Coaches and players were going nuts, family members and frenzied fans were off the chain. And the players on the field weren't backing down, thrilling everyone with their hard-nosed football, exciting all the disciples of local color in this sometimes boring little town on the plains.

Up in the booth the coordinators for each team brought their own styles of intensity to the game. They traded insults, sucking down mugs of hot coffee and munching on beef jerky. One guy was chewing tobacco and spitting into a Dixie cup, another was blowing billows of cigar smoke over the throng. Each man for each team, whether on offense or defense, was shouting out directions into his headset, encrypting plays on the fly so that the other team's scouts wouldn't decipher their particular systems. It was an unfortunate arrangement up in the booth, but there was only a chain-link barrier between each side. The sophistication of both offenses and defenses was obvious. Most people listening in thought it was all gibberish.

In the second quarter, Oak Springs scored again on a busted screenplay. The score now stood at 14-14. Then Echo fumbled the kickoff return. A huge groan rumbled through the stadium. Fans threw their hats to the floor in disgust. An Echo cheerleader found tears somewhere and began to weep with ominous foreboding. Dan and JD just shook their heads. As a result of the fumble, Oak Springs managed to kick a field goal just as the two-minute warning for the first half sounded. The celebration on their sideline and in their stands was momentous. Their kicker was mobbed by his fellow players like he'd just won the Cotton Bowl. The score was 17-14, Oak Springs.

Echo received the kickoff and ran it back to the thirty, then went into their two-minute drill. On the fifth play from scrimmage, with only thirty seconds left in the half, Chip ran a bootleg and was tackled at the forty. Flags rained down when a linebacker flew in late and crashed his helmet into Chip's unprotected legs. People in the stands leapt to their feet. Boos rattled off the superstructures. A time out was called. Echo's star quarterback was hurt.

After a moment Chip stood with the help of one of his big linemen, and began to hobble to the sidelines. He couldn't put his weight on his ankle. He would have to sit out the rest of the game before he would know any more, but he knew that it was a sprain at the very least, not good news for the home team.

Parrish ran down the sideline trying to find Chad Stone, the backup. *Where is he? What's he doing?* Dan found him facing the stands, flirting with a cute freshman blonde in the first row, unaware of the drama unfolding on the field. And there was only twenty seconds left to get someone out there. He was mimicking a phone call to the girl when Dan grabbed him.

"Chad! C'mon, man, you're on!"

Chad grabbed his helmet, confused. Suddenly guys were slapping him on the back, offering him words of encouragement. He looked across the bench and saw Chip being helped by the trainer, his shoe being removed, his ankle being wrapped.

Chad looked back at Dan. "But, uh...Coach. I'm not ready, Coach—"

"Well, get ready, son!" commanded JD Bobbitt, thundering up the sideline. "Get *real* ready. Like, NOW!"

Chad yanked his helmet on and adjusted his chin-strap. His heart must have been pounding. He took one step onto the field when Parrish grabbed him by his face mask, spun him around and said, "Twenty-one gun, FOX right."

Chad blinked.

"You got that?"

Chad didn't respond.

"Chad!"

A whisper. "Coach, I'm not sure this is such a good idea." His face was pale. Nausea was beginning to wash over him and his wobbly knees would have to be coaxed into service.

"Listen to me, kid," Dan said, placing his hands on Chad's shoulder pads and drawing him close. "You know how there are moments in your life that you never forget? Moments that last a lifetime?"

"Yessir." Chad gulped, hopefully.

"Well this is one of 'em." He turned the boy toward the field and shoved...

...which caused Chad to stumble and may have been a harbinger of things to come for Echo's number two quarterback. The first play had the team lining up in a shotgun formation. Dan had decided that it was best to keep Chad a few steps off the line, handing the ball off until he gathered himself and took control.

Chad must not have seen it that way, though, when he locked eyes with a big Oak Springs middle linebacker across from him. The guy kept mouthing nasty criticisms of his mother, his grandmother and a sister he didn't even have. When the ball was snapped it flew through Chad's hands, hitting him square in the chest, rebounding high into the air. It was recovered by an Oak Springs defensive back, but not before Chad was knocked senseless by the big linebacker just as time expired.

For Chad, time slowed, then stopped. He lay on his back, eyes glazed. Somebody removed his helmet. Blood trickled from his mouth. The team had wasted no time huddling around him, looking down, when Bobbitt and Parrish broke through with the referee.

Bobbitt knelt down beside his second damaged quarter-back. "Chad, you okay, son?"

Chad clamped his hands over his ears. His expression was far away. "Please stop blowing the whistle," he demanded. Nobody was blowing a whistle. A murmur arose among his teammates. One of them snickered. Dan silenced the guy with a look.

Bobbitt held up three fingers. "Chad, how many fingers do you see?"

Chad squinted, focused, re-focused. "Six." His voice cracked like the honk of a pubescent duckling.

The ref traded looks with JD and Dan.

"Son, who is the president of the United States?"

Chad was quiet for a moment. Overhead the lights buzzed and he squinted at them, puzzled. He refocused on the guy who was speaking behind the roar. "Justin Bieber!" he exploded, ostensibly over the roar in his ears.

The ref turned to Bobbitt and Parrish. "He's done."

Bobbitt sagged. "C'mon, Sam, he'll be good as new after half-time—"

"Justin Bieber!" shouted Chad again. He was a player on a game show. He almost giggled. He must have been sure he was right. Then he frowned: he'd forgotten to frame his answer in the form of a question.

The referee crossed his arms and arched his brows. Bobbitt sighed. He turned to Parrish and behind him to the head trainer, who stood in the shadows reading a notebook with concussion protocols printed in bold and underlined in red. "You heard the man," Bobbitt said.

Dan and the trainer collected their damaged boy and helped him off the field. There was a smattering of weak applause from the grandstands. People were already grouping together in front of the concession stand, talking about the tragedy. What would the team do? Who would replace Chip?

The smells of popcorn and sugared syrups wafted in the still night air. High above the field, bats circled in the halogen aureoles, picking off thousands of rapturous insects swarming in the artificial incandescence.

The first half was over and done. And for all intents and purposes...so were the Cougars.

CHAPTER 32

Inside the Echo JC locker room the air was dead and the mood was worse. Most players sat on the benches with their helmets between their feet and their shoulders slumped. No one dared to say anything. A few stood and leaned against their lockers, looking through the glass of the coach's office, wondering what was going on in there. The animated discussion never got loud enough to escape into the larger area, but arms were gesturing more vociferously than the players had ever seen, so they knew there was trouble.

Coach Bobbitt paced the floor. Dan Parrish and the other coaches were locked in full squabble. The Cougar's starter was injured, their backup was out with a concussion, and the only other once-upon-a-time quarterback on the team hadn't thrown a ball since junior high. He was eighteen, a small kid, and most days worked with the kicker. So the guy who might have to take snaps was a tyro towel boy who held balls on the ground with his finger for the extra point toe. Prospects were dim.

Bobbitt stopped pacing and snapped his fingers. "What about Jumbo? Or Reggie?"

A chorus of groans filled the room. Jumbo Carter was a lineman from Benton, Kentucky, who practiced with the centers. He knew how to take snaps. Reggie Fry was the second team running back. He couldn't throw or catch, but he was big and could pound the rock for three or four yards on most downs. Neither was a viable candidate for running the team.

Dan said, "Maybe Chad—"

But Bobbitt cut him off. "Forget it, Dan. Just look at him."

They all turned and stared through the office window at Chad, now lying on his back in front of one of the trainer's volunteer assistants. They could almost hear the wind whistling through his ears.

Dan shook his head. "I can't believe we only have one backup."

"This ain't Div I, Dan! We can't give out scholarships like the big boys!"

JD was mad now and didn't like the idea of Dan cutting his legs out from under him, especially in front of the others.

"I got one full-time center! One paid trainer! One defensive coach!" JD settled down some but not much. "On Sunday mornings I come in and mow the grass. My wife sews patches on the uniforms with her Singer. To get mouthpieces for the boys I have to beg. The state prisons have better weight rooms than we do!"

Things were heating up. Nerves were jangled. An undefeated season was circling the bowl. *Any* kind of successful season was circling the bowl. Without a QB the team was on the rocks.

"What're we gonna do, JD?"

Bobbitt wiped his forehead and sat down hard. There was a knock at the door. They all turned and watched Chip Hunter enter the room on crutches.

"How's the ankle, son?" asked Bobbitt.

"Doc Hatfield says high-ankle sprain."

"How long?"

Chip shrugged and swallowed the lump in his throat. "Few weeks," he said.

The coaches groaned. Their season in the sun was over.

Bobbitt said, "We are in serious trouble."

Out in the locker room some of the guys were stirring.

There was an entire half yet to play and nobody was standing in front of them making adjustments or berating them for sloppy play or slapping them on the backsides. It felt like a tomb. C'mon, man, they hadn't lost yet! It was a three point game! Ku'uipo Kawananakoa stood up and started pacing the floor, frowning and shouting at his teammates. He squinted into the faces of the players, doing his best JD Bobbitt imitation. His efforts fell short, though, when he opened his mouth. "Fo' real, brah," he said to Jimmy Durr, "You looked like one panty out there! Suck 'em up!"

Back in the office, Chip leaned against the closed door. He had an idea. It was a crazy idea, he had to admit. Insane maybe. But what did they have to lose? Everything. The coaches were still bickering and clearly getting nowhere fast.

Against his better judgment, Chip decided to speak.

He cleared his throat. "Well, you know what they say..." The coaches fell quiet. The tiny refrigerator full of Yoo-hoo hummed. He had their full attention. He looked around the room, out through the glass at Ku'uipo, then back to his throwing coach. "...you can't run away from trouble. There ain't no place that far."

The men in the room exchanged glances. It was an obscure quote for sure, but so what? And why?

"Bear Bryant?" guessed JD.

Chip shook his head.

"John Wooden," Dan offered.

"Nope." Chip paused, then said, "Uncle Remus."

The coaches moaned as one, some of them actually angry at Chip for his inappropriate inanity.

Chip adjusted his crutches under his arms and stood and took a step away from the door. "Look," he said, "It doesn't matter who said it. Because it's true. We can't run away." He let his words sink in. He continued. "Because the real test of a person comes after adversity strikes and he has to overcome it." He pointed at Bobbitt. "Those are your words, Coach."

Bobbitt nodded, chastened at having one of his quotes turned back at him by one of his players.

Chip continued. "This—" he gestured at his crutches, "—is adversity. So we have to overcome it. And there's only one way to do that."

Chip paused again. The coaches stepped in a little closer, all ears now. If Chip had a solution, they wanted to hear it. He pointed at the chalkboard covered in Xs and Os. "Only one guy besides me really knows this offense. Only one guy besides me could go out there and pull off a W." Chip lifted a football off Bobbitt's desk and looked through the window at his teammates. He smiled at them, and with a no-look under-arm spin, shot the ball right into Dan Parrish's hands.

"Suit up, Coach. You're goin' in!" he said, beaming from ear to ear.

CHAPTER 33

"What the—"

Bobbitt leapt to his feet like a man just freed from bondage. "He's right! Dan, he's right!" JD did a pirouette in the middle of the office. He ended the spin move facing Dan, daring him to deny it. "You designed most of the damn plays. So strap it on, brother. You're going in!"

"And you're going nuts!" Dan fired back. "I'm a coach, JD. Says so right here!" He pointed at the word COACH on his shirt.

All the other coaches squinted at his chest.

"He's got a point, JD," croaked one of the coaches.

"Literally," said Dan, still pointing.

"A mere technicality!" Bobbitt scoffed, sounding like Foghorn Leghorn selling used cars. "You signed an actual scholarship cert, dude. You're a bona fide player according to the NJCAA." He raised his fingers in air quotes at the word *player*. Then he turned to the other coaches. "Right, guys?"

They smiled toothy smiles and nodded their heads. A weird sort of euphoria was sweeping through the room.

"There you have it. So get dressed, Dan. It's our only chance." Bobbitt crossed his arms and stood back on his heels.

Dan stood in front of the whole staff. "Guys, seriously, help me out here."

They all crossed their arms like Bobbitt. They stood and leaned back on their heels and grinned with painful dexterity, cheeks glowing in the dirty greenish neon.

Bobbitt said, "Look, budro, if you don't, we're dead. Why not go down swinging? For old time's sake?"

"Hah!" said Dan. "You mean old *timer's* sake."

"Whatever it takes."

Parrish closed his eyes and opened them and wiped his right palm on his shirt like he was getting ready to bowl. He understood the theory, all right. Give the game to a game manager. But he hadn't taken a hit in two decades. Throwing a ball when you're about to get steamrolled is a lot different than playing catch in the street. And a lot more painful.

Bobbitt raised the stakes. "Look at those kids, Dan." Bobbitt pointed out through the window at a now-aroused team listening to Chip's exhortations. "You wanna let them down?"

"Don't lay that on me, JD. That's not fair." He began to pace. "Besides, I'm a dinosaur." He made a decision on the fly. "And I'm not going in. There's no way."

Bobbitt stopped him with a hand on his shoulder. He faced him, looked into his eyes. If he could have worked up a tear he would have, but there wasn't time for that. He spoke out of the side of his mouth. "Guys, do you mind? I need a minute with Dan here."

The coaches filed out. Bobbitt closed the door behind them and turned back to Parrish, his face grave, a dramatic moue of wrinkles. "There's something I gotta tell ya, Danny Boy."

"Danny Boy? Oh fer Christ sake—"

"School president told me before the game—"

"You can't be serious—"

"—if we don't reach the state championship, this'll be my last year."

"GIMME A DAMN BREAK!"

"Dan, I'm serious." He looked down at his shoes. "My job's on the line." He looked up, his eyes wild and frantic. No more twinkle, no more smile lines. "I'm about to lose everything. This is more than a game, Danny. This is my life and the lives of my wife and the kids—Ashley needs braces and Lindsay's been saving up for KU..." There was a pause. "So anyway, maybe you could think about them, Dan. And do the big thing, the right thing. For all of us."

There was a long pause before Dan spoke. "JD, I had my chance. A long time ago. I blew it. End of story."

Bobbitt nodded, dropped his head. He put his hand on Dan's shoulder. "That's okay, old buddy. I get it." He removed his hand, then his eyes went dead. "Just so glad I was able to help you with your job and scholarship when you needed it." He turned and left the office, slamming the door so hard it rattled the glass front and the back wall...

...where an old photo displayed itself. A team—*the* team, with two guys grinning into the lens like they'd just conquered Everest. Dan Parrish and JD Bobbitt.

Footballers.

Winners.

State Champs.

CHAPTER 34

By the end of the half-time break, most people had reclaimed their seats and were shouting the typical insults and deprecations at the visiting team. The undercurrent, though was of a confused audience wondering who would take the field and lead the Cougars. And when the team filed out of the locker room, the crowd couldn't help but notice that Chip Hunter wasn't in uniform and Chad Stone wasn't even on the bench. Up in row twelve, Agnes, who wasn't a football fan per se, was intrigued. She couldn't imagine who the coaches would find to fill the shoes of such an important player as the QB. Dan had told her on more than one occasion that the team's prospects were dead if something ever happened to Chip and Chad. Now it seemed his fears had come to pass.

Both teams took the field amid a certain frantic-yet-reserved applause and the enthusiastic bouncing of the cheerleaders, and before long the kickoff was spinning into the end zone. Jimmy Durr carried it out and was tackled just short of the twenty-yard line. Ten Cougar players jogged out onto the field, confused and concerned, they stood in a loose huddle.

The seconds ticked off.

Where was the QB?

Rory Kromm, the towheaded ox who played tackle, groused, "Great. No quarterback, and we're about to get a delay of game penalty." Then the eleventh man appeared and trotted toward them. Nobody in the stands would have known who it was, except for the ponytail, a dead giveaway. Jaws dropped; euphoric, blind insects flew in circles high above; mothers wailed; hell, father's wailed, too.

Rick Hunter stood, so angry he actually vibrated.

Meanwhile, Dan jogged to the huddle and looked at his team, adjusting his helmet strap. He said, "You were expecting Peyton Manning, perhaps?"

Nobody said a word. The clock was still ticking. Jimmy Durr looked like he was going to puke. The others stood stock-still. No matter how you sliced it, it was a shock to see one of your coaches on the field in pads.

Ku'uipo broke the silence. "C'mon, guys," he said. "This is gonna be fun! Let's geev' 'um!" He clapped his hands together and rubbed them like he couldn't wait to get started. Dan appreciated the gesture.

The other team looked like leering wolves. They were salivating. They couldn't wait to dismember the old man.

On the first snap, Dan fumbled the ball. When he dove for it, three of his linemen gave up their blocks and dove for the ball, too, along with half the defensive line and two linebackers. Dan couldn't remember ever being hit so much, so fast, and so hard when he had played the game twenty years ago, but he was able to hold onto the pigskin. *I'm in over my head.* He dragged himself back to the huddle, shaken, and called another play.

At the second snap he dropped back, rolled right, and threw to a wide open Jimmy Durr. The ball sailed ten feet over Jimmy's head, and Dan's effort drew the first of a few tepid boos and groans from the stands. Agnes, one of the most rapt of watchers, realized she'd been holding her breath and literally sitting on the edge of her seat. Above her, in the VIP seats, Rick Hunter was delighted, thrilled even. The only thing better than running Dan Parrish out on a rail was seeing him getting thrashed on the gridiron by guys twenty years his junior. He could close his eyes and see a broken femur or a

140

torn ACL being served up next.

On the third play Dan dropped back and hurried a pass to 'Ipo. The ball sailed again and was picked off by a defensive back. The guy had a head of steam, too, and nearly returned it for a touchdown.

Rick Hunter leapt to his feet and led a chorus of boos. Dan trotted off the field, head down, miserable. Bobbitt greeted him as he came off.

"It's not gonna work, JD—"

"Hey! Listen to me!"

"—and the speed of the game—"

"Shut up!" Bobbitt stuck his face into Dan's. "You can't tell these guys to gut it out week after week, game after game, then trot off the field with your head down, tail between your legs. They may not all be able to read Shakespeare, but they can read body language."

Dan looked up and down the bench. All eyes were on him.

"You're right, man. Sorry."

JD slid his arm around Dan's shoulder pads. "That's okay, dude. Just settle down and let it flow. You got the jitters is all."

"I dunno, man."

"I do." Bobbitt turned his face up into the stands. Dan followed his eyes to a self-satisfied Rick Hunter, who was parading right and left above the throng, carping about the turn of events. Dan could hear him all the way down by the bench.

"Hear that? Nothing he wants more than for you to fold," said Bobbitt. "Don't you dare give that to him, Dan. You got that?"

Parrish's eyes locked onto Hunter's. *You are one stupid sonofabitch.* Something surged inside him—something deep and inexplicable. Maybe his ego was being jarred awake. Or maybe it was fear or pride or anger or all three. His heart began to pound and the blood rose to his face. His hands turned to fists and that's when he realized: he liked what he felt, the beginnings of competitiveness rising up.

"Yeah, JD, I got it," he said.

"Good. Now get back in there. They just missed a field goal." Bobbitt shoved Dan back out onto the field, then turned and blew a kiss to Hunter.

Go down swinging, Danny Boy. Only way to fly.

CHAPTER 35

At the beginning of the fourth quarter the score was 24-17 and aside from Oak Springs' touchdown and Echo's lone field goal, neither team had been very effective moving the ball. Both scores had been orchestrated by the defenses. Echo and Oak Springs traded punts, then Echo found themselves with the ball at their own thirty. In short order they ran a sweep, a dive, and a screen. The last play came up a yard short of a first down, so Dan called a time out and once again boos and cat-calls rained down onto the field, choreographed by Hunter. When Parrish trotted over to the sidelines to confer with Bobbitt, even he looked a little miffed.

"Why the time out? It's fourth down, man. We gotta punt."

"Hey, you said it yourself." Dan took a long drink off a bottle of Gatorade. "If we don't win this, we're through."

Bobbitt agonized. His face was twisted with unsettled thoughts. There was plenty of time left on the clock; they were not even to midfield yet; any sort of misfire would give Oak Springs beautiful field position. Still, though, you had to follow your gut, and Coach-Quarterback Parrish was pretty sure about the call.

Chip crutched up close and tossed his two cents into the ring. "Go for it, Coach," he said.

Bobbitt looked back up at Chip's father, standing, arms crossed, satisfied. He looked so smug, like he knew Parrish was going to hang himself. He seemed so sure.

"Do not be wrong, Dan," said JD.

Parrish nodded. He bumped fists with Chip so his father could see. As he started to head back out onto the field, Chip stopped him. "Coach!" he volunteered.

Dan turned back.

"You're releasing a little high. Remember what you told me? Index finger on the tip? Terry Bradshaw?"

Parrish nodded, moved by Chip's earnestness. The two were on the same page. A lot of things had happened during these last two months, some of them not so good. But this strange relationship with Rick Hunter's son was a plus. Dan liked the kid. He liked his spunk, even if it was misplaced sometimes. The booze had taken a back seat for Chip, too, and his mind was more on point. Dan liked the way things were coming together for him. He was really a good kid, trying his best in an environment that wasn't that easy. He gave Chip a thumbs-up and headed back to the huddle and called the play. The players broke the huddle with "Ready, Break!" and jogged up to the line of scrimmage. Dan looked over the defense. Processed it. Barked signals and the ball was snapped.

He dropped back, five steps. His receivers—Ku'uipo and Durr—charged downfield, breaking on their respective routes. Oak Springs' defensive linemen fought and kicked and scratched to get to Dan. They were closing in. He couldn't hold the ball forever. Dan scanned his receivers downfield and they were covered, blanketed by the defensive backs. He stumbled to his right, dodging one defender. The boo birds in the stands began their rite of failure. Another Oak Springs linebacker was closing in, about to administer the punishment, a sack and a loss of eight yards and a humiliating forth down failure...

...but then Dan saw Ku'uipo break free from his defender.

I remember this feeling. I remember it from before the fall. I remember being the king of the world and how it felt, how time stopped and an instant became an eternity, and I knew I

144

couldn't fail back then. I knew deep in my bones that my arm would be the best, an instrument of perfection, throwing a strike every time.

He patted the ball, tightening his grip and slipped his index finger to the tip of the stitching and gunned the ball downfield, a mirage of velocity and precision, whistling through the air twenty, forty, then fifty yards, bringing the people in the stands to their feet, bringing with them Agnes, who began to scream, her hands pressed to her cheeks, bringing Rick Hunter along with the rest of them, standing up, ready to explode with derisive gusto. *To hell with this guy, Dan Parrish! Him and all the imbeciles that coddle him!*

Rick Hunter needs this collapse. This failure. He has to have it. Yet beside him Katy stands and widens her eyes and hopes with all the hope in her betrayed soul that this would be the beginning of Dan Parrish's resurrection.

And the ball came down and landed with no sound and no vibration, a silent invocation, a testament...

...into Ku'uipo Kawananakoa's outstretched hands, he and the ball glued together, the boy and his prize, flying into the end zone, ten thousand Echo fans screaming "TOUCH-DOWN!"

...while Rick Hunter dropped down hard on the bleacher seat. 24-23. One point game.

And when quarterback Dan Parrish ran down the field and snatched Ku'uipo up in a bear hug, Jimmy Durr walked by, yanking at his chin strap. "Just plain ol' dumb luck," he said, loud enough for every player in the end zone to hear.

'Ipo and Parrish exchanged a look. Then 'Ipo got up in Durr's grille. "Eh, whose side you on anyway, haole boy?" For a second it looked as if the two would come to blows right there on the field. Dan separated the two and they all three jogged to the sidelines, 'Ipo and Jimmy shooting daggers back and forth.

Meanwhile, the Cougar kicker wobbled the ball through the uprights, despite a hard hit by an Oak Springs linebacker and had to be carted off the field.

24-24. The score was tied.

CHAPTER 36

At the two minute break, the score was still tied. Both teams had played their tails off for fifty-eight minutes, and the sweat and the fatigue in the eyes of every player was evident, even in the simultaneous holding of knees between plays and the number of guys being shuffled in and out from both sides of the field, victims of dehydration. Both teams' trainers and volunteer staffs worked tirelessly on cramping legs. The contest had become something more than just one game in a season of many. Oak Springs was giving it their all to upset the big bad undefeated Cougars, and Echo was feeling their way through the calamity of losing their regular signal callers, forcing themselves into crisis mode, praying for a little luck and maybe a break of some kind to extend this finest of years.

When play resumed the Cougars had the ball on their own forty-yard line. It was now or never.

"Okay, guys, we need sixty yards. You got it in you?"

"Hell, yeah!" barked one of the guys, and they all nodded their heads, ready to go to war for their old, long-haired field general.

Dan turned to 'Ipo. "How many time outs we got?"

"None." The huddle's collective face drooped as one.

But Dan would have none of it. "Good. Just the way I like it." He grinned. "Power I Right, Forty-Six Blast. On two."

The first play, a draw up the middle of the line, picked up twenty yards. Then Dan threw three consecutive passes, connecting on all of them, netting twenty more yards. Durr dropped a guaranteed six points on the goal line, then Parrish hit 'Ipo on a quick out route for ten more yards and a first down. There were twenty seconds on the clock. Dan and the Echo JC Cougars broke the huddle and moved to the line.

Parrish crouched over center and took the snap. The clock started. He dropped back and set up. When he did the line-backers and defensive backs mirrored his moves, falling back into coverage. The short field was alive with two arm-waving receivers, a running back and a tight end, all of them trying to see themselves clear. There was nowhere to throw the ball. Dan sneaked a look at the clock. Sixteen seconds. He made a decision.

Run.

The crowd stood as one and went berserk as Parrish broke free down the sideline. Five yards. Ten yards. It looked like a touchdown was imminent. And with only a few yards remaining he couldn't be stopped...

...until Luke Gayton, a rocked-up, all conference, tough-as-nails defensive back, snatched Parrish by his ponytail and yanked him clean off his feet, sending him cart-wheeling onto his back, and still in bounds.

The clock ticked away. Twelve seconds, eleven...

After the play, Gayton trotted by Dan and said, "You forgot something." Then tossed him a handful of his hair, laughing, and jogged back to the line of scrimmage.

Ku'uipo heard the taunt and gestured at the DB with an upraised forearm and fist. "Game ain't over, brah!"

Luke Gayton pointed to the clock and grinned.

Meanwhile, JD Bobbitt was losing it on the sideline. "SPIKE IT! DAMNIT, SPIKE IT!" Bobbitt screamed, spittle flying, as the clock refused to stop.

Dan and his teammates lurched into position. No time to

think. No time to scan the defense. Eleven guys facing eleven guys. Everyone racing the clock...

...and for Dan, time slows and he narrows his eyes and grabs 'Ipo by the jersey.

"Be ready. I'm gonna fake spike it."

"Uh...whut?"

Up in the stands Rick Hunter was mentally dancing a jig. A tie game was okay, he thought. The Cougars don't have a kicker. Overtime with this has-been throwing the ball will be fun to watch and more fun to commiserate over when he's able to get together with his town friends and begin to rip JD Bobbitt and Dan Parrish and every other clown on their side of the fence. He stole a look at his wife, who scowled at him. *To hell with her, too.*

Six seconds, five...

Dan turned to the referee. "Eye on the ball, ref."

On the nod, Dan said hut and the ball slapped into his hands. He took the cursory step back and pumped the ball toward the turf. The crowd took a breath. Except Dan never let go of the ball, slipping it behind his back. So twenty players stood there, waiting for the whistle as the clock wound down toward zero.

Yet because he'd never let go of the ball, it was live. The play had to be over for the game to be over. So Dan wandered to his left, head down, a picture of dejection. And then he looked up and produced the ball. Then fired a bullet to Ku'uipo, standing alone in the end zone.

The dazed Hawaiian looked at the ball in his hands, looked up, looked like he'd just been kissed by his mother. And then he grinned. And the ref signaled touchdown and the crowd erupted as the whistle blew.

30-24. Cougars win.

The entire stadium explodes into something more than pandemonium. Bobbitt stands at the sidelines stunned. Somehow they'd won. The Oak Springs coaches begin to scream at the ref, but it doesn't work. Agnes begins to cry. Katy begins to cry. Rick Hunter sits again, and takes another sip from his flask, blinking. There's not enough booze in the world to fix this mess, he thinks. And the band begins to play the fight song and the cheerleaders rock and roll and the Oak Springs defensive back who'd snatched the fistful of Dan Parrish's hair stands alone under the crossbar and drops his head and sighs.

"Brah," said 'Ipo to his QB, "where'd you come up with that?"

"A page right out of Dan Marino's playbook," said Dan.

"Remin' me to read dat book."

As the dejected DB walked by heading to the bus, Dan said, "Hey!" Luke Gayton looked up and Dan pitched him the ball. "You forgot something." Throwing the ball and the DBs own words right back at him. Then Dan and Ku'uipo laughed.

To his credit, the young DB smiled. "Well-played, Grandpa." Then held out his fist for a bump which Dan graciously obliged.

Then Dan's teammates hoisted 'Ipo up on their shoulders and carried him to the locker room. He'd caught two touchdown passes. And helped their long-haired QB save the day.

That night in the stadium, emotions were a complex thing for some. Chip Hunter was ecstatic for a minute, gesticulating at the howling, frothing fans in the stands until Jimmy Durr reminded him, "Too bad ain't none of that's for you."

Sure enough, Chip had been caught up in the moment, waving and smiling at the fans still in the stands. Now he dropped his hand. Suddenly he was uncomfortable. He looked at Jimmy, then across at his QB coach and was not happy with what he saw—a guy leading a parade.

A star.

And it was true. Dan was soaking up the back-slapping 'attaboys like a teenager. But at some point he paused and thought about the consequences. He'd been under the radar until then. He'd been just one of a number of guys helping the team from the cheap seats. He'd been a cafeteria manager, really. Now he was a hero. Dan ducked out of the mobbing crowd, and when he found a bouncing, schoolgirl Agnes in the stands, he hugged her like a lifeline. *This feels so good*, he thought. He'd dreamed it a thousand times. *But the press is here. I gotta bail. Before it's too late.*

Meanwhile, Rick Hunter sat alone, abandoned by his wife, scorned by his son, smoldering, wheels turning.

The quiet man stared. He stood and saw the bastard quarterback hugging the whore. He hurried out of the stadium to the parking lot, and into his stupid little car. He drove away, one man inside a long line of cars from the other team, the losing team, driving out into the night.

Sometimes the quiet man is so angry, he forgets himself, forgets to wash, forgets to eat, forgets his plan. He can't let that happen. He cannot forget his plan. Football has no business in his plans. He must stick to his blueprint. His blueprint of dark shadows. And blood.

CHAPTER 37

Who is Dan Parrish? That's what they'll want to know. And what's he gonna do for an encore? I'm not prepared for this. I didn't think this through. I didn't do my homework. I can't get my brain out of that concrete box. You're in the world now, buddy. You've just tapped the world on the shoulder. Don't think you'll get out of this alive. Don't be that naïve.

A few hours had gone by; the town of Echo was buttoned up; people here didn't dance in the streets after midnight or turn over cars after a big win. But it's true that they were thinking, "Who was that guy?"—the question on everyone's lips. Townspeople in their homes, getting ready for bed, all thinking, "Who was the old, long-haired, bearded guy who guided the Cougars team to victory?"

In the darkened locker room the smell of camphor and old sweat permeated everything. Dirty uniforms and bandages littered the floor. Not until tomorrow would anyone be in to clean things up. Most of the coaches and the trainer and even the volunteers had driven away in a caravan to the whiskey bar on the highway out by the lake. They would drink beers and shots and beam at each other and talk about offensive plays and defensive schemes, and the trainer would explain how he was going to get the kicker healthy or open tryouts for a new one on Monday.

Inside the coach's office Dan sat with JD, winding down. The adrenaline was still pumping through Dan's system. Sleep would have to wait. Who could sleep after such an extraordinary night? Sitting with his buddy shooting the breeze was a panacea. Maybe it would calm him down. Nobody knew what this had meant to Dan Parrish—nobody except JD Bobbitt. And he wasn't telling tales out of school.

"Rick...Hunter's...face," said Bobbitt. He looked across the desk at his friend.

They both busted up, laughing. They laughed until tears ran down their cheeks and their stomachs hurt, and even if they felt a bit childish and petulant and maybe somewhat self-satisfied, they laughed. Because in some cases it was a good thing to win one, to get over on someone who wished you harm. Dan hadn't felt such a release in decades. He didn't want it to ever stop.

"Can you believe it?" said Bobbitt, his voice hoarse from the strain.

"I really can't, JD. Nope, I cannot."

"Was it as fun as it looked?"

"Oh, God, JD. Oh man." He paused. "Yeah." He paused again, adding, "Although I might be thinking differently tomorrow." He faux-grimaced the onset of aches and pains.

"Do you know how many frustrated thirty-six-year-old ex-athletes there are out there who dream about doing what you just did? Do you?"

"Gotta be a zillion."

"Ga-zillion."

"You were always better than me with the math."

"Bite me."

Dan smiled, then lapsed into silence. He thought for a moment. The smile left his face. "I hope it all doesn't backfire somehow."

"Dude! Don't worry about Hunter. Just enjoy the moment. You earned it. And you deserve it."

Parrish rolled his shoulders and winced with the stiffness. "Deserve it," he said, trying to wrap his head around the concept. He grew quiet again and Bobbitt knew there was something on his mind.

"What? Out with it," JD said. He stood and retrieved a Yoo-hoo from the little fridge. He popped the cap and drank it down, as usual, in one long, sucking pull.

Dan watched in silence. "I just can't help but worry about what Billy Cox—"

"Billy Cox? Billy *Cox*? Are you kidding me?"

Dan blinked, shook his head no.

JD rolled his eyes so hard you could hear them. He tossed his empty bottle in the can beside his desk. "Look," he said. He held his hands wide apart. "Billy Cox left Echo eons ago. He is here." He wiggled the fingers of his left hand. "And we're here." He wiggled the fingers of his right. "Billy Cox does not give a rat's ass about you or me or Echo, Kansas. Trust me on that one."

"I hope you're right."

"I know I'm right."

A few hundred miles away, in a darkened office at a Kansas City newspaper, a world-weary journalist with thin hair and a pot belly sat at his desk, staring slack-jawed at his computer screen. He was fascinated by the tale now being sent across the web, a story about what just transpired at his old beat back in northwest Kansas—a town called Echo. He had found his first good story in there. The wire services had picked it up. So you could say he had cut his teeth in Echo. He could never forget the guy's name; it had become part of his DNA. Dan Parrish, the high school hero, was his first big break.

Billy Cox sat back in his chair and pulled a cigarette pack from his pocket and lit it. *What's going on?*

Out through his window blinds he saw the streetlights dim for a moment. A brown out—middle of the night stuff. Somewhere a siren wailed, the Doppler drop fading into the distance. He'd have to check the blotter. A fire or a crash or something more catastrophic. He missed the small town beat. The people coming together for things. The dust in the wind. The moths banging on the porch lights, the lightning bugs, and the folks knowing their neighbors.

Dan Parrish, he thought.

Well I'll be damned.

CHAPTER 38

Just after midnight Dan lay on his cot and stared up into the shadows, watching one of his spiders make its way from a dusty overhead junction box, along a tendril of web to one of the blackened trusses that supported the roof. He admired the spider's ambition, as well as its artistic style. It couldn't be easy to construct such webbed dinner traps. They were models of efficiency. Even as Dan watched, a tiny insect was dying, caught up in the mastic of the silken threads, putting to rest a short, desperate life in futile fits and starts until it was time to be eaten by the eight-legged king of the roof beams.

Dan couldn't sleep. He'd replayed every down of the game in his head, and there were several ways he knew he could improve. One stood out above the rest. It was something he should have done weeks ago. He realized it was late, yet he had no hope of getting any shuteye anyway. He threw back the covers, dressed, hopped on his bike and pedaled out the driveway and down the road.

The night was inky black, but Dan didn't need a moon. A few street lights cast long, cartoon shadows across his path. A cat started and dove into the hedges as Dan whizzed by. The self-generated bicycle breeze felt good as it flushed his face and hair. He rode down Anchor Lane then Captain's Row, turned onto main and headed for 8002 East Kenyon Drive. All of Echo seemed asleep.

* * *

Agnes Stankowiecz was for sure asleep. The knock on the door came from a thousand miles away. She rolled over and fell back into her dreams. Then a second knocking and her eyes clicked open. She hadn't lived in Echo for very long, but she knew by now that it was a quiet place where folks had the sense to live more sedate, diurnal lives that weren't complicated by wee hour escapades. It made for a predictable, almost boring existence, true, yet at this point in her life the benefits outweighed the drawbacks. The big city where she'd come from wasn't at all like Echo, which was one of the things that had convinced her to accept a job offer in rural Kansas. Life for her now was more predictable, even if it could be lonely.

She threw on a robe and padded to her door. As she reached for the knob, she stopped herself. How could she be so foolish? There was no telling who was on the other side of that door.

"Who is it?"

"It's me, Dan," came a voice from the porch.

Agnes turned the outside light on and pulled the lace curtain aside. She couldn't quite believe what she'd just heard. She peered into the haze at an abashed Dan Parrish, standing on the landing in a pair of cords, a baseball T and flip-flops. He waved at the shadows behind the glass. She dropped the curtains and cinched her robe tighter. What was he doing here? It was one in the morning. Her heart began to thump in her chest. She felt a vague sense of excitement. It had been a long time since someone she'd been seeing had come calling in such a way. Too long, she thought.

She straightened her hair, tested her breath, fluffed her hair again. She opened the door. Dan's smile was weak, almost apologetic.

She pushed the door all the way open and looked around and behind her shoulder. "Whattya know, Superman's here."

She folded her arms. Her dimples creased her cheeks when she smiled.

Dan was speechless. Apparently he had nothing prepared. No paragraph to explain his eccentric behavior, no emergency to relate, no dire warning to impart. The sky was not falling. No atom bombs or earthquakes on the horizon. He shoved his hands deep into his pockets and looked up, out past the yellow glow of the porch light and into the frantic clarity of a million stars. He would be hoping she didn't see the blush. He looked back down.

His face is red, she thought. *He's embarrassed. He's come calling in the middle of the night, and I'm pleased as punch. And my heart is beating and my skin is tingling all over like a little girl. But maybe I'll just ignore the red face and the way he's fidgeting and say something silly or informal or both.* She'd been hoping for this day for weeks now, and she didn't want to screw it up, even if it wasn't how she'd imagined it would happen.

"What are you doing up at this hour?" she said. She leaned against the doorjamb in her sexiest of poses. "Don't you have other small town football teams across the country to save?"

Dan nodded, up and down, not listening. Then shook his head no, confused. She leaned against the doorway in her Tennessee Williams robe, looking like a dimpled Marilyn Monroe and grinning up at him like she could see everything that was in his heart.

"I'm sorry," he said. "I know it's late. I was just too wound up to sleep."

"Can't say as I blame you. That was some kind of performance, mister." She pushed a lock of hair from off her cheek. "So," she continued, "is there something I can help you with?"

Being a quarterback was probably easier than this. "Yes," he said. "Actually there is."

Agnes felt the first signs of heat. Her palms moistened, her lips went dry. She didn't know what he was going to say, but she knew she had to help him somehow. She'd been thinking about this scene for weeks now, and here it was and she wasn't prepared, or not as prepared as she thought she was going to be. The man she was looking at had no bottle of wine, no flowers, no limo waiting in the street. So what was he going to say to her that could cause such trepidation for the both of them?

"I need something, Agnes. Bad."

She gulped. "What Dan? What is it you need?"

He licked his lips. Even the crickets ceased chirping.

"A haircut," he said.

Agnes blinked. "A haircut."

"Got some scissors?"

She grabbed his hand and pulled him through the door, into her enclave of secret desires. "You really know how to sweep a girl off her feet, don't you?"

A half hour later Agnes finished towel drying Dan's hair. As he sat on a wire-back chair in the kitchen, she combed out sections of lustrous locks, bobby-pinning them in squared off plats like a beauty shop pro. Etta James wafted from the stereo. The lights were muted and golden and the shades were drawn down. She leaned over him with the comb and pressed her warmth into the side of his face and thought how unfair this was going to be—a man was always a little boy first, especially Dan. Then she pushed the curves of her breasts into him, over his eyes, pushing her heat and her appetite and her determination into the point of no return, enveloping the man she'd grown to love and enlisting him in a covenant of mutual desire. When she bent down she felt his breath mingling with hers, and her neck stretched out and went long and creamy white in his eyes, and when he reached up she accepted his kiss and another. And so she leaned down and opened her lips to him as Etta sang...

I want a Sunday kind of love,
A love that will last...

She cut his hair then, carefully, with slow deliberate moves, long tresses falling to the floor, prolonging his agony. When she finished, she heated his beard with a hot, damp towel like her grandfather used to do. She lathered his face and began to shave him. When she was finished she wiped his cheeks and neck with another towel. She flipped off the kitchen lights and sat down on his lap, one knee on either side of his legs. Her robe came open and his shirt came off. Their bodies were limned by the glow of the stereo, as the sounds of two lovers' desperate coming together accompanied Etta James repeating the refrain...

I want a Sunday kind of love...

At nine o'clock Agnes rolled over to an empty bed. She wasn't troubled, though. Her heart was full to bursting. Dan had left an hour ago, but not before he nuzzled her awake, mumbling something about "Millie and the twins." She hadn't stirred; she didn't want to spoil the feeling. It had been so long since she'd been moved this way, so long since she'd held a man in her arms and luxuriated in the liquid passions of such a night. She could smell him on the pillow and on her body. She could feel the heat of him and she relived the gentle strength in his movements as he took her in his arms. He had slipped his pants on, and his shirt. She had heard the water running in the bathroom. When he left she pulled the covers over her head and fell back to sleep.

But now she was up. She stood and donned her bathrobe, trying not to smile too hard. The words of Etta James ran through her head. She began to hum, something she hadn't done in ages. It was too delicious. When she reached the kitchen, she stopped in her tracks and the smile she could not contain broke loose and spread across her face. The hair on the floor had been swept up and the table was set. There was a steaming mug of coffee waiting for her, beside it a glass of fresh-squeezed orange juice that Dan had extracted by hand, judging by the pulp in the sink. He must have just left, too, because there was a perfectly poached egg seasoned with salt, pepper and what looked like dill, resting on a plate of diced red potatoes. Beside it there was a handwritten report card.

Haircut: A+. Pantry: F.
See you Monday morning.
XOXO. Dan.

She sat down and sipped her coffee. No sugar. Perfect. He remembered. She picked up the fork and pressed it into the eggs. The yolks broke over the hash browns with lubricious opulence, like a four star meal at a café along the Seine. This was something she would have never made for herself. She was always in such a rush. A perfect morning with a perfect breakfast after a perfect evening. This was going to be a perfect Sunday. Nothing could spoil such a night.

She closed her eyes as she savored each bite.

When she was finished, she pushed back from the table and stood. She put her dish in the sink with the others. That's when she saw something on the floor by the refrigerator, almost hidden under the drip pan. She kneeled and picked it up and held it to her eyes. Her heart sank when she realized what it was.

She'd been wrong about nothing being able to spoil this day.

And suddenly her breakfast didn't taste so good anymore. Outside a dove cooed by her back door.

The only other sound was that of her heart splintering.

CHAPTER 39

Out on State Highway 406 there was a broken down hacienda-style establishment called Eloise's Beach Shack, which served liquor to anyone old enough to reach the bar. It wasn't a beach shack, really. How could it be? But nobody seemed to mind that the nearest actual beach was thousands of miles away. The owner of the place had attracted her clientele from towns as far away as the next county by building a sand pit in the back yard and calling it a beach volleyball court, and by offering wet T-shirt contests and other surf-side enticements like bikini bingo and Hawaiian luaus that seemed a bit overdone, what with the size of the hog that was featured as a centerpiece, apple in the mouth notwithstanding. The house band wore coconut husk bras and the everyday drink special was two-for-one mai tais made with cheap Hawaiian rum. And the waitresses had skirts so tight, the Saturday night upshot was of pouring hot oil on hormonally explosive stove tops. One or another of the sheriff's deputies' cruisers was constantly in the parking lot, the uniforms enlisted to put out the horny fires of late-night moral turpitudes before someone got hurt.

Eloise's was known for its sand-pit romances, but also for its resilience in the face of underage drinkers and for its beer sold by the pound. The sheriff turned a blind eye to the former, and enjoyed the benefits of the latter on his way through. He had been a patron of the place as a teen, and now he was reluctant to stop the parade. Besides, Eloise owned the mortgage on his house and he was forever in arrears on his payments.

Eloise's never closed, either, which meant that it was a handy place to nurse a hangover.

Darla Finch and Jimmy Durr sat at a table nursing mean ones that Sunday morning. The staple for those sitting at the bar was a drink made from beer and tomato juice and lime—a Red Eye—and it was a big seller during weekend mornings. Darla and Jimmy had already had a few. The evidence was stacked on the copper-topped bar when Chip Hunter limped in on crutches. He was annoyed at the behavior of his two former compatriots, but held his tongue. After all, he'd been here on lots of Sunday mornings. He knew the drill.

"Sorry I'm late," he said. "I was at—"

Darla interrupted. "Let me guess: Sunday school?" She looked up over her glass. Her eyes looked like two piss holes in a snow bank.

Chip leaned his crutches against one of the tables. He hopped across and sat on a stool. "What if I was? That a problem?" He didn't want to be irritated, but he was. He glared at Darla while Durr ordered another round of Red Eyes from a woman twice his size—the early morning barmaid from hell.

Durr turned his face to Chip. "Want one?"

Chip waved it off, a sudden rush of recognition lighting up his face. Jimmy had been trying to hide it, but someone behind them had opened the door and a big yellow ray of sunlight had splashed across Durr's face. He was sporting a shiner. A big one. A black eye good enough for the record books.

"Whoa! Looks like someone got him some Hawaiian punch!" said Chip.

"Yeah, right. I kicked his ass," Durr snapped back.

"Oh yeah? What'd you do, hit him in the fist with your eye?" Chip looked around the bar and chuckled at his ancient remark. He'd spent the last few weeks sober, and it was a mind-expanding exercise. Had he looked like this? Had he sounded like these guys? Did his breath stink of puke and poison when he slithered around town on early morning hangover exercises? Jimmy Durr hadn't changed his clothes in days, except to strap on a uniform. And his performances on the field were getting harder and harder to excuse.

Darla said, "Chip, it's not funny. Jimmy's been kicked off the team." Chip leaned in closer to Jimmy. "Serious?"

"Bobbitt called me this morning." He took a sip from his drink. "But it's all because of Parrish. *Coach* Parrish. He's an ass, ruining the—"

"You can't blame him, Jimmy. I mean you—or we—started the whole thing. And I told you this summer not to mess with 'Ipo. That guy's a gamer."

"'Ipo? Whose side you on, anyway?"

"I'm on the team's side, man."

Durr put his fists on the bar and hung his head. He had big hands, receiver hands. And he was fast. On the field he could do a good job of shaking and baking. He could work himself loose from most defensive backs, especially for a guy six-foot-three. But his heart was never where it was supposed to be. He'd been a star in high school. He expected the adulation of the crowds would carry him through. Yet that wasn't the way it was playing out. His grades had already cost him a scholarship at a four-year school. Now, it seems, he had washed out at the JC level.

Durr reminded Chip that he wasn't the quarterback anymore. His candid animosity leaked through with every word. "See if you're saying all that team stuff come November, when Parrish is still QB and you're on the sidelines."

"Yeah, right. That's not gonna happen."

Durr pushed a copy of the local weekly across the bar. Dan Parrish's grinning, bearded face was front and center. Under the picture it said:

COACH DAN, THE LION TAMER.
18 FOR 27, 2 TDs, 1 INT.

Chip glanced at Darla and felt a stab of jealousy. He covered it up by looking away.

"So? What should I do, quit?"

"Sure. Why not?"

Chip scanned the back wall: the liquor bottles lined up like sentries, the cute memorabilia from beachside spring breaks. He looked back at Darla, who was watching him, a curious smile twisting her lips. At that moment Chip knew there was nothing she would love more than to see him fold his tent. He had ambitions—that was for sure. But he was injured, and when the team does well it lifts everyone. Mocking and scorn never worked. He'd learned that over the past few weeks. He said, "Because there's no I in team, that's why."

"Yeah, but there's an M and an E," fired back Durr.

"Careful, bro. You're starting to sound like her." He gestured at Darla, whose eyes flared at the truth of the statement. She shook her head, too hungover to respond. Chip stood and hopped to the table where his crutches were resting.

When Chip hobbled off into the parking lot and the door shut behind him, Darla leaned across and touched Jimmy's hand. "That sucks, Jimmy, about you losing your scholarship," she said. "And we all know it's because of that new coach."

Durr looked down at Darla's hand on his. This was something new. He decided he liked it. "I hate that guy. He's a jerk."

"Yeah?" she drawled. "You think so?" She grabbed her Red Eye from off the bar and chugged it down. When she looked at him again there was a red mustache on her upper lip and a spot of tomato juice on the corner of her mouth. She looked downright predatory. "Well, you don't know the half of it." She reached into her purse, where she drew out a document. She handed it to Jimmy Durr and turned her back and left him at the bar to ponder the revelations on the reprint.

She shot a last look at him as the wash of morning light grew narrower and the door closed. These guys were so clueless. If someone wanted to play games, she could rack 'em up with anybody. She wiped the blood-colored stain from her mouth.

So let's see what Jimmy does with that document.

CHAPTER 40

On Monday morning Dan was still enveloped in the rosy glow of love's first bite, and with the success of the cafeteria and of his status on the football team. Things were on a slow ride to something like prosperity and contentment.

He'd gotten to the kitchen early that morning and spent the first hour teaching Jorge the finer points of braising. The kid was coming along well. The former hip-hop star seemed pleased with his new facility at the grill and the stove top and the chopping block, enough so that his love life with Tiny was ever expanding and delighting him. And the crabby cafeteria ladies were loosening up and enjoying themselves in their transformative new environment.

The bottom line had improved, too, which meant that the cafeteria was now making money—the first time such a thing had happened in years. As long as the trend continued, Dan Parrish was free to do as he pleased. Sam Blevins had given him the keys to the place. Even Sam was eating lunch in the pleasant new environment that featured delicious aromas from a busy kitchen, ferns in pots along the wainscoting, paintings from the art students decorating the upper walls, and Cougar news, Cougar scores and Cougar highlights on the two bulletin boards.

But as good as things were going in the cafeteria and on the gridiron, those pleasures paled when compared to one starlit night that promised to drop him into Agnes' gentle arms for the long haul. Dan Parrish had a new lease on life and an awesome haircut to go with it. As he walked down the halls to his first class of the day, he realized for the first time what a spring in his step meant. He smiled at the thought. He hadn't felt this great in, well, forever. And with his freshly shorn locks and hairless face, he looked almost exactly like he did when he walked these same hallways nearly twenty years ago. The similarity was, as the folks of Echo would later say, un-frickin'-canny.

Yet the spring in his step disappeared the second he walked into the confines of Agnes' classroom. The entire class fell silent. No one would even look at him. He panned the faces. Surely a new haircut wouldn't do this, he thought. Or maybe there was a touch of resentment for his heroics during the game. He stopped and knit his brow, confused. He looked at Chip Hunter and noticed the strange look on his face. Almost of anger. He followed the boy's eyes to the far corner of the rear wall. It was papered in photocopies of a newspaper article from eighteen years ago:

FOOTBALL STAR KILLS INFANT SON
DRUNK DRIVING THE CULPRIT

He stepped around the rows of desks and stood in front of the ancient indictment. Some of the script was highlighted in yellow:

JOHN HENRY. JUDGE HUNTER.
VEHICULAR HOMICIDE.
BLOOD ALCOHOL LEVEL.

At the bottom of the page were the words:

PROSECUTOR ASKS FOR 20 YEAR SENTENCE.

And the byline read: Written by *Billy Cox.*

In an ironic touch that nobody could miss, a freshly shorn and shaved Dan Parrish stared at his likeness. The photo was a mug shot, yet he looked the same; he still looked like the picture of the kid in the article, a kid staring out at an unseen audience, shell shocked and numb.

In real time now, and with a suddenness unforeseen, he was enveloped in his nightmare. He was on exhibit again. His life was a script, written long ago: no rewrites, no second chances. He stood at the back corner of the class, heart racing, blood rising to his face. He felt trapped. His mouth went dry and his lips stuck to his teeth. His ears rang. He had no idea how this had happened or who was responsible. Time seemed to stop. Each second was an eternity and the roaring in his ears belied any thoughts that made it to the top. The cacophony of emotions and, yes, fear, erupted like a geyser.

The summary of my sins has arrived, he thought. *Here it is. And now it will ruin me, cut me down with one huge swipe. And it won't be anything nice. This is a hanging courtroom, and the minutes will be read and digested. I'm done. I'll forfeit all my progress: my job, my spot on the team, my girl...I'll have to lie on the tired springs of a bed I made myself, and drown in a pool of my own blood. And someone will be there to say "so what, he was a child killer, he was a nobody. He was a drunk and a bum and the world is better off without him."*

And they'll be right.

He glanced around the room. Jimmy Durr's desk was empty. Darla Finch sat in the second row, her head down, a hint of a smile on her face.

He looked at Chip, who regarded Dan as if seeing him for the first time in his life.

Parrish thought, *Danny Boy...now you know the truth. If you dance with the devil, you don't get out alive. Ever.*

And then Agnes walked in. Like Dan, she stopped and

looked around. Her mouth came open, but no words came out. Parrish turned to her and she must have seen he was dying a slow death right there in the classroom. Before she could say anything, he dropped his books and bolted.

Agnes ran to the door and watched Dan tear down the hallway.

"Dan!" she yelled, a little too loudly.

But Dan Parrish was gone.

CHAPTER 41

Katy and Chip rode along in Hunters' shiny, black Town Car, Katy behind the wheel, driving, idling, turning, braking, rolling with slow precision through downtown Echo. They finally reached the outskirts of town, where businesses gave way to farms and ranch land, then to cottonwoods and stands of maple and larch.

They were quiet, each in his or her own thoughts, and the tension could be felt in the unnatural silence of the moment. On any given day, this was not the way things were between them. They were a team, joining together to protect each other from whatever came at them. Now, though, no words would come. When Katy turned onto the old highway that passed the little cemetery, Chip probably felt he had to say something, anything, to open the dialogue between them.

"You hear what happened?"

Katy sighed. "It's Echo, Chip. Everybody hears everything. Over and over again." She looked at her son, at his handsome, troubled face. She knew she was partly to blame for his confusions. He was just a kid, and she had tried to shield him from some of the harsher realities of their lives and a family history that wasn't always as sanitary as she would have liked. Maybe that had been wrong—who's to say?—but now there were issues between them and she would have to open up, at least enough so that he could deal with things instead of stumbling along in the dark.

"I can't believe you never told me—"

"You don't just get to know everything, Chip!" Her voice startled him. It even startled her. She composed herself and continued. "We all make mistakes. We all have secrets. Everybody. One day you'll have kids and you'll understand what I'm saying."

They were silent for a time, riding down the highway, the scenery killing the empty spaces in their hearts. Chip's mind was a dervish, whirling at warp speed, refusing to rest on what little he'd been told.

Katy had hoped her implied confession would be enough. She was wrong. "Were you guys...married?"

Katy couldn't answer. Her throat tightened and she was afraid she would falter. Her eyes were beginning the long dissolve into tears. She so much wanted to avoid such histrionics. She thought about a response; she thought about another. She stifled both. She'd been masking her feelings for years. She blinked back the guilt and the loneliness that only she could know. "This close," she said, gesturing with a thumb and forefinger.

Another silence filled the car. Chip said, "I heard he's leaving." He studied his mother's face, looking for any clue that his words held meaning for her.

They did, of course. Except there was no way to say what she needed to say and this was not the time. This was the time to put out the fire, not to refuel it. She suppressed her thoughts and said, "Can't say as I blame him." Then she threw the ball back in Chip's court. It was time at least to gauge the level of her son's concern for Dan Parrish. "Do you?" she said.

"No," he said. "But I don't want him to go."

Katy was relieved, even proud that she'd raised him in such a way as to make him think through things that he didn't understand. She knew how difficult it was for him to voice his feelings.

"Maybe he'd like to hear that from you, Chip."

Chip looked at her to see if she was serious. She returned the look. They continued down the old rural highway, passing mile after mile of sameness. Chip stared out the window, thinking.

"We used to go there, didn't we?"

Katy offered him a puzzled look.

"God's Little Acre. You 'n' me. When I was little."

Katy nodded.

"How come we quit?"

"Why do you think?" Her reply was a little too sharp and way too quick. She was referring to Chip's father, the reason for everything miserable in her life.

Then she began to cry, softly at first. She had to pull off the road.

Chip put his hand on her shoulder. "What's wrong with Dad, anyway?"

Katy sniffed and took a tissue from between the seats. "Ya got a week?"

They both smiled then, in spite of themselves, and Katy drove on, steeped in her own thoughts, as Chip was in his.

CHAPTER 42

At dusk the sun over northwest Kansas was a saffron dollop in the haze, standing sentry over miles and miles of order and symmetry and the sweep of a western history as rich and vibrant as any. A romanticist might claim that the muted autumn sun had placed its hand on the bosom of the Great Plains and blessed the land for its fortitude in the face of such history. Orange rays shot through the dust and formed a blanket that could be seen from a thousand miles up. And in the northwestern part of the state, in a little known cemetery on the outskirts of a little known town, Dan Parrish stood among the gravestones, in front of a marker that said John Henry, and he closed the book on his burgeoning new life of possibilities gone wrong.

After a time he collected himself and his few possessions, all packed in a duffel bag that said SGT. CARL PARRISH. He backed away from the grave he'd restored to respectability. He turned and walked up the path to the gate where, to his surprise, Chip Hunter was waiting.

The boy was leaning on his Jeep Wrangler, his crutches by his side. They locked eyes—the young man who so emulated his teacher and the older man who'd been living in the shadows for so long. The sun fell below the horizon. Neither knew what to say.

A minute went by. The air freshened and the temperature dropped with the passing of the day.

"C'mon, Coach. Don't."

Dan looked up at a darkening sky, searching for something to say. He needed a lie or an excuse, yet he realized only the truth would do. Only the truth worked. "I've been through this before, Chip. The looks. The stares. The whispering. I don't have the stomach for it."

Dan started for the road.

Chip felt a lump rise in his throat. He didn't know why, exactly, but he knew he had to stop this man from leaving. He knew there was more to it than a lesson about throwing a football. He knew that if he let his coach go he would regret it for as long as he lived. "What about me?" he said. "You promised me you'd get me to a four year school."

Dan's words floated in the air. "Sorry, kiddo. I'm done here."

"Done?" Chip raised his voice. "What you mean is you're quitting!" Dan stopped and turned.

Emotions are a funny thing. One minute you're contrite, the next you're angry. And Dan didn't like the tone of voice from his one-time protégé. And he didn't like the word quit, either. There were reasons for his decision that Chip wouldn't understand—he *couldn't* understand.

Chip gestured into the depths of the graveyard. He said, "Would you want him to know you're a quitter?"

"Easy now, Chip—"

"No!" He was angry now. "I mean, if anybody should be quitting it's me, right? Last year of JC ball and I'm stuck with these." He picked up his crutches and flung them to the ground. "At least you can play." Tears sprang from his eyes and ran down his face. "'You can't run away from trouble, Coach. There ain't no place that far.' Remember?"

175

Parrish took a step back and set his burden down. He hung his head. Suddenly he felt small. He realized Chip was right and he was humbled by the revelation. The student had explained something basic and universal to his coach. "Uncle Remus. Yeah, I remember." His smile when it came was weak, mirrored by Chip's.

"Good. When my ankle heals you go wherever you want. But until then...you're staying."

A gust of sundown air bent the trees and ruffled the leaves of the elms, sending a cascade of gold through the cemetery.

"C'mon, Coach. Let's go to practice. We got a big game Saturday night."

CHAPTER 43

The next morning Dan rose with the chickens as he always did, made breakfast for his housemates, and jumped on his bike. The air was cool—almost cold—and dark clouds rode the horizon like waves on a storm-tossed sea. A front was threatening, the first big one of the season, and everywhere trees danced in the wind and the lids of garbage cans came off and windows rattled with trepidation at the coming incursion of winter's trespass. Dan pedaled his bike along the streets, ignoring everything around him, head down, pumping fast and furious in an effort to beat the first spats of icy rain on dry concrete, a harbinger that had held off all night.

But when cars passed him, going to work, and the drivers pointed his way, he caught it. He knew. When kids on street corners stared and early morning dog walkers stopped and turned, he saw. He wondered if deciding to stay in Echo and tough it out may have been a bad idea.

Dan reached a stop sign and braked. He put his feet down on the pavement. Beside him a little boy walked hand-in-hand with his father. The boy noticed him and turned to his dad and said something. The man said something back, nodding.

"Excuse me, sir," said the boy, turning to Dan. "Are you the man...uh..."

Dan felt a rush of adrenaline course through his body. He didn't want to do this, not in public, not now.

"...are you the man who won the game for the Cougars

last Saturday?"

And Dan was shocked. With all that had happened, he'd forgotten the game. He'd forgotten how people cheered and how they stood and gaped at him, applauding.

The kid dropped his backpack and dug out a little rubber football. "Dad says it was you." He found a Sharpie and offered it to Parrish for him to sign. Dan hesitated, then took the offering and looked up at the boy's father, who said, "Go get 'em, Danny." It was Bobby Hollowell, a guy he'd known since first grade, now a dentist but first and foremost a father.

And a rabid Echo football fan.

And that was enough for Dan Parrish. He signed the ball and handed it back to the kid. Then he looked at the father and smiled. "Thanks, Bobby." He pedaled off to the cafeteria, hoping he still had a job.

Dan parked his bike and locked it to the railing outside the delivery ramp at the back of the cafeteria. He noticed Sam's car in the parking lot—unusual so early in the day. Not good. The old guy never arrived at his office before noon, and had lately been skipping Mondays and Tuesdays, coming in at the tail end of the week. Things had been going so well, Sam Blevins had been visiting the municipal golf course on Mondays to take advantage of the senior citizen special, twelve-dollar green fees until winter snows shut things down. Maybe the coming rain had convinced him to forget the golf for the week, although it wasn't likely. In inclement weather he and his pals just adjourned to the clubhouse and drank beer and discussed whatever political outrage had pissed them off that week.

Or maybe something else was in the wind.

The first low clouds raced across from the west and the first heavy drops hit the ground and dimpled the steam gutters at the rear of the building. Dan ducked and entered and strode across the sparkling linoleum tile floors of the kitchen. The ladies were already there, pulling big pans of fresh baked cinnamon rolls from the oven. The smells would make a dead man climb out of his coffin. He nodded to them, then glanced up the short flight of stairs and saw that Sam was in his office, at his desk, reading the local paper.

Dan took the stairs two at a time. "No golf today, Sam?" Blevins didn't answer, just folded his newspaper and gestured for Dan to sit. Dan took a chair. He'd noticed that his ladies—like jurists about to hand down a guilty verdict—wouldn't make eye contact. He noticed that Sam wouldn't either.

Sam Blevins got up and closed the door. "Dan," he said. He rubbed his face, unable to continue. He tried again. "Damn it, Dan, somebody called the state licensing commission. Told them we have an ex-con running the cafeteria. And, well—"

Dan held up his hand, stopping Sam's painful, prepared admission in its tracks. He understood. He was being fired. He nodded and smiled at the man who had been a good guy, a Good Sam. He knew that Sam Blevins didn't want to say the words out loud, and he wasn't going to make him. Outside, the rain was coming down in waves on the roof. Icy sleet rattled the windowpanes at the front of the cafeteria, dissolving in opaque sheets of water over the glass.

"I'm sorry, Dan. Really."

"I believe you, Sam."

They both sat and looked at each other. Downstairs Jorge had arrived wet. He was toweling himself off, joking with the ladies—something about big buns. Sam rolled his chair back and examined a pencil in his hand as if it were alien to him. Dan stared at the clock, listening to the noise from overhead.

Sam said, "So...I'm guessing that's where you learned your way around a kitchen?"

"Where?" said Dan. He figured he had the right to make his ex-boss say it if he was going to pry.

"Prison."

"Yep. Eighteen years. Started in the dish room scraping pots. Graduated to cook. I was allowed to use these big knives tethered with wire cables to the butcher tables. I had some pretty tough customers. One lump in the gravy and…" Dan drew a finger across his throat.

Sam dropped his pencil. "Really?"

"Nah," he said, smiling. "Gravy was the least of our palatability problems. Prison food is pretty basic. Things like boiled cabbage twice a week. We used to stir a big cauldron of it with a canoe paddle. But I studied a lot of old, donated cookbooks in the prison library. Made time pass." He glanced back down into the kitchen at the four ladies, now icing their cinnamon buns. Jorge stood apart, arms crossed. He knew something was up.

"By the way," said Sam, nodding toward Jorge, "How the hell did you get through to him?"

"Simple," Dan said. "I let him cook."

"Well I'll be dipped."

Dan stood and was about to leave.

"Whoa. Where you going?"

"Pound the pavement. No job and the state punches my ticket back to the joint."

"You didn't think I was going to just kick you to the curb, did you?" He handed Dan a slip of paper. "Greasy spoon on the edge of town. Ask for Waylon. He won't pay much, but it's job enough to keep the State of Kansas off your back."

Dan looked down and studied the address. "Cool, Sam. What's it called?"

"I told you," Sam said, annoyed. "The Greasy Spoon."

Dan offered his hand across the desk. The two men shook.

"Hate to lose you. You really turned this cafeteria around. We've got teachers and students lining up out the door. The women in there are singing and dancing for the first time in years. Balanced the books, too. You've got us operating in the black. It'll be hard to fill your shoes."

"I enjoyed the opportunity, Sam. You took a chance on me. I won't forget it."

Sam heaved a sigh of relief. He looked down at Jorge, who returned the look, glaring at him, hands on hips. "That kid is gonna miss you."

"No he won't," Dan said.

Sam looked at him.

"I'm taking him with me. That is, if it's okay with you."

Sam clasped his hands together and turned his eyes to the heavens.

"I take it that's a yes."

Sam nodded.

Dan turned, and opened the door and took the stairs two-at-a-time, down to the kitchen. He pointed at his little conscript. "You...me...outta here."

Jorge grinned. He took off his apron, bowed to the ladies, saluted to Sam, and hurried after Dan Parrish, who was striding down the hall like a man on a mission.

CHAPTER 44

By eleven-thirty the rain had moved on and the winds had abated some. The temperature had fallen and the dry, clear air behind the front had taken control. Agnes Stankowiecz sat on one of the benches by the little fountain in the commons, nibbling an apple and grading papers.

"Mind if I sit?"

She looked up. Dan stood in front of her trying to smile. She scooted over to the far end of the bench, putting her work in her satchel. She looked unsure of how to handle things. She didn't even know what Dan wanted anymore. The best option up to now must have been to ignore any percolating animosity she held and walk away. Still, as a professor she might just as well have taken some responsibility, not letting personal disappointments cloud her judgment. After all, Dan Parrish was still her student.

Dan gestured at her apple. "Give up on the cafeteria?"

"I should ask you the same."

"Touché," he replied then took a seat. "They let me go. You know how dangerous ex-cons in the kitchen can be." He feigned stabbing and thrusting with invisible knives.

Agnes didn't laugh.

"It was a joke."

She forced a smile. Parrish looked away. This wasn't going like he had planned. He looked down at the ground and clasped his hands together. He began to twiddle his thumbs until he realized he was literally twiddling his thumbs and stopped.

"Well…what do you think?" he said.

"About?"

"About the article. Or articles, I guess I should say. I heard they were plastered all over town." He tried to look at her but couldn't.

"It's none of my business, Dan."

"Sure it is."

She sighed, realizing that Dan had decided he wanted to talk. This was a new development. It wasn't just Agnes who had been mute about recent events. He hadn't spoken to her either, since that day he stormed out of class. And the quiet had been a blessing, because even though she'd pulled the damning reprints off her classroom wall and thrown them in the garbage, she didn't know what to say about the years-ago events that had destroyed Dan, or how to even approach the subject. And there were more things going on than just the article. There were issues that had not come clear yet.

She took a deep breath, let it out and began. "I think what happened was horrible, Dan. I think what the judge did was cruel and excessive. I think you must be living in a world of pain. I also think it was a long time ago and that you've more than paid the price."

Dan still didn't look up. The grass at his feet had worn through. He drew circles in the dampness with the toes of his shoes. The wind had pushed the standing water into shallow swales, and the falling leaves drifted onto the grass and formed reefs of gold and tan in lines slanting down the hill.

"I feel sorry for you, Dan. Really."

"Don't. There's nobody to blame but myself."

A gust of wind tousled Agnes' hair and she shivered. They sat without a word as the bells of the distant First Baptist Church chimed the noon hour. It didn't sound joyful as it had in the past. It seemed somber and chilly and hollow.

"Were you and Katy married, Dan?"

He closed his eyes. The question must have come as a shock judging by the look on his face. "Almost." He looked up and saw the pained expression in her eyes.

"You must really love her."

"Loved," he said. "Past tense."

"You sure about that?"

Agnes reached into her purse. Some part of her didn't want to do what she was thinking; she felt in her heart that pushing Dan was the wrong thing to do. She intuited his delicacy, and knew he wasn't as strong as he pretended. But something made her ignore all that when she handed Dan the photo of Katy.

"Found it on my kitchen floor."

Dan inhaled and found his tongue. "Agnes, I can explain—"

"No need, Dan." She stood and gathered her things. "A picture's worth a thousand words." She turned and left, walking briskly across the damp, dead grass and fallen leaves. She had to hurry, before he saw the tears welling up. She thought, *This is why I didn't want to talk about it. I seem to be able to think and say what I like about other people having poison memories and motives. Yet maybe I need to examine my own. We all have histories that color our lives. My past failures with relationships aren't as catastrophic as Dan's, but I still lock my door and peek out the window, even here in Echo. My world appears safe now, but my feelings aren't bulletproof.*

Dan watched her go, mad at himself for his misplaced loyalties and for his idiotic devotion to something that wasn't real. He looked down at the photo in his hand. Katy, the cheerleader. His first love. The girl he almost married. The mother of his only son, John Henry.

Rick Hunter's wife.

He crumpled the old photo and dished it to the wind. Somehow his past life was still getting in the way of his new life. He hadn't learned to move on. Eighteen years in that big concrete box had colored his perception of time and wouldn't turn him loose. Now it had cost him his position at the school cafeteria.

And it had cost him his girl.

The quiet man has been stupid, but no more. He watched the whore, his Agnes, hugging the hero in front of everybody. Now he sees them seated together on campus. What she called his insane jealousy all those months ago was not misplaced. And the hero quarterback is trying to destroy his plans.

The quiet man returned to his motel room and locked the door.

Better be safe. Don't be stupid anymore.

Remember the blueprint.

CHAPTER 45

Never was there a more appropriately named diner than The Greasy Spoon. It was apparent even from the outside. The old brick walls were covered with peeling gray paint and the doors—once red enamel and neon bright chrome from the sixties—were now mottled, dull and lifeless. The windows were dark with dust and the landscaping around the place was more a collection of weeds and split asphalt than anything else. The sign on the road—once an artist's pastiche in fiberglass of a buxom, apron-wearing waitress, tray in hand, big smile and lascivious wink on her face—was now a tumbledown ruin made famous by local teenage graffiti virtuosos.

Inside, Dan had been sitting for a half hour at a grimy Formica counter across from Waylon, the gruff, former biker who owned the place. The man was in his sixties, and wore a sleeveless leather jacket over his torso. His biceps still bulged. His hands were like platters. He wore a monstrous gray Fu Manchu over his upper lip and no hair at all on his head. Together the men were hashing out the particulars of Dan's new job, while Jorge examined the place, inspecting the fryer and the stoves and the other equipment behind the counter and in the back.

"I'll be by once a week to collect the receipts," said Waylon. He pointed a thick, calloused finger at Dan. "You have them ready for me. Don't do any skimming and we'll get along fine. Dig?"

Parrish smiled, nodded, chanced a look at a shrugging Jorge, who half-heartedly stuck a thumb in the air. "Dig," said Dan and the two men shook. Then Waylon slid him a set of keys.

"Just like that?"

"Gotta run, son. My old lady's got Alzheimer's. Last week I stayed late for a beer and when I got home she'd shaved the cat." He held up a thumb and forefinger. "She was this close to roasting him like a chicken in the toaster oven."

Jorge stepped around to the counter. "So, when do we start?" he asked, confused.

Waylon checked his watch. "One hour."

Before Dan or Jorge could protest, Waylon was out the door. A moment later they heard the hellish sound of a Harley pulling away and fading to nothing as it sped around the wide curve in the highway and was gone. Dan followed Jorge's gaze to the grease-spattered menu above the counter, every bit as dull as the plywood it was painted on.

"Yo, homes. That is some seriously tired chow."

"Well..." said Dan. He squinted into the corners and ran his eyes up and down the room. "Then it's our job to wake it up." His smile faded and flattened into a look of pain. Truth be told, he was overwhelmed by what he saw: dirty floors, neglected booths, the seats repaired with duct tape, broken light fixtures, a filthy kitchen that would have never passed any health department inspection that he knew of, including the monthly checking of the state prison system's kitchens. In fact, the prison chow hall made this place look like a bus station toilet. He heaved a deep sigh and looked back at Jorge.

"You ready for this?"

Jorge ran his finger along the lip of the griddle and came away with a thick curl of ochre colored glop. "I dunno, man. Are you?"

A rat scooted from behind one of the ovens. It chittered and stood up on its haunches like a small dog with his hackles up, challenging them. It turned all the way around, inviolable,

187

and made its way to an opening under the sinks. *Screw you*, it must have been thinking; *this is my house.*

"Brother, I don't have a choice," said Dan.

CHAPTER 46

The next three weeks were a blur to Dan Parrish. Between classes at Echo JC and football practice, Dan and Jorge were consumed with the cleaning and repairs of The Greasy Spoon, often working past midnight, sometimes sleeping in the booths. Dealing with the customers in those first few days was comical, especially listening to Jorge take orders in his unique brand of Spanglish. And Dan had to work with a whole new set of problems on the antiquated stove and griddle. Without Waylon, there was an immediate drop-off in customers. Some wanted their resident biker back; others disliked change and were irritated by Jorge and his ridiculous humor. But none complained about the food. In fact, many that quit the place came back once they heard about Dan's hominy cheese grits, buttermilk dinner rolls, crispy pig's-ear lettuce wraps and smoky, fried chicken skins served with hot sauce and honey.

Dan also started bringing in local beers like Blind Tiger, Great Loop Lager, Walnut River Wheat and the bestseller, Wichita Titty-Twister. And he relied on local farmers to deliver the freshest produce, the best cuts of beef, the sweetest apples and rhubarb. The folks of Echo took notice and began to trickle in. Jorge's girlfriend, Tiny Lopez, and Sandie, the young girl from the dime store took waitressing jobs, which solved the Jorge-as-resident-clown problem—he could work full time with the cooking beside Dan—and they in turn brought their friends and families in as customers.

Before long, The Greasy Spoon wasn't so greasy anymore.

In the classroom, though, Dan wasn't doing so well with Agnes. He was still getting the cold shoulder, and try as he might, he was unable to thaw the chill that had grown between them. The two were more apart than ever. Dan didn't know what to do about it—he had very little experience with these life issues—so he did nothing. He was a man used to being lonely. He gave up and concentrated on his grades, his griddle and the gridiron.

Echo continued to win, too. With Dan at the helm and Chip on the sidelines still using crutches, signaling plays, the Cougars ran off an impressive trio of victories that added to their luster, a shine that was unprecedented in recent history. Everyone on the team began to exude confidence in the new arrangement, and everyone in town was paying attention. Farmers and ranchers from the countryside began to come to the games. Temporary end-zone bleachers had to be installed to accommodate the overflow.

On one Sunday morning in mid-November, following a home game in which Echo scored more than fifty points, Bobbitt, Chip and some of the other players and coaches descended on The Greasy Spoon. With two gallons each of white paint donated by Sam Blevins, they painted the place from top to bottom. One volunteer and his father sprayed the roof shingles with silver oxide anodizing. A trio of players—self-professed auto body experts—put the road sign back together, gave it a layer of gel-coat, and painted the smile, the apron and the wink back on the ancient waitress. The place shone like it hadn't since its heyday.

On Thanksgiving Day, Dan put a CLOSED sign up and kept the doors locked except for those near and dear. There were reasons to celebrate. And he and his new friends were going to do their best. After all, his life was on the right track, his job was secure, the Echo JC Cougars were 10 and 0, and the entire town had become rabid fans and supporters. Business windows were draped in Echo bunting and displayed "Heart of Kansas Bowl" banners. Every intersection bore testament to Echo pride. Hats and sweatshirts were selling out at the campus bookstore. Dan Parrish, the grizzled old man from the past, had led them to their first bowl game in over a decade. Players' pictures were in windows all over town, too, because proud parents were everywhere. *Our Team is Kick-Ass!*

That afternoon at the Hunter household, the mood was dark, even tense, as Chip, Darla and Katy sat down to the table with Rick Hunter. He'd been drinking all day, and his self-styled poses and lust-filled remarks to the young girl that still enjoyed Chip's attentions had destroyed any feelings of holiday cheer. When he winked at Darla he didn't hide it. When he offered his slithery asides, he was obvious. When he sat at the table and said grace before the meal, his voice was slurred and his eyes were bloodshot. He laughed too hard. When he tried to carve the turkey, Chip had to take over for him. And to make matters worse, Darla couldn't stop flirting. She also refused to let up on her complaints about Dan Parrish and how rotten it was that he was allowed to lead the team. Halfway through the meal she was still carping. And Rick Hunter, the most volatile of men when he was in his cups, was listening.

"It's just not fair," she said, pointing a forkful of stuffing at Chip. "You've been cleared to play. You practiced all week. And this is the last game of your last year. You should get the start."

"It doesn't work that way," said Chip, annoyed at the length of the harangue. "Does it, Dad?" He was hoping to engage his father in something less caustic.

Hunter didn't answer. He looked over at Katy, who glanced away.

"Besides, Coach Parrish has the hot hand now," Chip continued. "So maybe he should be starting. He's earned it."

At the word *earned*, Rick Hunter blew up. "That's absurd!" He slammed his hand down on the table, rattling the plates and platters. The group fell quiet. The air was charged with venom and the beautiful meal that Katy had prepared had soured. Her husband took a sip of his scotch. His face was red, either from the alcohol or from internal fires impossible to bank.

Darla tried to steer the conversation to a safer place. "It's hard to believe we're still even talking about him." She shook her head. "I mean, you'd think after we posted those articles all over campus, he'd have left a long time ago." She laughed.

Chip was about to take a drink of his iced tea. The glass stopped halfway to his lips. "We?"

Once again the room went quiet.

Darla dropped her head, the word *oops* written on her face like a roadmap of discomfort.

Chip set his glass down with care. "What's that supposed to mean, Darla? We."

She didn't answer, choosing instead to stare down at her plate and move her cranberry sauce around with her fork. She tried her best to look young and virtuous. Chip reached over and stilled her wrist with his hand.

"Darla, I know that look."

Still, she said nothing.

Chip dropped her hand and turned sideways in his chair to face her. He raised his voice some. "Darla, were you involved with that crap?"

Darla turned to Rick Hunter, who looked away, reaching for his drink. He refused to acknowledge the eight thousand pound gorilla in the room. Thanksgiving dinner was officially over.

"Answer me!" Chip shouted, standing, leaning over her.

The words poured out in a rush. "It was just some articles, is all. I didn't know what Jimmy was gonna do with them—"

"Get out!"

Katy put her napkin down and tried to calm Chip before her mercurial husband started in. "Now, Chip—"

"No!"

Darla began to whine. "But it's Thanksgiving!"

"I don't care! Get out of here!"

Darla refused to budge. "The guy is a total loser!"

"You don't even know him!" Chip bellowed. "Now go, Darla, and don't come back!"

The grandfather clock on the dining room wall began to chime four o'clock. Rick Hunter, already drunk, stood and snatched Darla by her arm and began leading her through the house to the door. "C'mon, young lady—"

And at that Darla came alive, whipping her arm free, the sniffle vanishing, teeth bared at the disgusting middle-aged man who thought he was such a heart throb. "You! Get your damn hands *off* me!" She stood in the foyer, panting, face turning to each member of the Hunter household. "Okay, I'll leave!" She focused on Chip. "Don't you worry about that! And yeah, I gave Jimmy Durr those articles." She leaned against the archway that divided the dining and living rooms. Her voice went soft and low. She smiled like a killer. "But who do you think gave them to me?"

She looked at Rick Hunter, then back to Chip. She arched her eyebrows. Then she turned on her heels and left, slamming the front door so hard it jarred the photo of Hunter's father hanging on the wall.

Chip sat down hard and looked at his mother. Both of them gazed at Rick, who was now busy mixing himself a drink.

Chip found words. "You didn't..." His voice betrayed him. He tried again. "Did you—"

Hunter circled around and grimaced, losing his balance for a minute, almost falling. "I'll be damned if I'm gonna sit back and let that son of a bitch run my son's team."

Chip looked at his father as if he were a piece of excrement on a hot, summer sidewalk. He made a fist with his napkin and laid it on the plate in front of him.

"You are so pathetic."

He rose and left the house. Katy watched him go and turned to her husband.

"I couldn't have said it better myself," she said. She stood up beside the table and began to clear the dishes, refusing to look at the man.

Hunter stood in the ruins and sipped his whiskey. He stumbled back around through the arch and sat down in the living room. He clicked on the TV and pretended to watch Dallas and Detroit play football.

CHAPTER 47

The sign on the front door of The Greasy Spoon read:

HAPPY THANKSGIVING
CLOSED TODAY
Reserved for Staff and Families

Chip stood outside the front door and vacillated. He didn't know if he should go in...or knock...or walk away. He was neither staff nor family, and his own father had been responsible for something terrible that had affected Dan and almost ruined his efforts to succeed. Even though Chip had no hand in it, he felt answerable in a way, like maybe the thoughts and actions of the drunken father would rub off on him someday, and he would reap the whirlwind, using his own life as a bludgeon and ending his days in Echo, thinking small and acting small and being forever angry at whatever fates were thrown his way. He couldn't handle that.

He cupped his hands and peeked through the glass. There was a party going on. He could see an eclectic mix of people laughing and munching away. Coach Bobbitt was there with his family, 'Ipo was playing the ukulele along with some Hawaiian slack-key guitar music on the jukebox and some of the other Cougars from out of town were there, along with Parrish's house mates, Millie and the twins.

Chip turned the bill of his hat aside and pressed his face into the glass. He saw Jorge and his big girlfriend Tiny, sitting at a table with some people that could have been family members. In the back there were people that Chip didn't recognize, some of them up and dancing. He noticed Waylon, the owner of the place. The guy was partying with his wife, who had a leopard-skin leotard on and wore her bra outside her T-shirt like Madonna made famous. Along one wall, two counters were stacked with platters and plates full of stuff, meats and cheeses, dips and spreads that looked flat out delicious. A steam table full of other holiday edibles occupied the left of the display.

In the middle of the party, Dan Parrish stood as chief server, passing plates to those in line, smiling and nodding to his guests. The life that his coach was carving out for himself was going to succeed. Chip could see it. And he was pleased. To hell with his dad and Darla and Jimmy Durr. To hell with anybody that went through life burying themselves inside a crater of bitterness.

Dan looked up and saw Chip standing at the door, his arms hanging at his sides.

"Chip!" he shouted, alerting the crowd, hurrying to the door. He threw it open and dragged the boy in. Chip's face turned red. He didn't know what to say. He stumbled through the threshold and tried to smile. He did a slow pan of the crowd, everyone seeming to be happy he was there, people shouting his name. He laughed at Coach Bobbitt, sitting and patting his belly.

He waved to 'Ipo who was flashing him the shaka. And within the passing of the first minute, Chip knew he belonged.

In the living room of the Hunter house, Rick Hunter sat morose and unresponsive, his eyes on the TV, his mind numb, a drunken swirl of loathing encapsulating him like a shroud. The Thanksgiving dishes had been swept from the dining room table and nothing was left of the holiday but bad feelings. Katy blew by, her car keys jangling. She held her tongue, but her bearing was resolute and she didn't slow down except to open the front door.

"Where you think you're going?" Her husband's voice cracked.

"To find my son."

Dan Parrish sat, finally taking a break. He shared a booth with Chip, watching him eat. The boy had an appetite for sure. But the food was good, even if he did say so himself. In addition to the turkeys and hams, there was stuffing and mashed potatoes with horseradish cream sauce, plates of shiitake mushrooms and sautéed winter greens and cranberry-mustard relish. Four huge cast iron skillets had been filled with cornbread. And trays that used to hold bourbon-pecan tarts were now almost empty. There were three pumpkin cheesecakes, now almost gone, too. They had been frosted with Dan's own recipe.

"You make all this?" Chip asked, his mouth full.

"Me and him," said Dan, pointing at his assistant, Jorge, whose arms were wrapped around two-thirds of Tiny. They were intimately involved in a slow dance for the ages. Love could be a complicated thing, yet somehow Jorge and Tiny simplified matters.

Dan and Chip laughed.

"So...what's up, Chipper?" Dan asked. He knew Chip should have been home with his folks. "You okay?"

Chip didn't answer.

Dan sat back, crossed his arms and tilted his head askew. "C'mon, man, out with it."

Chip put his fork down. "You know those articles, the ones Durr put up all over town?"

Dan nodded somberly.

"He wasn't the only one responsible."

"I know."

"You do? How?"

"Let's just say I had a pretty good idea and leave it at that."

"Why am I the last to know everything?"

"Because you're a kid, Chip. It's the law."

Chip tried to wrap his head around it all. He poked at his dessert with his fork. "Why does he hate you so much? Is it just because you 'n' Mom…" he trailed off, unable to finish.

"That's part of it, Chip. But there's more to it than that."

"Like what?"

Parrish placed his hands on the boy's shoulder. He didn't want to appear condescending, but there was so much involved, this was not the time, nor was it the place to offer opinions or to proselytize. "I'll tell you someday, but not today, huh? It's Thanksgiving. And what's a day like this all about?"

Chip smiled. "Food…friends…fun…" His smile faded at the final alliteration. "…family."

There was a knock at the front door. Dan looked up.

"Speaking of which…"

Dan stood as Katy Hunter stepped through the door. When the people cheered she blushed. When JD Bobbitt stood and gave her a bear hug, lifting her off her feet, her resolve to be cool fell apart. She started to cry. Dan and Chip escorted her to their booth and offered her a seat. Nothing about this day had gone right for Katy until then.

CHAPTER 48

Dan bent and scooted into the seat opposite his former lover. *Being uncomfortable has its signatures and everyone knows them. Sometimes I think it's only me that wears feelings on my sleeve. Then I see my people, the ones that I love, attacked by the same sort of gauntlet. It's not easy to witness. Especially when I'm the cause of it all.*

"We were just talking about you...weren't we, Chip?"

The son nodded, probably embarrassed for his mother's tears, happy to see her just the same.

"And there's something we both want to know, Katy." Dan paused. The woman and her son looked at him. They were both afraid of what he would ask next. They showed it in their eyes. Dan leaned in close and summoned his gravest look for effect.

"White meat or dark?"

Katy flashed her smile, the smile that was surely the reason he'd carried that ancient photo around for so long. He stood. "Extra marshmallows on the sweet potatoes, right?"

She nodded, touched that he'd remembered. She looked at her son. "Seconds for you, big guy?"

"Hell, yeah!"

Dan headed off to fetch them some plates. Katy watched him go. Chip tried not to show what he was feeling deep inside, but the day had been complicated. And mostly lousy. But things were looking up.

* * *

And things were improving for Katy, too. And as long as Rick Hunter stayed away, the afternoon was going to be a good one. At least for her and her son. She knew that she was being scrutinized, too. *It's all part of the ticket I purchased long ago. Slow and steady wins the race. Don't berate your husband in public. Don't destroy the rest of the day with speculations and impossible dreams.* She decided to ask her son about the upcoming game...

...except he'd taken it into his head it was okay to worry the bone between them. "I don't know, Mom," he said, pointing to Dan. "He seems like a good guy to me—"

"Look!" Katy glanced around, concerned someone had heard the tone of her voice. She quieted. "I know where you're going with this; it's a road I've driven down a thousand times. And frankly, I'm sick of the scenery, Chip. You understand what I'm saying?"

He nodded, contrite.

"Things happen, Chip. Some good, some not so good. You have to deal with it the best way you know how, and don't look back."

"Like my ankle."

"There you go," she said, pointing at him with her fork.

Dan approached and slid two plates in front of them. He winked and went to fraternize with the other guests.

Katy crinkled her forehead and smiled into her food. "Now, if you don't mind..." She held up a mostly melted marshmallow on her fork.

"Go for it, Mom."

Katy sucked the gooey concoction off the tines and glanced around the room, focusing on one then another of the tables. In the far corner there was an old acquaintance, one that startled her. And the girl was staring at her. Katy put her fork on the plate. "Brenda?" she mouthed.

The girl nodded, waved and forced a smile. Then quickly looked away.

Katy had known Brenda Price since she was a little girl. She'd watched her attend the same school her son had gone to, coached her as a cheerleader assistant, knew her parents, Alice and Elam and her brothers, Leon and Willie.

She knew Brenda. She knew that look.

And something wasn't right.

CHAPTER 49

It was late. Everyone had left. Thanksgiving revelry had died and gone to bed. The Greasy Spoon was empty except for Dan and Jorge, washing the dishes, wiping down the place and mopping the floors. The music had been turned off and the only thing you could hear was the slapping of the mop against the baseboards and the humming of the refrigerators.

A car passed and for a moment its headlights lit the inside of the restaurant. Dan looked up, but his face fell when the lights faded away. He leaned on his mop handle and stared out the window. Jorge watched him from the kitchen area.

"Call her."

The voice startled Dan. He turned around and looked at his helper. "Huh?"

"Huh?" Jorge imitated his boss.

Dan stuffed the mop in the bucket and then into the ringer, pushing the lever down, squeezing the water out. He began mopping again.

"I say call her, dude."

"Nah. Some other time maybe."

"Whatevahs. But I heard she's moving away at the end of the semester." Jorge stuck his hand in one of the sinks and pulled the plug. The dirty water swirled away. When Dan leaned his mop against the wall, Jorge knew he'd hooked him. Without looking up, he said, "That's only two weeks, brism."

Dan stared at the counter, his mind lost.

Jorge reached into his pocket and pulled out his cell phone. He tossed it to his boss. Dan began to dial.

"Well, I appreciate you thinking of me, Dan. No, no, no, don't be silly. I've eaten, like, so much." Agnes looked down at the coffee table, at her half-eaten TV dinner. She'd never been a cook. And it wasn't easy to make a feast for only one mouth, anyway.

Dan listened to the quiet. *Remember, Danny Boy, what you'd said to yourself when you got out. You complained. You whined. You carped to yourself about yourself.*

But he was just now starting to understand—prison existence had been so obsessive and self-absorbing. The focus was always pointed inward. All he'd thought about was himself. Except now, that same kind of self-absorption wasn't working for Agnes, either. She felt alone in a strange land. *So what are you going to do, big guy?*

He turned his back to the dining room and lowered his voice. "Agnes...I, uh...I hear you're leaving Echo. Is it true?" *I'm being selfish again.*

Agnes did her best to sound cheerful. "Yeah, well, it's just that I have an awesome opportunity at this liberal arts school in New England. And, y'know, I just couldn't turn it down, Dan."

"Oh. Well, yeah...geez..." *What am I saying? She's drifting away.* "That'll be nice with all those russets and reds and pea coats and labstahs." *I am such an ass...*

"Oh, yeah, can't forget the labstahs." She forced a laugh.

The silence grew awkward again. The gulf between them had grown too wide.

"Maybe I should stop by? You know, bring you some dessert?"

But he knew she couldn't cave now. "No," she answered. "Like I said. Blimp city. But thanks, anyway, Dan. Awfully sweet."

Another beat passed.

"Oh well. Okay then…" *I am an idiot of the first order.* "…be safe."

"You, too, Dan." She hung up.

Dan tossed the phone back to Jorge, who'd been listening to Parrish's side of the conversation. Outside, beyond the hard shadows, the full moon bleached the neighboring fields with a patina of blue. There would be frost in the morning.

Jorge said, "Be safe? Be *safe*? Are you kidding me?"

"Lame, huh?"

Jorge hid his face in his hands. "Ai, ai, ai!"

Dan dropped his gaze to the floor.

"Bro, you told me the way to a girl's pants is through her belly—"

"I said heart, not pants, Jorge."

Jorge shrugged. "Heart, pants, same thing." He stepped to the banquet tables still piled with platters of leftovers. All of it was now wrapped in plastic, ready to go into the fridge. He picked out a few things, stacked them, and handed them to Dan. "Go. Before it gets too cold. And the food, too," he added with a wink and elbow to the ribs.

Dan closed his eyes. *I'm wrong, he's right. I need to get out from behind my old thoughts. Everyone can be a teacher sometimes. And my partner here knows more than I do about the real world.*

Jorge stepped back behind the counter. He tossed Dan the keys to his car. "And here, take my ride. Your ten-speed ain't gonna cut it."

CHAPTER 50

Jorge's Ford Fiesta was a masterpiece of insouciant inspiration. The car's exterior wasn't much, except for the LED mud flaps and the gnarly tires. But inside there were little white fur balls hanging everywhere and it smelled like someone had poured a cup of lavender perfume into the carpeting. The windows were tinted almost black and there was a fuzzy, powder blue headliner that Dan crashed his forehead into when he climbed in. Jorge had installed two-tone, saddle-shoe seats up front, and there were two mega-ultra bass blasters empowering the vacuum under the rear windshield, and two more in the trunk. It took Dan a few minutes to figure out how to turn off Pit Bull and his minions. By that time, his ears were ringing.

But before long he was lurching down the street toward Agnes's place. He was nervous for a couple of reasons. He hadn't seen Agnes except in class since the great unveiling of his life. And he hadn't driven a stick in decades. He also didn't want gravy to spill onto Jorge's seats. They weren't in perfect order; stains were evident; burn marks had taken the shape of amber hearts and flowers. Yet no matter, it was a loaner from his almost partner, and he didn't want to dishonor the ride.

When he was a quarter-mile from Agnes' place, he heard the distinctive whop-whop of a short burst police siren. He looked in his mirror and saw flashing red lights fast approaching. Then the cop car came up beside him and he pulled over. He wasn't speeding, but it didn't mean anything; any sort of face-to-face on the side of the road was dangerous for someone on probation. Dan's hands began to shake and heart began to race and suddenly he was working without a net.

The officer took his time. Dan's anxiety grew. In the moon-lit neighborhood, curtains were drawn aside and nosy residents peeked out to see what was happening. The flashing lights and the loud radio chatter must have awoken them from their Thanksgiving comas. When the officer finally got out of his car, Dan rolled down his window and offered the cop his best smile.

"Problem, Officer?"

"Tail light's out." He began snapping his fingers as he said, "License, registration, insurance."

The finger snapping shook Dan. It was a bad sign. The last thing Dan needed was a run-in with the law. If his parole officer got wind of this, he'd be in trouble. But hey, he told himself, a dumb little issue with a taillight couldn't be a real problem. He would fix it, pay the fine, move on. He handed the cop his driver's license and started rummaging between the seats for other documents, hoping Jorge had them stashed somewhere.

"Sorry, Officer. This isn't my car." He offered a little chuckle, then a weak smile. "I'm sure the registration is in here somewhere." He forced his facial expression into a sem-blance of calm.

"It better be," said the cop.

Oh boy. What's going on? He must be in a bad mood, having to work on the holiday.

The officer shined a light into Dan's eyes, blinding him. Then he began to reexamine the license.

Dan's hands fumbled through old receipts and pay stubs. He was fumbling with his thoughts. The responses from the guy didn't add up, unnerving to say the least, and no matter what a policeman's shift hours dictated, he was supposed to at least give lip service to the idea that he was serving the public. Dan sneaked a look at the name tag under the badge. The last name read: DURR.

Dan closed his eyes. No doubt this was Jimmy's older brother. He looked like Jimmy Durr, except shorter, not as rangy, a pot-belly starting to show. They both had the same straw colored hair, though, and round green eyes that were too close.

"Not good," Dan said under his breath. Except the cop heard it.

"What's that?" He trained his flashlight on Dan's face again.

"Nothing." Parrish shielded his eyes and looked down at his lap, trying to regain his vision.

"Nothing what?"

There was a pause. Dan's blood was beginning to boil. What was this? The old days? A prison hack riding his ass? Some kind of take down? Or did this guy get orders from someone? Did he follow Dan from the diner? Could Jimmy Durr have coerced his brother into some kind of standoff? This wasn't how a stop for a taillight infraction was supposed to be conducted. Anger began to replace fear, and Dan knew in his heart that anger would get him nowhere. *Calm down. This guy's running a game, and I better get in line.*

"Nothing...sir."

Then the worst possible thing happened. Still searching for the car's registration, Dan popped the lid on the glove box and a bottle tumbled out onto the passenger seat. A bone dry wine cooler bottle. Tiny Lopez's trademark fuchsia lipstick decorated the neck. For a moment neither man spoke. Then the cop's face broke into a malevolent grin.

"It's not what you think," Dan said.

Officer Durr wasn't listening. In fact, he was chuckling. "Tell it to the judge, Slick," he said. Then he gestured for Dan to get out of the car. Dan complied. "Now hands on the hood, feet apart. I'm sure *you* know the drill." He reached around to the back of his belt and produced a pair of handcuffs. Some of the neighbors had slipped out onto their front yards to watch. Who could sleep with all the flashing lights stabbing into the night? Who could sleep with all that radio chatter?

And wasn't that man Dan Parrish? The Cougar's quarterback? Drunk?

A few blocks away the quiet man sat in his car and watched the front door of Agnes' apartment.

Thanksgiving alone. She hasn't left her house all day.

He started his car and drove back to the motel. *Soon*, he thought. *Real soon now.*

CHAPTER 51

There was an old gas station on the outskirts of town that still looked like it did fifty years ago when Belden Ferguson's father Caleb first bought it. Caleb was gone now—he'd had a stroke—so Belden had taken over, letting his cousin Lonnie pump gas and change oil and rotate tires while he handled the books and all the auto repair duties.

Belden himself was a good mechanic—he had a reputation all over Punch Town and even into the white sections of Echo—so his mornings and weekends were filled with jobs that involved brakes and water pumps and rebuilding carburetors. He worked on cars during the times when he wasn't at the feed store. It kept food on the table and allowed him to pay the bank note on his twenty acres. There was also an old tow truck that had to be kept up.

On this cold Saturday morning Belden was the only one working when a customer that he recognized from many years ago stopped in for gas. The man asked him if he would check his oil. Belden did. He closed the hood and walked to the driver's window. Billy Cox handed Belden his credit card. Belden took the card but he was more than familiar with the name on it.

"Need to ch-ch-change your oil, Muh-Mister Cox. It's bu-bu-black. Too thick."

"Been meaning to get around to it."

Belden didn't say anything. He tapped the card against his

palm.

Billy Cox checked his watch, impatient. He had a deadline.

Belden said, " So...I'm g-g-guessing y-you're here to...uh... ri-rip Dan Parrish a new one?"

Cox removed his sunglasses. He stared into Belden's face. "Do I know you, son?"

"Belden Ferguson." He pointed to the sign that read Caleb's Sunoco. He didn't stutter when he said his own name. As a kid, he'd practiced. His father had told him if he was ever going to get anything right, make sure it was his own name.

"You're Caleb's kid?"

Belden nodded.

"It isn't my job to rip anyone a new one, Belden. They always seem to do that themselves. I just write about it."

"L-last time you jes' wrote about it, you r-r-u-ruined him."

"Whoa now. Wasn't me that put that bottle of Jack in his hands."

"Maybe it wasn't him, either." The words came out too loud, too hot, too fast.

Billy Cox, the consummate journalist, smelled something he hadn't smelled in a long time. It wasn't the gasoline. Or the ancient oil stains in the cracked concrete slab. It was something else.

He smelled a story.

"Meaning?" he said.

Belden took a breath. He looked around. It was early; the frost had yet to burn away; the big cottonwoods at the edge of the road were brittle with the chill and the dry air. This man had just appeared and he knew why. All the bad things that were being said about Mr. Dan. All the nonsense that was percolating to the top, no matter that Dan Parrish had been doing alright with himself, that he was coaching and playing football and working every day and being strong and doing good.

Belden was committed now. No turning back. He couldn't

pretend he hadn't said anything. He'd been waiting for this moment forever.

"Just suppose you got it all wrong, Mr. Cox?"

"Well, I suppose that's a whole 'nother story then, isn't it?"

"W-w-would you...would you write that story?"

Billy Cox studied Belden's face. A face like his fathers, absent of guile, honest. Belden wouldn't lie. Even so, Billy would have do his homework. He'd listen to what Belden had to say, but he would do his homework.

"What have you got in mind, son?"

CHAPTER 52

The Echo County Courthouse was a photogenic, heart-of-town centerpiece, with white marble columns and high dormer windows and eight steps up to the double front doors. The only metal detector was inside, a walk-through in front of the Honorable Judge's courtroom. There was a hand-held wand also, used by the officer at the magistrate's docket desk for unpredictable divorce participants, but it usually didn't work. The building itself was historic, but it had an unfortunate add-on in the basement. The Echo police department wasn't a big deal, and neither was the jail or the licensing office. But they had to be somewhere, and anyone having business with the city garage or the licensing bureau, had to forego the marble stairway and take the ramp down into what they called the catacombs.

On the second level, in the alcove that fronted the two courtrooms, the atmosphere was grim. Agnes Stankowiecz and JD Bobbitt sat together on one of the benches. She had just arrived, bundled up against the cold, and was visibly upset. JD was consoling.

"...it'll be okay, Agnes," he said. "I've got my attorney working on it. We'll get him out." He patted her arm and smiled at her but he wasn't exactly confident about the last part.

"But it's just...absolutely insane, JD. There has to be more to it."

"Trust me, there is."

Agnes sat quietly for a moment, a tiny door opening in her brain. "This is about Splinter City, isn't it?"

Bobbitt looked at her. His eyes receded into his squinting face and became tiny little glimmers in the greenish neon light. "Who'd you hear that from?"

"A Belden something or other—"

"...Ferguson. Belden Ferguson. That figures." He issued a wan smile as he recalled the kid from years ago. "Belden followed Dan around like a little puppy when he was a kid." He fell silent. The heat cycled on and somewhere a fan rumbled. Time stood still.

"Well?" said Agnes.

"Well what?"

"Where the hell is Splinter City?" she nearly yelled, then immediately quieted herself.

Bobbitt shifted his eyes around, looking for a way to explain. Finally he pointed down. "You're sitting on it."

"A bench?"

Bobbitt nodded. The two locked eyes for a moment. Agnes closed hers, opened them, flattened her right hand and performed a whoosh-over-my-head gesture.

"Riding the pine?" JD said.

"Still no," she said, shaking her head.

JD rolled his eyes, agitated. "You know, Agnes, you should get out more. It's about *being benched*. As in a wooden bench. As in Splinter City."

A light bulb went on. "Ah. I get it. A metaphor." She looked down at the oak bench. "Demotion."

"Yeah."

Agnes nodded. "But still—" The hand flattened again, reprised the whoosh-over-the-head.

Bobbitt sighed and looked heavenward. "*War and Peace* or *Reader's Digest* version?"

"Tolstoy fan here," she said, raising her hand like one of

her students.

"What's a Tolstoy?"

Agnes grabbed Bobbitt with both her hands. "Just tell me the damn story, JD."

"Oka-a-ay." He stopped to collect his thoughts. He was a small town person, now charged with explaining a concept that's true in all walks of life, except only in a small town could it reverberate for generations. How does he say this? *One sentence at a time.*

"Splinter City is a euphemism our old high school coach used for being benched." JD looked at Agnes to see if she was following along. "You see, when Dan and me were juniors, Richard Hunter—you remember him—was the starting QB at Echo. And, man, he really looked the part. Spoiled rich kid, shiny new convertible, his daddy the big county judge. He dated the prettiest girl in school, who was also captain of the cheerleaders—"

"Katy."

Bobbitt nodded. "He was all the time talking about college scouts and how much he'd be recruited his senior year, yadda yadda yadda."

"Big man on campus."

"With even bigger plans," Bobbitt added. "State championship, headlines, scholarship offers—the whole nine yards, pardon the pun."

Agnes rolled her eyes.

"Only one thing he didn't plan on."

Agnes snapped her fingers and pointed. "Let me guess. Dan Parrish."

"Exactly. First game of the season, Hunter chokes, throws four interceptions in the first half."

"Ouch. Splinter City for Richard Hunter."

"See? You're not so dumb."

She whacked him playfully on the arm.

"So in comes this skinny-ass junior named Dan Parrish.

His father was a nobody war vet, didn't own squat but a little white house, mother bakes cookies. And Danny throws six TDs for about four hundred yards. The town falls in love with him and when the dust settles, he's set all kinds of state records on his way to leading our school to the state championship."

"I'm guessing the Dick Hunter wasn't exactly doing hand-springs?"

"Never recovered. Never played another down. No head-lines, no scholarship offers, nothing. Became a full-blown drunk. Even lost his girlfriend—"

"—to Dan."

Bobbitt nodded.

"Yikes. Did I say demotion? More like castration."

"Yup. And Hunter laid all the blame on Dan, of course. Still does."

"But that's ridiculous. I mean, clearly it wasn't Dan's fault."

"On the contrary. It was Dan's talent. And Rick knew that down deep. But his father didn't see it that way. And he never let his son forget it. And Rick absolutely idolized his father."

Agnes thought for a minute. "Hunter's father, he was the judge that sentenced Dan for the accident?"

"Yessir. Absolutely hated Dan for what happened to his son. So when he got his chance—"

"—he made Dan pay," Agnes finished.

"Boy, did he ever. For eighteen long years. And the reper-cussions were everywhere. They're still rolling in. Dan's mother and father grew apart. Grief and later cancer took them both. Before Carl died, Rick Hunter snatched the house just to spite Dan, just because he could. Now this. And it won't end here."

Agnes rolled her spine into a curve and put her elbows on her knees, stunned. She felt sorry for JD, who was leaning back against the wall, almost winded. Dredging up the past had taken its toll.

"Who would ever guess that a simple game could cause so much heartache?" she said.

"I know. And yet, every year, in thousands of high school football programs across the country, some junior is taking some senior's place. And that senior either rolls with it or he lets it eat him alive. Unfortunately, Rick Hunter was the former."

"You mean the latter."

"Never could keep those two straight."

Just then a bailiff poked his head out of the courtroom doors. "Dan's being arraigned, JD."

So here it was. Agnes and Bobbitt stood together and stepped to the door. They were about to witness the next chapter in the caustic, on-going saga of Echo. Agnes tapped JD on the back of his shoulder. "One more thing, JD. How does the whole Splinter City dynamic have anything to do with what's happening today?"

JD led them through the large oak doors. They were both struck by the sight of Dan Parrish, shackled and unshaven, standing at the defendant's table. The bailiff boomed, "ALL RISE!" Everyone stood. A chamber door opened and the judge strode in. He took his seat behind the bench. That's when Agnes saw it was not just any judge; it was The Honorable Richard S. Hunter, County Judge.

Bobbitt turned to Agnes. "That's how."

CHAPTER 53

Across town, a few hundred brave Echo residents stood outside Judge Hunter's house protesting. It was snowing—the weather had turned—and a few held signs demanding the judge free Dan Parrish. They chanted "Let Dan Go!" Among them there were some of the parents of the football players. There were students, also, and Sam Blevins and the cafeteria ladies, and some folks from Punch Town. The twins were also there, both wearing hoodies, dark pants and sneakers. They huddled in the shadows.

"You ready?" said Booker to Baker.

"Hell, yes," said Baker to Booker. "Let's do this."

The pair bumped fists, donned sunglasses, and slithered over to Hunter's Town Car. They each dropped to their knees, one on the left, one on the right, and began to let the air out of the tires.

As they were finishing with the rear wheels, Chip Hunter pulled up in his Jeep, slammed on the brakes, and pushed through the crowd as best he could on his way to the front door. The sound of a motorcycle caught his ear and he turned just as Jimmy Durr pulled up to watch the melee, Darla Finch behind him on the seat, her arms wrapped around Jimmy's waist.

"Perfect," Chip muttered, shaking his head. He threw the front door open and entered.

"Where is he?" he demanded from his mother.

"He's in his study. Chip, he's been drinking—"

"What's new?"

Rick Hunter swung his door open and stepped into the lighted bar alcove and began pouring himself another drink. Chip closed the distance between the two in a few big strides and stopped. "Why? Just give me one good reason!"

"I strongly suggest you back up and start over, son," said the judge. He seemed calm. Too calm.

Chip ignored the warning. "Fifty-thousand-dollar bond? That's insane!"

Hunter slammed his glass down on the bar cabinet, ignoring the spill, dispensing with formalities. It was time his family got in line. "He's a felon, on probation, for vehicular homicide I might add, and got caught with an open container—"

"A month-old, empty, lipstick-covered wine cooler bottle inside a car he doesn't even own, *I might add*—"

"My hands are tied." Hunter took a drink from his highball, then pared his lips back over his teeth. It was a strong drink, just the way he liked it. He gazed out the front window, where the crowd was gathered. Up and down the street some of his neighbors had already put up Christmas decorations. The muted lights did nothing for his mood.

"So untie them!" said Chip.

"It doesn't work that way."

"Hah! Since when?"

Hunter stuck his finger up in Chips face. "Watch it, mister, you're treading on thin ice."

"So?" Chip stepped around in a little circle and finished in his father's face. "What are you gonna do, take my wheels? Excuse me, *your* wheels! Kick me out of your house? Go ahead, I'm outta here anyway!"

The judge spread his feet and tried to stand tall, but he was wobbling. He was shorter than his son by two inches, even in boots. He decided to be a teacher. A preacher. A mentor. He licked his lips and narrowed his eyes into what he imagined was a pose of infinite wisdom. "Be careful how you use proud words, son. You can't always call them back." Then he fell into a drunken sermon that sounded a little like his usual claptrap from the bench. "They wear long boots. Hard boots. They walk off proud. They can't hear you calling."

Chip couldn't believe the irony of what he was hearing. He looked out the front window at the protesting mob. He saw his father's car had melted into the snow, the tires flat. He turned back to his dad. "Do you realize what you've done? You've got everybody in town thinking 'Poor little Chip. His daddy has to step in so he can play in the big game.'" Chip raked his fingers through his hair. He'd learned some things since the beginning of school. One of them was that perception was nine-tenths of truth. When he'd acted like an ass on the first day of class, it followed him. And if His Honor the Judge acted like an ass, the people of Echo would hear the story. They would equate the two. The narrative could never be fixed. "It's humiliating!"

Hunter sipped his drink. He'd had enough sass from his kid. Way more than enough. He raised his hand. "What's humiliating is watching a washed up, alcoholic ex-convict outdo a twenty-year-old nobody."

There. It was out. Hunter knew it. Katy knew it. Chip knew it. Irony of ironies. And like those proud words and hard boots he'd just been referencing, Richard Hunter could not call them back.

A cloud settled over the room like a noxious blanket. Chip was in slo-mo, instant-replay mode when he stuck his face to within inches of his father's. In the past, the act would have been unheard of. Chip would have been frightened. Now, though, the fear was gone, replaced by resolve. All the tumblers had fallen into place for Chip. He was going to open the lock and expose a world his dad thought he knew nothing about.

"C'mon, Dad," he hissed. "This is all about *you*." He couldn't help a slight grin twisting at his mouth.

"I don't know what you're talking about," said the judge. His voice was flat, his eyes dead. Katy stood by the dining room table, her breath shallow, one hand clasped over her mouth. She steadied herself by leaning against one of the chairs.

"Sure you do!" bellowed her son, hands wide apart, as if all the world was in on his old man's little secret. "I read all those articles! The ones you gave to Darla. And I read between the lines." He lowered his voice. "And you know what all that stuff told me?" Suddenly the smile disappeared. Chip inched closer to his father. "You're jealous."

Hunter tried not to swallow. He opened his mouth, but nothing came out. He cleared his throat, and swallowed anyway, the lump surely going down like poison.

"And, really, you *should* be jealous," Chip continued. His voice was barely a whisper. "Do you know why?"

Hunter said nothing. He felt sick and his face was red, and he knew his heart was racing, which made him dizzy sometimes. The booze was to blame. He needed some air. He could go outside, but there were all those ignorant people out there, all those stupid, idiotic Echo morons messing with him, and now his own son in his face, never on his side, never *listening* to his side of things...

Chip moved in for the kill, his stilted enunciation a denouement.

"Because," he said, "you couldn't carry Dan Parrish's jockstrap when you were in high school." Chip curled his upper lip in an approximation of Rick Hunter's petty scowl. "And you still can't!"

Hunter's fist crashed against the side of Chip's face, knocking the young man back.

Chip rubbed his jaw. His smile, when it reappeared, was tight and knowing. "And now, I know why. Because you hit like a damn girl." Chip spun around and left the house, slam-

220

ming the door on his way.

Outside the chants were muted, muffled by the snow falling and the drifts piling up on the hedgerows and the lawns, blanketing the trees in an apron of white. The Town Car in the driveway squatted on her rims in the snow like a rabbit snuggling into cedar shavings. Jimmy Durr and Darla Finch had motored away several minutes ago. The people watched as Chip got into his Jeep and started the engine and roared away.

CHAPTER 54

The grandfather clock in the dining room chimed the hour as Rick Hunter refreshed his drink. In the front yard people were still assembled, holding signs, chanting slogans. The neighbors' Christmas lights were hard to even see now, muffled by the still-falling snow. The cold was coming on stronger.

Pigs and simpletons. They're all pigs and simpletons, my son included. Echo isn't a town, it's a sty. And my son has officially joined their ranks—the retard brigade, full of people that dream in pastels and think Dan Parrish has come back from the dead to save them from their pathetic little lives.

Katy spoke first. "Proud of yourself?"

"That kid's a loser."

"*He's* a loser?" She wheeled and approached her husband. "Look in the mirror lately?"

Hunter snorted.

"I mean, even *Brenda Price* thinks you're the one that's a loser."

At the mention of the girl's name he blanched. He could feel the blood rushing from his face.

"What's the matter, Rick, cat got your tongue?"

Hunter felt dizzy. He licked his lips and, because he was afraid he might lose control and drop his glass, he set it down on the counter.

"You remember Brenda, of course. That pretty clerk of yours who—" Katy shaped air quotes with her fingers, "—

inexplicably quit last spring?"

He leaned heavily against the bar. He wanted to walk away, except he felt paralyzed by Katy's words. If it ever got out that he had been using the little black bitch, he would never again be able to command respect in Echo.

Katy must have sensed blood. She put her face in the line of fire. She had never done this, never been this brave, but years and years of tyranny take a toll, she must have thought, and her husband needed to know, not everyone around him was there to service him. So she was joining the ranks of those who'd had enough. She changed gears and her voice became light and airy when she said, "I ran into her a couple nights ago. At Dan's restaurant, of all places. Isn't that ironic?"

Katy let the irony set in. "Anyway, we got to talking, Brenda and me. You know how women are. Don't you?" Gone was the smile now. She was showing her anger at being the woman scorned.

"And she told me everything, man. All of it. And I mean all of it. Every disgusting detail." She moved in closer, her nose inches from Rick's. "You know why she told me, dear husband of mine?"

A pause. She could smell his breath. He had been chewing that damn toothpick like a cud, and he hadn't eaten in hours. The liquor had taken control. His nose was shining with flop sweat and she could see the broken capillaries on his cheeks.

"Because she felt sorry for me, Rick. Because everybody feels sorry for me. Because everybody knows, you dumb son-ofabitch!"

Hunter stepped forward and slapped Katy hard, a stinging blow. She staggered back. But she didn't cry out. And she didn't whimper. Instead she smiled. Because she knew—and Richard Hunter knew—that it would be the last time he would ever slap her.

"By God, you will regret that."

She grabbed her purse and her jacket and headed for the

door. Then she stopped and turned. "And Chip was right," she said. "You do hit like a girl."

CHAPTER 55

It was after midnight. The protesters had left and quiet had descended on the Hunter household. The TV was on, but the sound had been turned off. Rick Hunter slouched low in his leather recliner staring at a patch of wet on the rug where he'd spilled his drink. His gold toothpick was parked in his mouth. His caiman skin boots were on. His hair was perfect. There was still glass scattered around, glittering in the soft light. *Let her clean it up*, he thought. Then he spoke the words out loud to the empty house. "Let her clean it up." His throat was raw, his mind designing solutions to this new problem even as he raged. He began to cough. He spit his toothpick into his hand and jammed it into his shirt pocket. He had to sit up in the chair until the fit subsided.

The phone rang, startling him, jangling his already frayed nerves. He found it lying atop a stack of hunting magazines. *This is Katy, for sure. She'll be wanting to talk. I have to tell her how much she means to me, how much I love her. How sorry I am. I can't let things get out of control about the black girl. At least no more than they have. And I'll have to go see the bitch, too. Force her to take some money.* Hunter cleared his throat. He looked at the caller ID and frowned.

It wasn't Katy. It was the jail. "Yeah," he grumbled into the phone.

* * *

In the basement of the courthouse Sergeant Mike Mathias, the desk man, was making a call he dreaded. Somehow he would get blamed for this. "Shit rolls downhill," his father had told him probably one thousand times. He was right.

"Sorry to call so late, Judge."

"What do you want?" Rick Hunter tried to control his slurred voice by speaking slow. He took a sip of his drink and waited.

Mathias heard the ice clinking in the glass. "Well, sir, I don't know quite how to say it—"

"Say it!"

Mathias held the phone away from his ear. He looked across the room at Officer Nic O'Meara, his nephew new-hire, who had clamped his hand over his mouth to keep from laughing. Mathias flipped him a bird and continued.

"Fact of the matter is…we had to kick Dan Parrish loose."

Hunter fell back in the recliner. His heart began to race again, blood pounding in his ears. "You did what?" he bellowed.

Mathias knew what was coming. And he also knew the judge was drunk, so maybe he wouldn't remember. He'd been forced to make these calls before. "Had to, sir. He made bail."

"Impossible! That sonofabitch doesn't have a pot to piss in!"

"True, Your Honor." He ran his eyes down the hall, where Katy Hunter, Dan Parrish, and a teacher named Agnes Stankowiecz were kibitzing with a bail bondsman. "But your wife does."

The silence over the phone was like that of a tomb. Like the quiet after a shot goes off or after the end of a sermon. At the jail Mathias waited. When Hunter said, "The hell she does. I manage the finances around here." Mathias was as ready as he could be, given the circumstances. He'd been at this job for thirty years. He had been born and raised in Echo and had, on more than one occasion, been browbeaten by the megalomaniacal Judge Hunter and his father before him. So he had no problem delivering the next line. In fact, you could say he enjoyed it.

"That's probably why she used your house for collateral."

Mike Mathias could almost see Hunter's face. The histrionic ass would be standing up in those stupid cowboy boots and raising his arms. His voice would begin to shake like it did sometimes in the courtroom.

"She said it belonged to Dan Parrish, anyway," said Mike.

CHAPTER 56

A few hours later Dan Parrish leaned his bike on the breeze-block rail in front of room 12 of the motel, behind a blue Ford Focus. It was still dark, sunrise just around the corner. Dan knocked. After an interval he knocked again. When a crack appeared between the door and the frame, Dan pushed himself into the room so forcefully that the privacy chain popped loose. The man fell onto the bed and began to shout.

"Shut up," Dan said, pointing a stern finger in the man's face. He closed the door behind him.

"What are you doing here?" said the man, gasping for air and holding his chest.

"You know why I'm here."

Against the back wall an overworked heater rumbled and spat. The air in the room was fetid and stale and too warm. A suitcase on the dresser was open, displaying dirty clothes and sundry items. The garbage can by the bed was full of fast-food detritus from the night before and the night before that.

"You got a lot of nerve," said the man. "I'd suggest you leave now." He shot his hand into the space between his pillow and the mattress, pulling out a pistol, fumbling with it just long enough so that Dan quickly disarmed him, a move so fast it seemed like a scene from an action movie.

Dan popped the clip and ejected the round in the chamber, then tossed the gun into the open bag and the full clip into his jeans pocket.

"You don't know me." He sat down purposefully in the little chair at the foot of the bed. "But I know you. And lots of other guys just like you that took their pathetic little broken-hearted stories too far. I saw you that day, across the street from the drug store. I saw you on campus. And your car. Everywhere she was. On her street. Outside her house. I *watched* you, dude. I've been watching you."

The quiet man placed his palms flat on the cigarette-burned comforter and began licking his lips. His eyes darted around and finally rested on the gun in his bag.

"Look at me!"

The man looked at Dan.

"I'm not going to waste a lot of time here because you don't deserve it. What will happen to you if you persist in this thing, is either you'll die or, worse...you'll *live*." Dan let the last word percolate with the man.

"And you'll spend the rest of your life in a place I'm familiar with. A place you could not handle for one day much less one lifetime. A living arrangement that will rot your soul without actually killing you. Trust me."

The man tried to speak.

"Shut up. You've already said too much with your pitiful little gun." Dan paused for a beat and took a calming breath. "*Now look at me*. Think about your selfish ideas. Go ahead. But listen, this is important. Where you're going to be, where you will end up...the stink of it will erode you. The desperate man in the bunk below you, the desperate men in the cells beside you, all those guys *are* you. Self-absorbed victims. And they're all bigger and stronger and meaner than any men you have ever seen. Think about a place where's there's no way out. A place where taking a shower is an adventure. Eating lunch is a fight. Sleeping is an exercise. A dog on a chain, snowbound and starving, has a better chance than you will."

At first the man said nothing. Then his bottom lip began to tremble and it all broke loose. "I hate that bitch!" The man started crying.

For a minute Dan thought about his own recent history and his years of unsettling thoughts. He constructed a silent prayer and sent a thank you to God that he didn't go crazy and become a subject of a restraining order somewhere.

"Yeah? Well, grow up."

Dan stood to leave. "I'm gonna call back here at noon. If you're still here, there'll be trouble. And if I see you again, you'll be sorry. You got that?"

The man sniffed, nodded.

"She's not yours anymore. She doesn't belong to anybody. Nobody does."

A few minutes later, Dan Parrish watched from across the street as the sobbing man got into his vehicle and drove away west. In a few seconds the little car was a tiny spot on the horizon.

CHAPTER 57

The room was dark and chilled and spare in the way of older folks, who chose to fight clutter in their lives. There were no crocheted doilies or knitted afghans. Or knick-knacks and decorative ashtrays from decades past. The few pieces of furniture were dated, but spotless. A plaque with the Lord's Prayer was hung on the wall over a piano that was rarely played except at Christmas. The other wall spaces were adorned with a few dated impressionist prints and some black and white family photos. There were potted plants in some corners and the woven rug on the oak floor was oval and as clean as the day it was bought some thirty years ago. The only recent decoration was a little fir tree in the corner, hung with festive lights and homemade ornaments.

Chip Hunter lay under a quilt on the couch across from the large front window. Curtains had kept the light out, but now it was eight o'clock, so they were drawn open with a flourish and the morning invaded, assailing Chips eyelids, causing them to flutter open. He looked across and saw a pretty woman in her sixties smiling at him. She was still in her bathrobe, even though she'd been awake for hours. She had trouble sleeping through the night now, ever since her husband died five years ago.

"Mornin', Grandma," Chip said, smiling sleepily.

Chip's grandmother nodded, flashing a smile that some years back had carried her to the finals of the Miss Kansas pageant. "It's game day, Chipper. Your eggs are getting cold." Behind her Katy stood, also in a bathrobe and wooly slippers, holding her coffee mug with both hands like an offering to some obscure god of wakefulness. She blinked into the sunlight. She, too, had just gotten up. Both women turned around and waddled away into the kitchen.

When Chip followed a few minutes later, he found a committee of sorts waiting for him. His mom and grandma sat at the table. But Coach Bobbitt was there also, along with one of Chip's professors, Ms. Stankowiecz. And at the stove, Dan Parrish was putting the finishing touches on something that smelled unbelievably good.

"What are you doing here?" Chip said, looking around.

Everyone stared at Chip. "Is that how you say 'good morning' around these parts?" Dan replied.

Bobbitt stood and clapped Chip on the back. "Came by to go over the game plan with our starting QB. You got a problem with that?"

The room resonated with the words.

"I'm starting?" A shocked Chip Hunter locked eyes with Bobbitt, who nodded.

Dan put his pan down. "You kidding me, Chip? This is your team, man. Always has been, always will be."

"But I thought...you—"

"That was a ruse, man. JD didn't want Kilgore to know which one of us to prepare for. That's why I practiced all week. But he and I knew all along it would be you. Saving the best for last," he said with a wink.

Dan gestured for Chip to sit. The boy virtually floated to a chair. He marveled, *the game of football is so darn complicated. Like some kind of adventure novel where you don't know who the good guy is or what the plan is, but you know you have to read every word or you'll miss something. Secret meetings and Xs and Os and Dan Marino plays that save the day.* He was suddenly so excited the others could feel the vibes bouncing around the kitchen. "I don't know what to say," he mumbled.

"Don't say anything," ordered Bobbitt. "Just listen up. We got a ton of stuff to go over before kickoff."

Dan shoveled some eggs onto his plate. Chip looked down at the concoction and beetled his brow. "What's that?"

"It's a frittata," Dan said.

"A frittata?" He poked at it with a fork.

"It's I-talian, Chip," said Bobbitt.

"Kind of like an omelet—" said Katy.

"—with a Ph.D.," finished Grandma.

Chip dug in. He decided that he felt better than he had in weeks. The others joined him, and Dan brought over a pan full of chipped beef gravy and a basket of sourdough biscuits. Coffee and orange juice were administered to the needy.

A few minutes went by.

"I'm just gonna say it: Gravy is my life," said Bobbitt.

"I know," said Dan. "Everyone knows." He touched spoons with his good friend and sat down to eat breakfast.

CHAPTER 58

Across town the day was breaking differently for Richard Hunter. He'd been up the entire night, mostly in his study, drinking expensive whiskey and staring at walls lined with shelves full of law books. His eyes were dry and shot with blood, his head fuzzy with booze, his mind an olio of recriminations and denials.

I'm the victim here. I've spent my life taking care of this town, feeding their need for order and logic. But the needs of a town are sometimes too much for the people to ingest. A firm voice is beyond their abilities to understand. They think special considerations should be granted to certain people, even when those people are tearing everything apart. This town needs me. We were doing fine. It doesn't need Dan Parrish.

He shuffled through the morning rays of light sneaking in from around the curtains. He found the center of the house and turned down the hallway, opening the closet door at the end. He rummaged in the hanging coats and forgotten clothes until he found what he was after. He lifted it out and examined his find at arm's length. The old letter jacket was still in good shape. He put his nose to the leather and drew a deep breath, his mind falling backwards in time to a place where everything was good. He unzipped the jacket and put it on.

On the inside of the door there was a full-length mirror. He clicked the light on and examined himself...

...and a transformation took place.

For a moment Richard Hunter was a teenager again. A handsome kid with a thick head of dark hair, clear eyes, an athlete's jaw and a dazzling smile. He stood there, remembering the days when he held the town of Echo in the palms of his hands and was the envy of everyone. He was adored by the girl of his dreams and had the world by the tail.

A knock at the door spoiled the image. He scowled. Once again he was the mean drunk he'd been for ages. He squinted at his image and groused aloud when the knocking continued. He strode to the front door and flung it open, ready to tear into whomever was disturbing him at this early hour.

Belden Ferguson stood on the porch—the last man on earth Hunter expected to see. And come to think of it, an opportunity, here, to unleash his fury. *This imbecilic Punch Town baboon dares to come here at all.* Hunter's blood began to boil.

"Well, if it isn't B-B-B-Belden F-F-F-Ferguson," he spat.

Belden was beyond nervous. He'd been thinking about this moment for a lifetime, and now it was here. But despite his butterflies, he wasn't about to allow Hunter's snide mockery deter him. That's when he noticed the jacket Hunter was wearing. And how pathetic it looked. And the nervousness suddenly left Belden with a whoosh. He decided at that moment that nothing this man could do was worth the pain of the last two decades.

Hunter must have realized he'd never removed his old letter jacket. It was loose in the shoulders and tight in the stomach, and he looked like a fool. He ripped it off and threw it across the room. He stood erect and tried not to wobble.

"What do you want?" Rick Hunter used his judgeship inflections. He was an expert at the intimidations he'd learned from his father. But this time they fell flat. There were no echoes of righteousness, nor was there an audience in the gallery. And he was much drunker than he allowed himself to be in the courtroom, which diluted the presentation.

"The truth," replied Belden, his voice even. There was no stutter. Only two words, but still, they had meaning beyond the syllables...

...and in that moment, both men were transported to another time twenty years ago.

It was a springtime dawn—there was still snow on the ground—and a nineteen-year-old Rick Hunter was driving his Mercedes coupe through the outlying streets of town, feeling sorry for himself. The car had been a gift from his father a year and a half ago. It had cost a lot of money, but as the judge explained at the time, there was no way he was going to allow his son to be seen in anything less. That was before Rick had destroyed his chances at college ball with his performance in the first game of his senior year in high school. Since then, his father had been hard to live with. The whole Hunter household had been a theater of allegations and finger pointing. At least he hadn't taken the car away. And at UK he'd been able to disengage and forget Echo for a while.

Rick was back in town for spring break, though, and the evening at home hadn't gone well, and now he was drunk. After last night's fight with his father, he'd gone to Eloise's Beach Shack and tipped a few. He'd ended up staying all night, but he just couldn't go home yet; his father had been unreasonable. Still unreasonable, after all this time. And with only two of them in the house, no power on earth could have assuaged the scene at the dinner table.

Last night early the old man had begun drinking scotch, and soon he was starting in on him about Parrish, who had led Echo High to another Kansas State AAA title last fall. Sitting down to eat in that cavernous dining room was torture. They began to shout at one another. He was an unappreciative burden. His grades were terrible. Sigma Alpha Epsilon had to be forced to accept him. Couldn't hold his own against anyone, let alone Dan Parrish.

He left.

So this morning Rick Hunter didn't want to go home. He didn't want to face the judge, whose belittling of him never seemed to end. It was the incalculable measure of his father's disappointment, he knew, that fueled the rage and the verbal reprisals. He remembered the aftermath of that first game. The man was so mad he made Rick walk the three miles back to their big dark house, alone, through the silent streets of Echo then up the hill under the street lights and along the curved drive. When he got there the front door was locked and he had to go around to the maid's kitchen entrance and wake her up. She'd seen he'd been crying. She sat him down at the breakfast table and made him a cup of cocoa. The next day she was fired for it.

"Coloreds don't run things around here," said the judge. "I do."

Rick Hunter hated that big house. It was a prison.

So Rick was driving around with a half-full bottle of Jack Daniels, unwilling to go home. He was wearing his two-year-old letter jacket—a reward for his work as a junior standout. He hadn't been awarded another starter chevron for the sleeve, though. He'd sat on the bench last year.

Splinter City.

He stopped at a stop sign and watched incredulously as Dan Parrish drove by in his beat-up sedan, heading in another direction. What's he doing up at this hour? What's he got, a *job*? He's such a nervy bastard. He's a nothing from the sticks who had stolen Rick's girl and all his damn chances. There was nobody he despised more, and when he listened to the diatribes from his own father, the judge, he got so mad at Dan-super cool-Parrish, he could kill him. And then last spring Katy got pregnant and they had that kid. Should have been *his* kid.

There were no other cars on the road that morning. Echo was still asleep. Saturday morning. *Everyone's still asleep.*

Rick made a face and hit the gas, tearing around the corner, falling in behind Dan Parrish. He took a pull from the Jack. He smoldered as he watched his rival drive slowly down the tree lined, rural road. Hunter capped the bottle and set it down on the passenger seat. He pulled up alongside the old beater and began honking his horn, looking over, shooting Parrish the finger. *Screw him. Screw him and the horse he rode in on.*

Dan looked over, waved like nothing had happened, sped up a little to get out of the line of sight. He was late for the photos. The wedding was tomorrow at the Methodist Church, Katy was doing something at the florist's, and he was late. He didn't have time for Rick Hunter's histrionics. *He's probably drunk.*

To tell the truth, Dan felt sorry for the guy. Nobody should have a father like that.

The bastard's a coward, too. Won't even fight me. Steals my girl, claims he feels sorry for me.

Hunter was enraged, now. He'd taken enough. He stood on the gas. As he screamed past the older car he yanked his wheel hard over to scare Dan...

...except at that moment, Dan was half turned, looking at something else: his infant son, John Henry, belted into a second-hand car seat in the back. When Dan spun his head back to the road, all he could see was Hunter's car veering toward him.

"What the—"

Instinctively, he swerved to avoid contact. The morning sun hadn't been able to find the ice in the shadows of the big trees, and Dan's tires lost purchase. All of a sudden the little Chevy wouldn't respond. The boy-man and his son sailed off the road and smashed with incredible force into the six-foot-wide trunk of a one-hundred-year-old oak tree.

The sound of the crash was deafening in the morning quiet. Then everything went still. Steam began to pour from the radiator of the smashed car. Dan had hit the tree head on and rolled up, and the engine pushed through the firewall and halfway into the front seat. Dan lay unconscious, slumped over the wheel, blood pouring down from his forehead. He never heard the sound of approaching footsteps.

CHAPTER 59

Standing back from the open door, looking at Belden, Judge Richard Hunter almost lost it. Admissions of guilt were not a part of his life, now. He had no time for treacle and postures of guilt. But a certain internal agony was still in place. He couldn't help that. It couldn't be helped. If only he could get someone to understand. Back then he'd been forced to do the things he did. There wasn't an alternative.

The young Rick Hunter opened his car door and stepped out onto the cold Kansas ground. He ran to the side of the little Chevy and saw Dan and the blood and the glass scattered over the scene. In the back, the baby John Henry was on the floor of the sedan. His skull had been fractured. He was dead.

Hunter's mind was a whirling spasm of booze and sleep deprivation. He had to act fast, to do something, but what? Think. This will ruin you. People will think you killed the kid on purpose. Your life might be in the toilet now, but just wait until this thing explodes across the landscape of Echo, Kansas.

He turned and retraced his steps back to his car. When he returned to the wreck he was carrying his half-full bottle of Jack. He snatched Dan Parrish's head back by the hair and pried his mouth open. He jammed the neck of the bottle down Dan's throat, nearly drowning him.

When the bottle was empty, Hunter wiped it and tossed it

on the floorboard and ran back to his car. As he pulled away, he took one last look around. And his heart went to his throat. He began to vomit. The space around him contracted into another snapshot.

He sees the road and the snow-capped berm and the ditches on either side of the road. He sees the big oak trees and the yellow sunlight trying to peek through the bare limbs. He smells a field on the other side of the trees, freshly plowed, a scent of hay, the earth smell reaching up and across. He feels the shape of the scene and how it's encapsulated, like a painting.

His eyes focus. Across the road there's one of the big trees, ugly, like a many-limbed monster of power and force and discipline and a symbol of solidity. A giant troll. A tolling bell. His executioner. Sitting on one of the lower limbs there's a boy, a little black boy, and his eyes are big as baseballs. He is watching. He sees everything. He saw everything.

Belden Ferguson had seen everything.

"I had no idea that child was in that car!" Hunter bawled. His voice cracked and he had to clear his throat of phlegm. The alcohol had destroyed his ability to reconstruct the past so people would understand. He was having trouble seeing. He had to squint to focus.

"I believe you," said Belden. "Maybe a jury will, too. But you got to tell 'em."

Hunter whispered. "Like hell I do." He took a step toward the black man. "Like hell."

Belden didn't budge. He wasn't at all cowed by the demonstration. He was inexplicably composed. Cool, even. He said, "Then I'll do it for you."

"Hah! Nobody will believe you! Not then, not now!"

"I'll take my chances."

Belden started to walk off. Hunter grabbed his shoulder and spun him around.

"Now you listen to me—"

No way, sir. Not anymore.

And once again the two of them were transported back to that fateful day.

There was a row of sharecropper tenements on Fortenberry Road in Punch Town, a mile or so out of Echo proper. The places were small and separated by dirt alleyways, and they were run down. In front of a little porch at one of the units an older man, a genteel southern gentleman by some accounts, Judge Harrison Hunter, dressed in a linen suit and sporting a white goatee, stood gesturing and nodding at a frightened black man and his equally-frightened little boy. In the corner of the judge's mouth there was a gold toothpick. His eyes were shaded by black glasses and he kept glancing down at the uncharacteristic mud on his heeled boots. He looked like some absurd caricature of Colonel Sanders.

The judge had decided to come to this disreputable place of hovels and odors to straighten some things out. He was old for the father of an nineteen-year-old, but he hadn't been lucky with children. He'd lost one son to heart disease—the boy had an undiagnosed fibrillation caused by a bad valve in his aorta—and his only daughter had died of leukemia. God had smiled upon him, though, one last time when Rick was born. He and his wife Abigail—now dead—had raised Rick to be something special, a boy to carry the family banner.

And now he would be damned if he was going to let anybody or anything take his only son away. Including Caleb Ferguson, the man standing before him on this hardscrabble yard.

"Now you listen to me!" he thundered. He seemed not to care who else heard him, as long as the words were understood by Caleb. He paused. He removed his toothpick and extended a long, elegant finger, reaching across to Caleb. He tapped the black man on the chest when he spoke. His words were metered. "I'm only going to say this once, you common, one-way, son of a bitch." His eyes were small and mean and bored into Caleb like fires, like devil's eyes, like coals in a greasy-white furnace from another world. Biblical eyes. "Say a word about any of this," he whispered, "and I will turn you and your entire family's lives into ashes. There will be no more Fergusons, Caleb. Ever."

He stood back a step. "You like that decrepit little gas station, Caleb, you make sure and shut your mouth, hear? You want a life for your kids, you keep quiet. You want to live to a ripe old age, you tell this little monkey of yours to do what's right." He pointed down at Belden, who was clutching the leg of his father's overalls.

The boy was crying. His face was dirty and there was snot coming out of his nose. He knew he'd done something terrible, but he didn't know exactly what. He ran his eyes along the ground and followed them out to the passenger seat of Judge Hunter's shiny, black Lincoln. Rick Hunter was sitting there. Rick looked up from his lap and their eyes met, then he pointed a make-believe pistol at the boy and pulled the trigger. Belden turned and ran to the broken screen door, opened it and disappeared into the dark interior and buried his face in his mother's apron.

The grown man, Belden Ferguson, large and imposing in his own way now, took a step toward Rick. "That stuff worked once, a long time ago, Mr. Hunter. But my old man's gone now. Yours, too. It don't work no more. I'm gonna do what's right."

When Belden turned to go, Hunter grabbed his shirt.

"Take your hands off me," warned Belden.

Hunter didn't. He couldn't. His world was imploding. He was numb.

"Now!" shouted the black man.

Hunter dropped his arm. His life had irrevocably changed. *I hate this town. I have always hated this town. I hate it for what it did to me. My own father saved my ass that day, and until he died he never let me forget it and he never let me leave this God-forsaken hole in the Kansas prairie.*

"I'll kill you, Belden."

"No, you won't. You don't have it in you. You never have."

Belden walked out onto the lawn and across the driveway to his car.

CHAPTER 60

A few hours later, in one of the booths at Mulligan's, Belden and Billy Cox sat and listened to a digital voice recorder. Their coffees were untouched, cold. When the voices ended, Cox hit the OFF button and sat back. Even though he'd listened to the facts as Belden Ferguson had explained them, he was still stunned at the impact of the revelations. And even though a coerced confession was no good in court, especially when the confessor was drunk, the impact of the words could not be ignored. Judge Hunter was guilty of vehicular homicide, tampering with evidence, assault and DUI manslaughter. And Dan Parrish had spent eighteen years in prison for something he didn't do.

A long moment passed before he said, "I'll be damned."

He began to think about the story, always the story. He'd been writing uninspired pieces for years, the last ten of them written almost by rote. He'd used every cliché, every trick he could muster to keep readers in their seats. But he hadn't cared about that lately. Water under the bridge. If anyone wished to know, he'd tell them he cared about long walks with his wife, a good meal, a little down time with his grandkids. He hadn't penned anything worth a damn in ages.

Now, with the discoveries he'd just been privy to, all that retirement stuff had changed. Suddenly he was thinking about what his editor would say, what all the young reporters, plebes just out of journalism school would say. He was thinking about real impactful writing again.

About the Pulitzer, for Christ's sake.

Belden said nothing. He drew in a deep breath and let it out and looked out the window. Cox looked at him, worried. He reached over and touched his arm. "You okay, son?"

Belden turned to the man. He thought about what he'd just done, about all the years he'd bottled up the truth. About the nightmare his silence had caused Dan Parrish. His own nightmares, too. The bedwetting. The stammering. The guilt.

"Mr. Cox, I haven't felt this good in forever."

CHAPTER 61

Echo was closed. At two o'clock the Chat & Chew put a sign in the window:

IT'S HERE!
WE'RE NOT!
GO COUGARS, BEAT KILGORE!

It was the only establishment that had in years past been open, so when the Chat & Chew shut its doors, that was it. The town was locked and loaded for the game.

In the parking areas around the stadium, the cars and busses and vans had already arrived, clogging the access ways. People from Echo and the surrounding towns were milling about, lighting grills, painting their faces, dressing their dogs in Cougar red or Kilgore green.

At four o'clock the place was packed. The sheriff had prepared for the overload by requesting help from law enforcement agencies all over northwest Kansas, but even then they had all they could handle directing screwball fans into a semblance of order and decorum. The date was December 16, and the event was what they called the Kansas Bowl, and it was the biggest, most stupendous thing in most of these peoples' lives.

At four-fifteen, a chorus of *BOOs* arose when the caravan of green-painted busses carrying Kilgore's players and coaches

and cheerleaders and the band circled the stadium like inter-
lopers, accepting local tributes like thrown mud and chicken
wings as their due. A topless Mindy Detwiler tried to distract
the driver of the first bus. Tubby Wells, clad only in boxers
and boots, threw himself into the path of the second. Nobody
was arrested. After a second whirlwind orbit, the busses of the
Green Machine filed into the parking lot adjacent to the visi-
tor's locker room and began to unload. The team from Kilgore,
Kansas was the reigning football champion of the high plains.
They were the favorites, according to Vegas odds makers. But
because the Cougars had the best record this year, the Green
Machine was forced to accept an away status. So they were
doubly pissed at the venue. Which, of course, made Echo proud.

For the first time since their third game, the Cougars were
underdogs.

When the visiting team gathered in front of their locker
room, the majority resembled what you'd expect from any
junior college. Most of them weren't as big or as strong as
Division I players. These were the players Division I passed
over. These were the guys that had all the hopes and dreams
but lacked the brawn and raw talent. They loved the game to
distraction, but they didn't quite have what it took to compete
on the Division I level.

There were exceptions, though. Sometimes a blue-chip kid
from Florida or Nebraska or UCLA was sent down, so to
speak, to work on his grades or his maturity, or because he
couldn't stay out of trouble. The history of Kansas JC football
is peppered with Division I stars and NFL greats who started
out in these small towns.

The gargantuan, onyx-black linebacker Royal Huckabee
was one such player. Miami had dropped him from its program
as a freshman, during his red-shirt year. Too crazy, they'd said.
And there was the trouble with the guns and then with the girl.
"He needs some time to think about what he really wants" was
the statement issued by the UM public relations office.

So in the milling throng of Kilgore players, Royal stood out, literally head and shoulders above his teammates. His body was an atlas of muscular definition. At six-three and two-forty-five, he was the ideal size and weight for any program in the universe. He could run as fast as most wide receivers. He'd made JC All-American two years running and had gone so far as to dump Miami in favor of Alabama. He'd signed a letter of intent to that effect.

To Royal Huckabee, the game wasn't so much about winning for his team or for the JC championship or for his friends and family. The game was about one thing only. Royal Huckabee.

ESPN had a trailer set up at the landing in front of the spot where the busses parked. When Royal stepped off the bus, he spat on the ground in front of the camera crew. A small boy ran up and asked for his autograph. He snarled at the kid. As the top-ranked JC footballer in the nation, with four-year schools still calling every day and Miami crying the blues and Alabama in the catbird seat, Royal was entitled to a little display of dirt. After all, being disrespected got old fast. Each game was a chance to prove himself. A chance to rectify a wrong. An opportunity for "I told you so."

And it got worse. At a Kansas news affiliate he'd delighted fans by saying, "That's right, I am temperamental. I got ninety percent temper, ten percent mental. So what? I had some problems with the law. Who ain't? Football is good, man. A good way to get rid of aggression wit'out goin' to jail. Knowwhatimsayin'?"

Later, during pre-game calisthenics, he tossed out this gem to a TV journalist. "Football ain't a sport. It's a frickin' concussion! I like to think my best stuff borders on felonious assault. Knowwhatimsayin'?"

JD Bobbitt had a tape of Royal's interview for a piece that had earlier aired on ESPN 3. At five-thirty, when the Cougars assembled in the home team locker room, he turned down the lights and played it. Dan, Chip, JD and the rest of the staff and players sat huddled around the screen as Huckabee went on and on about the game that would take place in just over an hour.

"Echo in for some serious (BLEEP). I'm'a jus' wrap my arms around that whole backfield. Peel 'em one by one till I get to Chip Hunter. Him I keep."

Dan and Chip exchanged looks. Chip smiled. He was nervous. Dan patted him on the back and winked.

Huckabee continued. He looked straight into the camera and at the entire Cougar team: "And God help that geriatric Jesse James, Dan Parrish, if dey put him in. Knowwhatimsayin'?"

JD hit the power button and the TV went black. The lights came up in the locker room.

CHAPTER 62

JD turned to the entire team. "That's Royal Huckabee, guys. Number 55. We beat him, we beat them." He paused. "Knowwhatimsayin'?"

Nervous laughter rippled through the room and died. Bobbitt stood atop a bench and faced his warriors. "Enough about him, though. Guys, tonight you begin the tail end of a journey that you started a long time ago. That was the day you picked up your first football."

JD tossed a few footballs into the group for emphasis. Some of the boys felt of the leather, trying to recall that moment in time.

"Part of the journey involved your buds. Some have left along the way. But those of you who stayed are a part of something special. You stayed for a reason. You stayed because you care about your town, your school, your teammates and yourselves." JD picked up one of the balls and gave it a squeeze and studied it.

"You care about football."

He wandered his eyes over the group, letting his words sink in. Goosebumps ran up and down the spines of his kids. Dan's heart began to thump in his chest. Chip's heart began to do the same.

"There comes a point in a guy's life when he asks himself, 'How do I want to be remembered?'" He turned and began to pace, three steps right, turn, three steps left. "It's not always fair, life...but part of your future and how you'll be remembered will be decided by what you do tonight."

Again JD paused. It was gut check time for the team and the staff. Players were visibly upset, youngsters searching their souls, wondering how they'd do. All year Coach Bobbitt had forced them to look into themselves, to draw strength from each other, to deal with adversity when it comes, yet to stay positive and strong and resilient. So now it was time, and the mettle that would be tested could echo through the rest of their lives.

"Look at your teammates."

All of the players did as they were told, some of them seeing guys they'd known since kindergarten. Their parents knew each other, too. Some of the parents had played bunco, bingo and bridge with one another, worked together, helped each other on their respective roads through life. And everyone had a story. Some of the players were rich, some were poor. A few were from out of town, but were now part of this thing. All of them were linked irrevocably on this day, joined together by a town and a school and a past and present and future called Echo.

"How do you want these guys to you to remember you?" JD asked. "How do you want your folks to remember you? Your classmates?" He gestured outside. "How do you want all the wonderful people of Echo out there to remember what you do tonight? Are you going to be remembered for something ordinary? Or something amazing?"

JD paused again and took a breath. He knew there wouldn't be forty superstars. He knew that not everyone would be extraordinary. Yet he also knew that with a group of guys such as this, a group of guys that had made it this far, there was an indefinable logistic at play that couldn't be codified and couldn't be catalogued. Only occasionally in a man's life is he granted the privilege of coaching such a collection of stout hearts. He knew his team wouldn't be the most talented on the field that afternoon. He knew that Kilgore attracted better players. But he also knew that these guys were special. And that they'd proven it time and again over the course of the season.

JD continued. "And while you're at it, wrap your heads around this: for most of you this will be your last football game. The final game. Your last chance *ever*, to participate in something so good."

Another silence. Testosterone meters were pegged. Hearts were starting to pound.

"So…play as if this were your last day on earth."

The team erupted.

JD began to shout. "Own this game! Don't let anyone or anything take it away from you!"

Cheers.

"NOBODY!"

Some of the boys stood and began to jump in place.

"NOT THE FANS! NOT THE REFS! AND DEFINITELY NOT *ROYAL-FRICKIN'-HUCKABEE!*"

The team screamed! They were ready. They'd whipped themselves into a rabid froth, some of them going hoarse already. On the other side of the door a few of the bystanders even became alarmed. It sounded like they were killing a goat and drinking its blood.

"Ready?" shouted JD.

"ONE, TWO, THREE…"

The entire team finished with, "HUSTLE, FINISH, WIN!"

They charged out of the locker room, almost breaking the door down. Dan grabbed Chip and pulled him aside.

"They're gonna be after you all night, son."

"Yes, sir." Chip jammed his helmet on his head and affixed the chinstrap.

Dan curled his fingers around Chip's face mask. "Be the hammer, not the nail."

Chip nodded. He had no words. The time for talking was over. It was time for action. Time for football.

CHAPTER 63

To say the atmosphere in Hunter Stadium was charged would be a considerable understatement and a disservice to the cliché. There was so much electricity in the air that had the circuit breakers blown for the stadium lights, the lights just might have stayed on.

On the visitors' side, the players for Kilgore were going through fits and spasms. They slapped one another's bodies and beat chests and clashed helmets and roared their hatred for everything Cougar Red. Fists were clenching; neck veins were popping; rage was in the air. One of the sports writers later likened them to Huns preparing to destroy the Visigoths. The yellow sideline grass was stomped into divots of dirt and frozen slush and the game hadn't even started. The head coach, Randall Hewitt, six pieces of Juicy Fruit in his mouth, stormed through his players, yelling into their faces, spittle flying, nose bubbling. When he turned his back, Theo York, a Kilgore cheerleader who waxed his arms and chest, got so worked up during the school fight song he threw up on Royal Huckabee's shoes. Some of the players had to intervene on Theo's behalf to keep the big linebacker from turning the puker's nose into blood pudding.

On the home team side it was the same—complete pandemonium. JD Bobbitt went down his list, ignoring the noise. He ran last minute checks on his communication gear, Gatorade levels and the first aid station. He roared at his volunteers to pay attention. He checked the supply staff, making sure longer cleats were available should a typhoon appear, and on and on. His red shirt was already matted to his back with sweat, no matter the mid-forties air temperature, and his mouth was moving like an auctioneer. He wasn't allowed to chew tobacco in front of the town, so he, too, had filled his cheeks with licorice-flavored Black Jack chewing gum, given to him by his grandfather who'd managed to keep a case of the stuff long after it had been discontinued. JD called it his good luck gum. His wife Mary called it disgusting.

The stands were also alive. And the throngs of people swelled and groaned and seethed like a colony of angry ants devouring a carcass. Red and Green men surreptitiously sipped whiskey. Red ladies shook their fists at Greens. Fathers threatened other fathers. Little boys streaked up and down the stands; little girls screamed for no reason; middle-school kids tried to text each other and look cool. A twelve-year-old boy named Barney Ketteringham was the first casualty of the evening. He tripped and fell as he was bounding down the stadium seats and had to be rushed to the ER. He wound up with ten stitches in his tongue and made it back to the game by half-time, only to be returned to the hospital for biting into a hot dog and ripping out his new sutures. Before the first whistle there were two fist fights in the north end zone men's room and a dustup involving twelve Cougar crazies, a Green Machine convertible sedan and a Ziploc of watered-down cow pies from Old Man Granger's pasture.

Again, no one was arrested.

There was personal drama, too. In a remote corner of the stadium, Julie Alie, the prettiest fourteen-year-old girl in the entire county—she'd just won the Little Miss Imagination's Rock Around The Clock Pageant—told her thirteen-year-old classmate, Andy Corrigan, that he so *bumfuzzled* her she couldn't think straight. When she said it, his heart took off like a bottle rocket. He immediately turned pale with want and had to sit down to keep from fainting. He had no idea what bumfuzzled meant, but he knew it was something good and committed it to memory. That night he spelled the word over and over on the roof of his mouth and decades later he would repeat the term to their grandchildren.

Meanwhile, a quiet fell over the stadium as the fans watched the captains from opposing teams trudge out to the middle of the field for the coin toss. Gamesmanship started early. Huckabee and Chip shook hands, but when it was time to unclasp, Huckabee held on and squeezed. Just as Chip was about to yank his hand loose, Huckabee let go and Chip's arm flailed wildly, knocking the referee's hat off. Laughter circled the stadium and Chip's face blazed crimson.

Kilgore won the toss.

Huckabee looked at Chip and drew his hand across his throat.

"Knock it off," barked the referee.

"Oh, I'm gonna knock it off, all right. I'm gonna knock it *clean* off!" Royal Huckabee said then trotted off the field.

Chip tried to come up with a zinger of his own but drew a blank. He watched as the big linebacker jogged away. He realized that for the first time in his football playing life...

...he was actually scared.

CHAPTER 64

The first few minutes of the game were fairly predictable, a virtual see-saw contest with neither team achieving much of anything. Chip was sharp, though, even spot-on perfect with his execution. Yet Huckabee was a beast, managing to break up every play, wreaking havoc all over the field, flattening running backs and receivers and destroying blocking schemes that had been designed specifically for him. Time and time again he was in someone's face at the critical minute. And he was getting to Chip, too, between his ears. Huckabee's instincts for the ball bordered on the supernatural.

Then it happened. Chip under-threw a screen pass and Huckabee anticipated the trajectory of the ball, snagging it out of the air and taking it to the house for a pick six. Chip tried to chase him down, but all he saw was Huckabee's 55 and all he could hear was laughter and taunts as the Kilgore star crossed the goal line.

Seven-oh, Kilgore.

'Ipo took the ensuing kickoff deep in the end zone. Against Bobbitt's commands, he headed upfield. He managed to duck a few tackles, but was tripped up on the ten-yard line and fell forward to the eleven. A groan surged through the home crowd. Chip trotted onto the field and entered the huddle strong, calm and focused. But Huckabee's relentless assault was starting to take its toll. Some of the offensive linemen were beginning to grumble and whine.

"Hey!" warned Chip. "Go hard or go home! Got it?"

The linemen nodded. It wasn't the first time they'd been chastened by their quarterback's tone. But never this early in a game.

"Pro Right, thirty-eight quick-pitch on two," said Chip and they all clapped in unison as they broke the huddle.

Echo ran the play—a sweep—but Huckabee had their number, shed several blocks, and dropped the running back for a ten-yard loss.

Another groan was drowned out by the Kilgore fans. Two plays later, Echo punted.

The Green Machine got the ball in good field position. Their play calling was flawless, and the execution was silky smooth, the QB going five for five. Before you could say "Huckabee" they scored.

Fourteen-oh, Kilgore.

Although no one from Echo had given up, there was a discomfort settling into the pits of their stomachs. Players and coaches and the entire town of Echo were put off by the lightning turn of events.

On the Kilgore side of the stadium, however, men were laughing and spitting, slapping each other on backs and wishing aloud they'd bet more on the outcome. Cheerleaders were thrombotic in their gushing fanaticism—some of them already trying to decide on which post-game party to attend. And coaches were trying not to laugh out loud and were wondering if it would be ribs or steaks at The Ranch House off Highway 6 on the ride home. There would definitely be beer.

The Echo fans were of course worried. Most of them worked to prop each other up—they'd seen such things many times in the past, and the team had been able to regroup and go on to win—but still. And none of the other foes had made it look this easy.

Agnes and Katy sat together just down from the press box, high up in the stands, sharing a thermos of smuggled chardonnay and talking about recipes, weather and politics, anything but what was happening on the field. Every once in a while one of them would sneak a look. As the quarter ended, they both looked up and saw that Chip and Dan were conferring on the sideline.

"It's like he's in the damn huddle!" blurted Chip, referring to Huckabee across the field.

Dan nodded. His thoughts exactly. But before he could respond, Bobbitt approached and told Chip to stick to the game plan and to "Stop making excuses!"

Chip nodded, strapped on his helmet and walked along the sideline, rallying his troops. Bobbitt watched him go, then shot a look at Dan. The look said, "What the hell is going on?"

Dan arched his brows and shrugged. He was fresh out of ideas, almost a believer now in the Huckabee hype. *It can't be that simple, though. It just can't.*

In the middle of the second quarter the score was still fourteen to nothing. Chip barked out his signals and took the snap. He dropped back deep and realized his receivers were blanketed by the Kilgore defenders. Chip decided to run. He turned upfield and raced to the sideline. He was three yards from a first down when he got mugged by Huckabee, flying in like a wild man, tossing him like a rag doll to the turf under the home team bench.

Flags flew like yellow confetti. *BOOs* descended from the Echo bleachers. Even the Kilgore fans were taken aback by the ferocity and the unsportsmanlike venality of the hit. Katy jumped to her feet, eyes ablaze, screaming at the top of her lungs and spilling her wine. Bobbitt threw down his headset and began to run out onto the field, until Dan stopped him.

"We need you, JD. Stay put!"

JD snarled and picked up his headset and leapt along the sideline to watch as his teammates helped Chip get up. The resilient QB for the Cougars stepped back onto the field with a hint of a limp and the crowd applauded. He raised his hand to the people to let them know he was okay. Bobbitt and Dan were worried, though, when they watched him try to run in place. His ankle had not been tested in such a way. There was always the chance that it wouldn't hold up. After the referee paced off the fifteen yards, everyone sat and waited for the next play. The kid had pluck. You could tell that. He wasn't going to go down without a fight.

The center snapped the ball on the next play, and at once Chip wished he had it back. He'd executed a perfect seven-step drop but just as he was releasing the ball, Huckabee managed to grab Chip's jersey and spin him to the ground. The pass wobbled off like a wounded mallard and fell into the arms of a Kilgore defensive lineman. He rumbled sixty yards untouched for a touchdown.

And just like that it was twenty-one zilch.

Then Kilgore, convinced the Cougars were in disarray, lined up to kick the ball. The onside kick tumbled and rolled, bounced and caromed and ended up in Kilgore's possession. Bobbitt slammed his headset to the turf for the second time. Another touchdown was soon in the books.

The score now stood at twenty-eight to zip with five minutes on the clock until half-time.

There were no moans, no groans following the two scores. Now there was just a murmur. The entire Echo sideline exchanged anxious looks when the chanting started.

"PAR-RISH! PAR-RISH! PAR-RISH!..."

Chip's eyes immediately began to swim and his chest began to heave. He'd never felt this low in his life. He turned his eyes to the stands and found the face of his mom. He looked away.

Parrish saw what was transpiring and jogged up to Chip and slid his arm around his shoulders. "Chip—"

But Chip didn't want to hear it. He was in no mood for a pep talk, especially from the guy everyone was crying for, a man twice his age and worse...

…an ex-con.

Parrish watched as Chip stalked off, his heart breaking for the kid. Then he turned his eyes back onto the field.

Something just isn't right.

Parrish stood on the fifty and squinted into the lights, his brain on fire: *The coaches prepared for this game. We went over everything. We slaved. Yes, we were aware of number 55, but this was not on the menu, this uncanny ESP thing. We'd watched him play a number of teams, none as good as the Cougars, and he was mortal. He was good. But he was mortal.*

Parrish tossed his headset aside. *Something's wrong. What the hell is it?* He bounded away. In twenty seconds he was at the door to the coach's booth up in the press box. The coaches were crammed together in their metal chairs, staring down at the slaughter with long faces. Dan burst in amongst them. On the field Kilgore kicked off.

"Better suit up," said Gerald Carter, the offensive line coach. "Chip's flat as a penny."

"It's not Chip," said Dan.

The other coaches all exchanged looks, stepping back to make room for Dan as he stared down at the field. He watched the next Echo series play out. *First down: Chip runs a dive play, Huckabee stuffs it. Second down: Chip runs a screen: Huckabee lays back and almost picks it off.* Dan looked harder. He was missing something. Yes, the guy was good. Real good. But this performance fell into the too good to be true category.

Parrish snatched up a pair of binoculars and glued them to his eyes. He twisted the center dial until the lens filled with Royal Huckabee's face. Then he panned the field to take in the action. He watched as Bobbitt signaled the play to Chip. He watched as Chip nodded and entered the huddle. He turned his attentions back to Huckabee. He watched as Huckabee fired a look to the Kilgore sideline.

Dan followed the linebacker's eyes and settled the lens on their target. He pulled the field glasses from his face.

"Son of a b…" and the rest was drowned out by the roar of the crowd as the referee's whistle signaled half-time.

It was full dark now. High above, in the halo of the big halogen lights, the bats had arrived. They were having a field day, picking off the insects that had been attracted to the glow.

CHAPTER 65

The boys from Echo straggled into the locker room, grousing and finger-pointing, some of them limping, others sullen and dispirited. The beating had taken its toll, and they would have to endure another half. This would be a massacre for the record books if things didn't change fast. Something good had to happen. And a few of the players were taking way more than their share of the poundings. 'Ipo had a long, crimson scratch across his throat and Chip had the beginnings of a fat lip. Everywhere you looked, players and trainers were tending to small injuries.

Team managers, once called water boys, passed out fresh bottles of Gatorade, while the coaches gathered before a white board for the chalk talk. Even they looked puzzled, almost dazed. Their body language translated to "hmmm," "uh oh" and "oh no." Bobbitt immediately, almost frantically, began drawing Xs and Os on the board. He didn't know what else to do.

That's when Dan walked up and interrupted him. "Whoa!" The word came out louder than he had intended. Then he reached for the chalk and offered a tiny smile and a wink. "S'cuse me, JD." He turned to the team. "Guys, this isn't about Xs and Os."

The room fell silent. You could hear one of the showers dripping; you could hear the blower fan in one of the back windows; you could hear a few people milling around outside the door. Yet on the benches in front of the white board there was silence. Confusion, even. JD looked annoyed. He pushed his hat back on his head and scratched his ear.

Dan had the room's attention. Then wiped the chalkboard clean. "It's about this." He spelled the name D-U-R-R on the chalkboard in big, bold letters. He faced the team. He searched for Chip's face and found it.

"That's right." He pointed at Chip. "Your old buddy, Jimmy Durr, is picking off our sideline signals. He's made up some signs to give to Huckabee. I watched the whole thing."

The players went ballistic. Bobbitt, too. Even the rest of the coaches and the trainers and the managers. Dan stood in front of everyone, arms crossed, letting them vent. He decided he liked the sudden energy. A little excitement and a few chest poundings would be good for the team. Somebody yelled, "Kill him!" and Dan rolled his eyes. Finally Bobbitt blew his whistle, nearly rupturing Dan's eardrum.

"Sorry," he said, abashed.

"What do we do now, Coach?" from Chip. He spoke for everybody in the locker room.

Dan traded eye blinks with Bobbitt. "May I?" asked Dan.

"Please do."

Dan grinned mischievously, clapped his hands then rubbed them together greedily. *How does a real coach do this? When you spend eighteen years in prison, you're exposed to a steady stream of drama, real episodes that involve life and death and a newsreel of human emotions. I've seen men bleed out. I've seen men beaten to death. I've seen rape and retribution, fear so stark that you could smell it on a man, I've seen it all, in the cloistered society behind the wall and the razor wire. So when I look at these guys, I have to keep in mind that this doesn't compare to all that...*

...except in the way an incident like this impacts lives. After all, this is Echo. And Echo, like in that little pride-soaked town, Lebanon, Kansas, "Center of the Continental US," like them,

these guys see themselves as ambassadors of a sort. To fall on your sword because you're clumsy is inexcusable. To be beaten because you're an egotist resonates. It could mean something down the road. It could cause those same emotions that I saw in prison, those same hatreds and feuds and later, some sort of middle-aged self-loathing, divorces even, and decades of personal confusion. They have pride.

But to be beaten because the other guy cheats is redeemable. It can be fixed. And it's all involved in a game, nothing more. A game, and a rat.

For these players, this IS the center of everything. Not just forty-eight states, but the entire universe.

"What do we do? Why, that's easy, Chip. We show run—" he paused, making sure he had every ear in the house. He pointed at Chip, "—then we let you air it out."

The team erupted into cheers. They stood and circled their field general and pounded him on the back, slapping fives, all of a sudden rejuvenated at the thought of a little deception of their own. Cheating sucks; everyone agrees with that. And it's worse if it's one of your own. So a little payback was just what the doctor ordered, and everyone in the room was ready to dish some payback out. Enough of this getting your ass whipped. Enough of this confusion in the ranks.

Dan gave Chip a private smile and called him over. There was work to do before the start of the second half.

CHAPTER 66

The second half began with a good one-third of the stands empty. Either the people were still milling around, or they were at the concession stand or they had decided to leave and avoid the pain when the final whistle blew. Some of the Kilgore team managers were already passing out Green Machine T-shirts to their fans, who put them on over their sweaters and jackets:

KILGORE JC
KANSAS BOWL CHAMPS...
...AGAIN!

At the concession stand Susan Royce, the mother of Kellan Royce, the starting left guard for the Cougars, had been forced to ration the Sno-cone syrup and was snapping at anybody stepping to the window in Kilgore green. She had earlier resisted the temptation to pour salt in the coffee of one of the Kilgore coaches' wives, but she had no problem selling the cold, wrinkled, over-cooked hot dogs to anybody wearing the offending T-shirts. She saved the fresh dogs for the Echo faithful. Twenty-eight to nothing might signal the death of Echo, but you could never get Kellan's mom to admit it.

On the field, Chip entered the huddle, strapping on his helmet. He stepped back and glanced at the sideline, and JD flashed him a signal. Across the field, Jimmy Durr stood against the fence, his tiny hunting binoculars glued to his face. He picked up the signal from Bobbitt then signaled the play to Huckabee, smooth as oil.

While the Cougars were still in their huddle, Royal Huckabee nodded to his own teammates. "Strong Side Dive," he mumbled, over and over, running up and down the line. Then he took his place, licking his chops.

Chip and his teammates broke the huddle and lined up.

"Your ass is grass, boy!" shouted Huckabee. "And I'm the lawnmower!"

With a hike, the ball slammed into Chip's hands and Echo faked the dive play. Huckabee and his teammates bit, hook line and sinker, plowing head-long into the gridiron mosh pit...

...while Chip stepped to his right and looped a pass to 'Ipo in the very spot Huckabee had vacated. The speedster from Hawaii high-tailed it, eighty yards for the touchdown. The Echo crowd erupted, slapping and screaming and pounding each other on the back. Some of the fair-weather fans out in the parking area heard the roar and began digging into their pockets for their ticket stubs. Katy and Agnes cheered. Other mothers cheered. Fathers roared their relief. At least it wouldn't be a shutout.

Twenty-eight to seven, Echo was on the board.

After the kickoff, Kilgore attempted to mount a drive, but every play resulted in a loss and they wound up on their own ten, staring at a fourth down and twenty. They now faced an invigorated Cougar squad, and they weren't up to the challenge. During the series, Huckabee stood atop his visitors' bench and stared daggers at his confidential informant, Jimmy Durr.

Durr apologized with a shrug. Huckabee was scary. He was huge when he was mad. Hell, he was huge when he was happy and he was never happy. Not even on his birthday.

Meanwhile, at an upper corner of the Echo bleachers, Belden Ferguson and Billy Cox sat side by side, Cox taking notes and both enjoying the momentum shift.

Below them and to the right, Katy kept looking around for her husband. She'd hoped he wouldn't show, and so far he hadn't. Good. She hadn't needed his usual bellicose tirades and his I-told-you-sos during the first half of play, and she didn't need him now, belittling what progress the Cougars had made.

Kilgore punted, a real boomer. Echo's ball, first and ten on their own thirty-six. Chip trotted out to the huddle and the whole process repeated itself. Bobbitt's signal, Durr's intercepting the sign and lateraling off to Huckabee, running up and down the line. "Weak side sweep! Be ready. Kick ass!"

Echo lined up at scrimmage. Brent Cullinan, the Echo center, said to Huckabee, "Yo, lawnmower! Better sharpen your blades!" The entire Echo team laughed.

"I'll show you some blades, Whitebread."

When the ball was snapped, Chip faked the sweep pitchout to his tailback, then bootlegged it the other direction. Huckabee and company fell for the fake and massed as one to the weak side, causing a pileup. Chip had the ball, though, and he was on the other side of the field. He stopped, planted his back foot, and fired a deep bomb to Ku'uipo for another score.

The Echo fans went crazy once again. One woman screamed so loud she fainted dead away. The cheerleading squad ran in circles, their hands clapped to their faces, laughing. Folks cursed and jumped up and down and kids ran the stadium steps, and even though the score wasn't close yet, some of the people were starting to have a little hope. One little boy asked his father if he could change his name to Chip. A few rows below the press box, the face of the mother of the quarterback—Katy Hunter's face—folded into wrinkles of joy. She bit her lip. Tears sprang from her eyes. On the bench next to her, Agnes gobbled two Rolaids.

Two other developments of note. When 'Ipo caught his second touchdown pass, most of the Echo teenagers stopped texting each other, put their phones away and began to pay attention. While on the other side of the field, more than a few green Kilgore-as-state-champs T-shirts came off and went into purses and backpacks.

Meanwhile, high up in the top corner of the stands, Belden Ferguson exploded, raining strawberry soda down on Billy Cox and staining the reporter's porkpie hat with red, sugary goo.

On the Kilgore sideline, Royal Huckabee stood atop the bench and locked eyes with the hapless Jimmy Durr.

This isn't good, thought Jimmy. *The guy's a freak. And he's pissed.*

And he knows where I live.

Darla Finch looked at Jimmy's face and watched his Adam's apple bobbing like a yo-yo. "What's the matter, doll? You look scared."

"Shut up, Darla."

Twenty-eight, fourteen, Kilgore.

CHAPTER 67

By the time the fourth quarter started it was nine o'clock. Clouds had appeared from the west and the wind had come up, dropping the temperature ten degrees. This was the high plains, though, and people were used to the vagaries in the weather. The smell of snow was once again in the air, and people could feel it coming. They hoped it would hold off. Even if the game was still a two-touchdown rout, the Cougars had kept Kilgore off the scoreboard for the entire third quarter. Anything could happen. Both teams had been battling, but clearly both teams were wearing down.

The upshot was that a fourteen-point buffer looked to be enough for Kilgore unless something changed. But who knows? This was football. It wasn't a funny-shaped ball for nothing. The outcome was as unpredictable as the bounce.

And at the moment, Echo had that ball at midfield. For the last few minutes Echo's receivers had stumbled. They had dropped balls they should have caught, and Chip's patience was wearing thin. He didn't chastise them, though. He decided to take a page out of Coach Dan's book. He encouraged them.

"Trust your routes, guys. And hold on to the ball. We're almost there."

The players nodded. They were tired, Chip knew. They were sucking wind around their mouthpieces.

"Pro left, slot right, end blast. On two. Ready? Break!"

The team moved to the line. The trash talk had disappeared. Oxygen was now at a premium. The ball was snapped and Chip dropped back. Royal Huckabee gave a hard forearm to the Echo guard, sending him sprawling. Huckabee stomped onto then past him, his eyes locked onto Chip's.

Chip planted to throw. When he did, his back foot wobbled sideways, aggravating his ankle. As he released the ball, aiming toward his tight end, Huckabee dropped back in coverage with an incredible athletic move and picked off the pass. He was tackled immediately. Still, though, when he got to his feet he grinned at Chip. He pointed and said, "I got your number, cracker."

Chip stood and took a step, then another toward the sideline. He was limping. Dan waited for him, palms skyward in a what-the-heck-happened gesture of impotence. When Chip stepped over the sideline chalk he delivered the news that Dan didn't want to hear: "He's onto us, Coach."

"Figured." Dan looked across the field and saw that Jimmy Durr was gone. "How's the ankle?"

Chip lifted his foot and rolled it around. He shrugged. "Hustle. Finish. Win."

Parrish slapped him on the back. "Atta boy, Chip."

Nine minutes.

The clock continued to run and the game became a back-and-forth battle of defenses. Two good offensive teams that couldn't score against one another.

Six minutes.

Three downs and a punt repeated itself over and over. And Royal Huckabee continued to get his licks in, knocking Chip to the ground on every play. He knew if he stopped Chip, he would stop Echo. And it was working.

Two minutes, twenty-five seconds. Kilgore's ball.

The Kilgore center snapped the pigskin and the QB handed it off not to his tailback, but to the big man up front, the full-back, a guy named Joe Daniels, two hundred twenty-five pounds of Midwest muscle. And inexplicably, for the first time in two years, Daniels missed the handoff and fumbled. The ball bounced and tumbled and was scooped up by Echo's blitzing safety and stalwart, undersized good guy, Johnny Barnini, the fastest Cougar on the squad. And he left no doubt about his speed as he blazed down the sideline untouched and into the Kilgore end zone, flipping the ball to the referee as the crowd went crazy.

Barnini was mugged by his teammates, so he couldn't see his father in the stands—Johnny Sr.—holding his chest, sobbing. He'd been watching his son play football since Pop Warner—always on defense—and had never seen him score even one point. He remembered saying to his neighbor that he would give his left testicle to see his son score a touchdown. He quickly jammed his hand in his pocket to make sure it hadn't happened. He counted two. "That's my boy!" he screamed. "That's my boy!"

Twenty-eight, twenty-one, Kilgore.

The teams lined up and the clock whistle blew. The kick sailed high into the air, past the goal line, past the end zone— touchback. It was Kilgore's ball on their own twenty and there was mass confusion on Kilgore's side of scrimmage. Finally the Cougars were establishing themselves, which on the next play translated into movement on the offensive line and a five-yard penalty. Then the air horn sounded for the two-minute warning.

During the time out, radio announcers could be heard recapping the game and lauding the efforts of the Cougars. They'd made a game of it, and even if they lost now, they could hold their heads high. As the coaches for both teams released their players onto the field, the wind came up a notch and the first flakes of snow began to fall.

On first down and fifteen, Echo stuffed the run to the outside. Out of bounds. The clock stopped.

One minute, fifty-five seconds to play.

Second down, Echo stuffed the run again. They took their

first time out.

One minute, forty-nine seconds.

Third down was an outlet pass. Incomplete. The clock stopped.

One minute, forty-four seconds.

Kilgore punted.

When Ku'uipo fielded the punt, he juked left, then right. There was nowhere to go, but he lunged forward anyway and was clotheslined by a Kilgore player for his efforts. He wasn't one to turn the other cheek, though, so he smacked the offending player in the helmet. Both teams rushed in. After offsetting penalties, the Cougars had the ball at their own twenty. Everyone, it seemed, was mad. In the stands, some Echo high school kids dared the Kilgore kids to "settle this under the bleachers." Sheriff's Deputy Will Lemke put his handcuffs on display and arched his eyebrows. The teens scattered quickly, most of them secretly thankful Officer Lemke stepped in.

Echo managed nine yards on two plays, both passes to the near sideline. Chip kept the ball on a sneak, and picked up the first down.

On the next play, Chip dropped back to pass in the face of a full-on blitz by Kilgore. They poured in from every angle and Chip went down. Worse, several of the Kilgore players piled on. One of them was Royal Huckabee. He used the opportunity to seek out Chip's tender ankle...

...and as the whistle blew, the big man twisted.

Chip howled in pain. One of the officials saw what Huckabee had done and threw his flag. Again, another fracas followed, both teams wailing away, both teams having to be separated. But this time Chip was unable to bounce back. He required assistance to limp to the sidelines.

He was finished for the night.

Katy stood and watched her son slump to the bench. Her hands went to her mouth. Agnes, beside her, rubbed her back. Neither could speak. The crowd of people around them stood and allowed themselves to mourn, a silent picture of dejection. The epitaph would be written. The Cougars were done. Echo had two more time outs, but no more quarterbacks.

One minute, sixteen seconds.

CHAPTER 68

Bobbitt and Parrish watched as Chip hobbled toward them. They traded grim looks. So close. They had come so close. And now the season was over.

The head referee jogged over and made it official. "One minute, Coach" was all he said. It was all he needed to say. Doomsday had arrived.

Dan dropped his eyes, looked back up and sighed. "Now what?" he said to Bobbitt.

"Beats me," snorted his old friend. "You were the genius that refused to dress for the game."

"Geez, JD, even if I wanted to now, we don't have time. The locker room is too far away."

Bobbitt shook his head. He watched the seconds tick off. Then his face lit up.

"Then let's bring the locker room to us!" He called out to the team. "Guys, circle up!"

So with thirty seconds left on the injury clock, all of Echo JC gathered around their head coach. Dan was still confused, but when he heard JD say, "Drop trou, Dan," he figured it out fast.

At first, Dan didn't move. There was no way JD was serious.

"Take off the friggin' pants, Dan. Now!"

The players began to hoot. "Go for it, Coach!" "Yeah, baby!" One of the trainers yelled, "Nudey fruity!" The snow was coming down and everyone was grinning at Dan, staring, but only for a moment. Chip had seen what was going on and he stood and hobbled to the group and pushed his way into the middle of the pile. He smiled and gave Dan a thumbs up.

"What the hell," said Dan, and down came his pants, just as Bobbitt called their second time out. The snow began to fall harder.

Bobbitt led the resurrection. "Rigney, your helmet. Farmer, your pads and pants. Moffett, shoes." The trio shed themselves of their uniforms and tossed the stuff into the middle of the huddle. They grabbed Dan's clothes as he removed them and each took what he needed to keep from freezing. Bobbitt turned to one of the injured players. "Frenchy, jersey." Then he turned to Flip Lyons, a pimply three-hundred-pound mountain of sweat and Twinkies.

"Lyons, gimme your jock strap."

"Now, wait a dang minute, JD—"

"I'm KIDDING! Just keep dressing."

When Dan Parrish trotted out onto the field, nobody was clear about who he was. After all, his numbers were wrong and he'd been out of any uniform, dressed in coaching clothes, and this time he didn't have a ponytail and a beard, and the snow was impeding everyone's view. But when they figured it out, people could hear the pandemonium two miles away on Main Street.

And Royal Huckabee deduced it, too. And was up in Dan's face in a flash.

"Old man, I'm gonna eat your ass alive," he hissed.

Parrish smirked. "You're gonna eat my ass? That's really gross."

Game on. It was now or never for the good guys.

CHAPTER 69

Dan Parrish knelt down and his team huddled up. He looked around and tried to connect with everyone. He thought, *Most of these terrific young loggerheads are in their teens, fresh-faced guys who still think snow storms are fun and who haven't been around long enough to have failed at something or to have their hearts broken by somebody or to live or die by someone's sleight of hand or pound of a gavel. Most of them have never left the state except on family vacations to places like Galveston or Yellowstone. Their eyes are forever open, their dreams intact, their lives just beginning to get interesting. And now, for the moment, their futures are dependent on what's going to happen in the next seventy-six seconds.*

Dan was their leader. He wasn't so sure he belonged there.

"Coach? You okay?" said Ku'uipo.

"Yeah," Dan lied. He was this close to throwing up. The butterflies were making him sick. His heart hammered like a conga line and he had trouble seeing into the lights and into the faces of his teammates and across the field through the slanting snow. *Was I like these guys when I was their age? It's snowing, for Christ sake.* He called the play, his voice cracking, betraying his conviction. The players exchanged looks. *They might be young, but they ain't dumb.*

The team moved to the line of scrimmage.

Slam! The ball was in his hands. He dropped back. His legs were rusty and cold and they betrayed him right out of the chute. He sailed the ball over his receiver's head just as Royal Huckabee dragged him down into the snow-covered mud at midfield. Before Dan was released by the big Kilgore star, he was forced to endure a massive fist into the small of his back. It was as close to a punch as was legally allowed.

In the stands, Agnes thought she would faint. She stood, clutching her sweater at the neck. She hadn't realized she was digging her nails into her palms until the half-moon dimples began to sting.

"It's okay, honey," said Katy. "I got your back." She began massaging her new best friend's shoulders.

The clock began again, its relentless, single-minded compulsion. Fifty seconds...forty-nine...forty-eight...

Snap! Parrish went into his five-step drop. This time he got it right. He set up and threw the ball, connecting with 'Ipo on a slick sideline pass. Echo cheered; Kilgore groaned. The Echo fans took breaths; the Kilgore fans began trading worried looks amongst themselves. They reasoned that Kilgore was still okay, but this old fart QB was a pain. Anything could happen. After all, this was football.

...forty-one...forty...thirty-nine...

Parrish took the ball. And he somehow stripped away the rust. He connected. Boom. First down. Then, as the clock ticked down, he connected on two more sideline passes— boom, boom, first downs. The Kilgore fans were having trouble swallowing. Smiling was not an option. The only thing going for them was that Royal Huckabee continued his onslaught, knocking Parrish to the ground on every play.

Echo gathered at midfield. Twenty seconds on the clock. The Cougars were all but done, really. There was too much to make up. But Kilgore was sucking wind like nobody's business. Anything was still possible.

Dan scanned the field and eyeballed his players. They were winded and beat and the odds were stacked a mile high against them. Except there was this indefinable shape to their faces and a quietude in their eyes that said, *Let's do this, man. Let's kill these guys. Let's screw their feet to the ground. Let's make this night special. One for the ages. A night to remember, and we'll force the world and the city of Echo and the state of Kansas to see us. And some will say I was there, I saw it with my own eyes, I know it's nothing to you people, but it's something to me and to my family, the night in the snow and all the mud, in the wind, in the face of all those impossible odds, the night when something impossible happened.*

So Dan huddled up. "Trips left, strong slot right." He looked at Ku'uipo. "X fly."

The Hawaiian grinned.

"I need a good head fake, 'Ipo. I want to see that DB's jock lying on the ground."

"You got it, brah."

And the Cougars nodded and set up on the line of scrimmage.

High up in the stands, tenured news reporter Billy Cox pushed the button on his phone to turn it off. He'd just received the word from his editor at the *Star*. Judge Richard Hunter had confessed. He was being transported to Wichita to be formally indicted.

Overhead the bats kept flying on nothing but instinct and radar. Bright lights meant squat to them. They were feeding. Surviving. Doing their thing. Killing bugs.

Like Kilgore, as they lined up against the Cougars.

CHAPTER 70

Dan Parrish ran his eyes along the line of scrimmage and settled his eyes on Royal Huckabee. Parrish winked. Huckabee seethed.

And the ball was snapped.

The big, mad linebacker charged across the line like a violent storm. He timed his rush so that the brace of linemen in his way went down like bowling pins. The Cougars' fullback, Tank Pendley, planted himself in front of Huckabee and was cast aside like an afterthought. Dan was cool, though. He'd taken just one-and-a-half seconds to set up and commence his progressions. He'd watched Ku'uipo streaking down the sidelines, a pair of defenders on his ass. He'd watched Ku'uipo swim left, then head fake to his right. He'd watched Huckabee closing in.

But then he watched the defenders as they were faked out of their shorts by another slight head feint, one of 'Ipo's small-guy moves coupled with Dan's own deft pump-fake.

He saw the giant Green Machine linebacker closing in, his arms held high, his face a storm cloud of hate, his teeth glinting like pearls of Armageddon...

...and Dan threw into the feathery sheet of white coming down, just as Huckabee fell on him and slammed him to the ground, and his shoulder turned forward and high and ripped itself out of its socket...

...and the bats fell on the moths as they flew into the

lights...and the ball sailed high into the air, spiraling through the snow...

...and time stopped. And the people were silent watchers. Silent. No sound. No concession stand noise, no cop sirens, no screams, no ticks, no noise at all.

Just snow.

And Ku'uipo ran under where he thought the ball should be. He looked back into the falling snow and reached his hands out, and out of the white there it was, and he received the ball and held it to his chest, and he fell into the end zone. Touchdown.

And the stands exploded.

Twenty-eight, twenty-seven, Kilgore.

Parrish tried to stand, but his shoulder hurt so bad he had to fall back down on the field. His teammates circled him and the trainers ran out. One of them said, "Coach! Raise your arm up!" He grabbed Dan's arm with both hands. He yanked down on the wrist and pushed up on the shoulder and the assembly went pop...and Dan's shoulder was back in its socket, albeit useless in any sort of football way. He got up and jogged to the sidelines.

JD Bobbitt rushed to get the extra point squad onto the field. There was no time on the clock, but by the rules, the scoring team was allowed to go for the extra point, or for two. And a point by Echo would send the game into overtime.

"Whoa," shouted Parrish, waving his good arm. "Don't even think about it, JD. Go for the win!"

"Are you nuts?"

"My arm's done, JD. Chip's ankle is shot. We gotta end this thing now. I'll never make it through overtime."

"Why not?"

"Uh, because I'm OLD!" Dan exploded.

"Oh. That."

Bobbitt called his last time out.

"That was your last one," said the referee.

"Gee, Hobie, thanks for the reminder."

"Hey, don't shoot the messenger." Hobie Stevens jogged off to confer with the other officials.

Bobbitt gestured for his players to gather 'round. Closest to the center were Chip and 'Ipo. Everyone leaned in, hanging on Bobbitt's words.

"Better make it a good one, Dan," he said.

Dan Parrish nodded, grim. He turned to the team. He knew the air would be sucked from their sails if he stammered. "Okay, listen up. Flea-flicker. Me wide left as decoy. 'Ipo wide right. And you—" he pointed at Chip, "—are taking it to the house."

"What the..." he said. "But, Coach, my ankle—"

"Exactly. Last thing they'll be looking for is you running it."

"Running it?" blurted JD. "Dan, the kid can barely walk."

"Doc!" shouted Parrish. He shot his eyes up and down the sidelines until he found Doc Hatfield, the seventy-five-year-old volunteer doctor for Echo JC and Echo High School, a volunteer job he'd had for almost fifty years. The man stood and grumbled and approached the group.

"Doc, we need a shot of cortisone for Chip's ankle. Pronto!"

Hatfield nodded and led Chip over to the bench where his battered medical bag sat. He began to rummage through the interior. Parrish sat down beside Chip.

"Pull your sock down, Chip, and look away. This one's gonna hurt. Needle's way big."

The boy nodded and looked away. Hatfield gave him the shot. Chip winced.

"That ought to do 'er," said Hatfield.

"Stand up, Chip. It works fast."

Chip put his weight on the balls of his feet and rose. He

put his full weight on the bad ankle. "Man, you weren't kidding," he beamed.

Just then the ref entered the arena. "On the field and hiking the ball in thirty seconds, or it's delay of game."

Parrish nodded. Stared at Chip and 'Ipo. "You ready." They both looked at him. They nodded and the three of them bumped fists. "Let's do it, then."

They jogged out onto the field, leading the rest of the offense. The crowd roared their approval. Most of the people in the stands seemed to want the game to end here and now, so when they saw that there would be a try for two, they were thrilled. Agnes and Katy, though, shared a worried look. Something was wrong and they knew it, and they knew that there was nothing they could do about it except watch and hope.

Down on the sideline, Bobbitt turned to Doc Hatfield. "I didn't even know you had cortisone in that bag."

"I don't." He showed Bobbitt a bent-open paper clip. "I poked him with this, and let his mind do the rest."

JD frowned.

"Hey, don't give me that look. It was Dan's idea. I did the same thing to him twenty years ago in the state championship."

Bobbitt shook his head, said a silent prayer, then turned his attention to the field. He watched as Dan rallied the other ten boys around him, just as he had when they were teenagers. He could remember times when they had been in dire straits, the clock winding down, the odds stacked miles high against them. And yet Dan always remained calm; his voice never wavered, his confidence always off the charts.

CHAPTER 71

Echo broke from the huddle. To a man, they were grim and determined. A lot was riding on the next play, so much that none of them spoke as they walked to the line. Kilgore was silent also, each man taking their positions, snarling, setting their jaws. Every player had promised to themselves that they would give their all, that they would not fail, that they would be damned if they would be the goat.

The crowds on both sides of the field stood silent. Then the chanting started. The Echo people began to pound their feet to the thrum of the stands, boom, boom, boom...and the terrifying noise grew even worse when Kilgore began their own shrill ululations. A lot of kids grew quiet. They'd never seen their parents act like savages.

Ku'uipo found his spot wide right, then looked back to Chip and nodded. Chip looked at Dan wide left and got the go-ahead. Then Chip stared into the face of Royal Huckabee. The guy was frothing at the mouth. He was ticking and moving from foot to foot and his eyes were big and round and crazed. He was a rodeo bull. He was a caged animal. He was a man given enormous talents, who was allowed into this arena of lesser men. And he was going to administer justice and save the day. That was the plan.

The ball was hiked.

The defensive line charged like wild steers. The offensive line dug in their heels and summoned every ounce of strength they could muster. Chip turned right and fired a strike to 'Ipo, who caught it with one hand before he took a step toward the end zone. Huckabee saw the little receiver take the ball and blazed after him...

...so 'Ipo turned, planted and threw the ball back to Chip...

...who snatched the ball out of the air and nearly dropped it. The crowd gasped. You could almost hear the squeal of brakes as Huckabee and the entire Kilgore team stopped and changed direction. Chip tucked the ball under his arm and began to hobble for the far side goal line.

An angry mob of green jerseys swept en masse after Chip...

...lugging along at a snail's pace.

Yet along the way, offensive linemen began taking out their defensive counterparts one by one. Bodies piled up.

Chip continued his painful stagger, reaching the four-yard line...

Kellan Royce, nicknamed "IHOP" for recording a league-leading number of pancake blocks—flattened one of the Kilgore gorillas.

...the three-yard line...

Jay Beardahl, the Echo tight end, took out two Kilgore fatsos with one wide sweep of his arms and legs.

...the two...

Echo's center broke his helmet and his collarbone when he lifted the Kilgore nose tackle off the ground and onto his ass.

...but Huckabee somehow was still on his feet, and he had made up the distance he'd lost when he bit on the pass to 'Ipo. He had the angle, now. He had the steam, now. He lowered his head and fired his legs and sailed through the white, across two yards of dead turf...

Time stood still.

Chip would not get to the goal line. He could barely walk. Royal Huckabee was going to make sure of it. Royal Huckabee was going to flatten the boy at the one and take home the trophy and the glory and he was going to go off to Alabama as a legend, as the baddest, most ferocious player ever to suit up on the High Plains...

...until old man Dan Parrish flew out of the wall of snow and blindsided him with such force, he took the giant out of his shoes. The shot was so loud, some folks said it was heard in Kansas City.

And as Huckabee rolled across the thin blanket of white into the dead grass and the mud, Chip dove over the plane of the goal with the tip of the ball and the ref signaled two points. And the snow came down and the stands erupted and Chip Hunter was mobbed by the entire team.

Parrish took his helmet off and stood over Royal Huckabee, who was still on his back, dazed, blood trickling from his nose.

"Who won?" asked the Kilgore star. His voice was almost child-like, the bravado gone. He sounded like the teenager he was.

"We did," said Dan.

"You shittin' me?"

"I wouldn't shit you, Royal Huckabee. You're my favorite turd."

In an unmarked Kansas Department of Law Enforcement Ford, two deputies drove east through the inky darkness. They were just ahead of the snow, somewhere in the middle of the state. One of them reached up and turned the radio off. They'd just finished listening to the Kansas Bowl. The driver shook his head. "Wow, that was one helluva game."

"I'll say," said the other deputy. "Too bad you couldn't make it."

Both officers turned and looked back through the cage at Judge Richard Hunter, handcuffed, face plastered to the window.

He blinked his tired, bloodshot eyes and watched the Kansas landscape fly by.

CHAPTER 72

The stadium was rocking. Nobody had left, and the band was playing the fight song and the cheerleaders were erecting human pyramids and the families of the victors were getting drunk on I-told-you-sos with the people who'd left and had to come crawling back.

JD Bobbitt was giving an interview with the sports guy from a west Kansas TV station when he saw Dan limp by. He rushed over and snatched him up and gave him a hug and kissed him on the face, spinning him around in his arms, slipping on the snow, the two falling in a heap.

"You did it, you sly old dog." He rubbed Dan's nose with his own, like an Eskimo.

"Yeah, I guess your job's safe for at least another year, huh, JD?" He stood, careful to put his weight where the pain wasn't. His shoulder was a mess, his rib cage was blue, and now he'd aggravated an old foot injury.

The smile left JD's face, replaced with a puzzled frown. "Whatchu talkin' about, Willis?"

Dan said, "You told me you were toast unless you made the finals, remember?"

JD rolled his eyes. "Dude, you kidding me? I was totally lying."

Parrish stared at his friend.

Bobbitt said, "Like I explained before, you always were a naïve s.o.b." He winked and backed up a step, just in time to get mugged by his wife and kids. He went down in another heap.

Parrish walked away from the scrum, still shaking his head but smiling. He turned to the stands and saw Agnes standing there, hands folded before her, staring at him from a few yards away. For a second neither of them moved. Then a smile broke across her face and she sped through one of the gates and ran and jumped into his arms and planted a big kiss on his battered face.

A few yards away, Chip was being administered to by Katy, the kisses and hugs raining down, making him laugh. "Mom, c'mon, knock it off."

"I'm just so proud of you, Chip." She let go of him and tousled his hair.

"Couldn't have done it without him," he said, hitching his thumb toward Dan.

Katy smiled as she watched Dan and Agnes. She was truly happy for the pair. "Well," she said, "you guys make a heck of a duo, you and Dan."

Chip must have felt a wave of pride surge through him. "You think?" And with that tone and that inflection, and the way he looked at Dan, it had to have broken Katy's heart into a thousand pieces.

"He's a real good guy," Chip said, nodding to himself.

"Yes he is," Katy agreed. Her voice was soft. Both regarded Dan from the distance of a few yards. Neither spoke.

"You know, Coach Bobbitt says I throw just like him."

Katy nodded.

"Says I have the exact same motion as he does."

Katy smiled and nodded again, unable to speak.

"The guys tease me all the time, say I look like him, too."

Katy glanced over at Dan again. Her lip began to tremble. "There's a reason for that, Chip," was all she said.

Chip looked at his mother.

A tear ran down her cheek. Then another. And another.

Shawn Corridan & Gary Waid

"Are you saying—"

She nodded, too overcome to speak.

Chip was stunned. His vision went silver and there was a roaring in his ears and he sat heavily on the bench, afraid his legs might betray him. His entire world was changing at lightning speed. He swallowed and found his tongue. "Does he know?"

Katy shook her head, her hand clutched over her mouth. "Nobody knows but us, Chip."

"Not even...?"

"Just you 'n' me, baby. I've never told anyone. Until now."

Chip stood up again. He stared at Dan.

"You okay, Chipper?" Katy asked.

Chip turned to her. He smiled. His eyes filled with tears. He nodded. "Can I tell him?"

"I was hoping you'd say that."

Chip hugged his mother and turned and limped across the field toward Dan and Agnes. "Yo, Coach!"

Billy Cox and Belden Ferguson stood at midfield, their hands shoved deep into their pockets, wrapped in a silence, watching as a number of familial moments unfolded around them. They watched Dan grab Chip by the shoulders and let go and turn and stumble backwards a step.

"What do you suppose that's all about?" asked Belden.

"Don't know, Belden. Can't be squat compared to the story we're sitting on, though."

"You think?"

They both looked over the field, at the now departing people and players. The snow was beginning to pile up in drifts on the bleachers.

"I *know*. Now let's go. I got me one hell of a story to write."

CHAPTER 73

It was near midnight on Christmas Eve. The air was brittle and clear, with a billion stars spread across the sky like broken glass on velvet. The forecast had called for a white Christmas, but the snow had held off. The parking lot at The Greasy Spoon was full to bursting.

Inside, a party was well underway. Employees were toasting one another for their good sense, and Echoans from all walks of life were joining them in their celebration of life.

In one of the booths, Agnes sat, showing off her engagement ring to a clutch of ladies...

...among them Tiny Lopez...

...who arched her brow at Jorge...

...who blew a kiss using his favorite spatula.

Katy and Brenda Price were off in the corner drinking tequila.

Booker and Baker, both drunk, were trying to drag Millie under the mistletoe. She was resisting. But only half-heartedly. She would get there eventually.

Belden Ferguson, Billy Cox, and JD Bobbitt talked football at the bar...

...while Dan and Chip read over Chip's scholarship offer from Emporia State. Dan looked up for a moment. Through the plate glass he could see beyond the neon sign and the Christmas lights, across the street and over the wheat-stubbled plains, awash in the glow of an engorged Kansas moon.

The first dusting of snow began to fall.

ACKNOWLEDGMENTS

Thanks to Waldo, Jimmy and Leon for setting the bar so high.

We'd like to acknowledge Eric Campbell and Lance Wright, the publishing team at Down & Out Books. Thank you for rolling the dice on a novel that did not fit any publisher's paradigm but will hopefully fill the hearts and minds and memories of many readers.

SHAWN CORRIDAN grew up in the shadow of Cape Kennedy, his father a NASA engineer. A high school football star as well as a surfer, he attended the University of Hawaii on a football scholarship and for the opportunity to surf the North Shore. After graduation, he got married, traveled the globe, sailed the Caribbean, was rescued by the Coast Guard twice, wrote market research reports for Wall Street, and worked in pharmaceutical sales. Corridan also won the Final Draft Big Break Screenwriting Contest and is a member of the Writer's Guild. He divides his time between Los Angeles, Honolulu and Merritt Island, Florida, a stone's throw from Gary Waid, co-author of *Gitmo* and *Goliath*.

Born a Navy brat in San Diego, GARY WAID has done almost everything there is to do in the water, from commercial fishing to operating tugboats to repairing yachts. He has also been a roofer, a carpenter, a musician, a tractor-trailer driver, a writer for magazines—as well as a guest in the federal prison system for smuggling marijuana. Waid lives in Cape Canaveral, Florida, on a sail-boat with his wife, Patty, and their two dogs.

BOOKS

On the following pages are a few
more great titles from the
Down & Out Books publishing family.

For a complete list of books and to
sign up for our newsletter,
go to DownAndOutBooks.com.

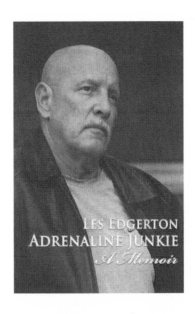

Adrenaline Junkie: A Memoir
Les Edgerton

Down & Out Books
November 2018
978-1-948235-41-9

Adrenaline Junkie is more than a renowned, multi-award-winning author entertaining with his life history. Les Edgerton understands that backstory matters. It influences the present. So he journeyed through his past seeking answers for why he was the way he was. Seeking answers for his thrill-seeking, devil-may-care, often self-destructive, behaviors. Seeking a sense of personal peace.

So settle back. Meet a real-life, twenty-first-century Renaissance man. A real-life adrenaline junkie.

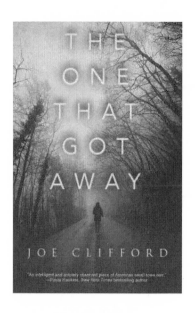

The One That Got Away
Joe Clifford

Down & Out Books
December 2018
978-1-948235-42-6

In the early 2000s, a string of abductions rocked the small upstate town of Reine, New York. Only one girl survived: Alex Salerno. The killer was sent away. Life returned to normal. No more girls would have to die.

Until another one did…

Repetition Kills You
Stories by Tom Leins

All Due Respect, an imprint of
Down & Out Books
978-1-948235-28-0

Repetition Kills You comprises 26 short stories, presented in alphabetical order, from 'Actress on a Mattress' to 'Zero Sum'. The content is brutal and provocative: small-town pornography, gun-running, mutilation and violent, blood-streaked stories of revenge. The cast list includes sex offenders, serial killers, bare-knuckle fighters, carnies and corrupt cops. And a private eye with a dark past—and very little future.

Welcome to Paignton Noir.

The Hollow Vessel
An Errol Coutinho/Big Island of Hawaii Mystery
Albert Tucher

Shotgun Honey, an imprint of
Down & Out Books
978-1-946502-93-3

Everyone wants a piece of wealthy young Rhonda Cunningham, which dooms her plan to disappear into the rainforest of the Big Island of Hawaii.

Detective Errol Coutinho needs to find out how her expensive tent ended up on the Kona side of the island.

And is that her blood in it?

It's getting crowded in the rainforest, and the shakeout will be murder…

Made in the USA
Middletown, DE
25 April 2019